Sage Parker dragged himself up from an alcoholic pit and now focuses on rebuilding his ranch on the Lakota Sioux reservation in South Dakota. He's rebuilding his life and helping others do the same by forming a recovery group that honors the Lakota tradition of seeking the Red Road, walking *in a good way*. And Sage knows his way around roads. Ranching is his hope for the future, but road construction pays the bills now.

Into his life walks Megan McBride, white and blond and idealistic. She's an engineer; she's there to build a much-needed road on the reservation. Sage struggles with his attraction to her just as he battles his addiction—one day at a time.

They're from different worlds. He's embracing the tribal heart, defending his people from the forces that threaten to destroy them. There's no way she'll stay with a lightning rod like him, once her job is done. And yet she's the courageous soul mate he's always wanted—and exactly what he needs.

Their slow, simmering, red-hot romance builds to a heart-wrenching question—what happens if he can't live up to his ideals and her dreams?

But That Was Yesterday was a finalist in the prestigious RITA awards, given annually by Romance Writers of America.

Praise for Kathleen Eagle

"Kathleen Eage is an author without peer."
                                    —Tami Hoag

"Kathleen Eagle crafts very special stories."
                                    —Jayne Ann Krentz

The Novels of Kathleen Eagle from Bell Bridge Books

This Time Forever

The Last Good Man

The Sharing Spoon

Night Falls Like Silk

Sunrise Song

You Never Can Tell

Reason to Believe

What the Heart Knows

But That Was Yesterday

But That Was Yesterday

by

Kathleen Eagle

Bell Bridge Books

This is a work of fiction. Names, characters, places and incidents are either the products of the author's imagination or are used fictitiously. Any resemblance to actual persons (living or dead), events or locations is entirely coincidental.

Bell Bridge Books
PO BOX 300921
Memphis, TN 38130
Print ISBN: 978-1-61194-628-4

Bell Bridge Books is an Imprint of BelleBooks, Inc.

Revised and updated copyright © 2015 by Kathleen Eagle

Published in the United States of America.

A mass market edition of this book was published by Silhouette Books, New York, 1988

We at BelleBooks enjoy hearing from readers.
Visit our websites
BelleBooks.com
BellBridgeBooks.com
ImaJinnBooks.com

10 9 8 7 6 5 4 3 2 1

Cover design: Debra Dixon
Interior design: Hank Smith
Photo/Art credits:
Couple (manipulated) © John Wollwerth | Dreamstime.com
Horses (manipulated) © Maria Itina | Dreamstime.com

:Ltby:01:

Dedication

For my family,
both sides now.

Prologue

SAGE PARKER hated being locked up. He clenched his jaw when he heard the steel door clank shut behind his back. More than one judge had declared just the sound to be enough to convince a man to mend his ways. It was a sound that chilled the blood, all right. That sound, combined with the taste of stale cigarette smoke and the smell of dirty socks, never failed to start his gut churning. But neither the sound nor any part of this place had ever convinced him to do anything.

Sage glanced over his shoulder at the man in uniform, who jangled the keys on the big key ring and jerked his chin toward the cot near the far wall. "He's got ten minutes before he goes to court, Sage. You know the drill."

Sage knew it well. He nodded as he shoved his hands into the pockets of jeans faded honestly through years of wear. No matter how many times he'd been here, no matter what the circumstances, it never got any easier. He dragged his boot heels against the cement floor as he approached the cot.

"How're you doing, Jackie?"

The man sitting on the cot had heard the sound of the cell door, too, but he didn't budge. He hung his head, stared at the patch of floor between his feet, and hugged himself around the middle. The question went unanswered.

Sage looked down at the top of the man's head and struggled against the urge to turn around and walk out. This was the drunk he most hated seeing—the one who had fallen off the wagon after a period of sobriety. It had disgusted him at first, but he knew the feeling was a cover-up. Truly, it scared the hell out of him. Finally, it humbled him. He laid a hand on Jackie's shoulder and sat beside him on the cot.

"Got the shakes, huh?" Jackie didn't have to answer that question, either. Sage felt the man's tremors under his hand. The tribal judge would commit Jackie to a detoxification program, but shock was a danger at the moment. "Are you going to make it, Jackie?"

Jackie shook his head slowly. "I dunno, Sage. I dunno. I don't feel too good. I just dunno." The litany became a hoarse whisper.

With a glance, Sage acknowledged the watchful eye of the closed-circuit camera. The officer at the front desk had seen the bulge of the airplane bottle Sage carried in his breast pocket when he made calls like this. Nothing was said. There was a tacit understanding that Sage Parker knew what he was doing. He drew a deep breath and exhaled slowly.

"You think a shot would straighten you out enough to get you to detox?"

Jackie turned his head and let Sage see the hope his words had sparked in bleary, bloodshot eyes. Sage scorned that false hope, but he couldn't help sympathizing with the man for being sucked in by it. He pulled the bottle from his breast pocket and broke the seal. About a shot and a half—enough to share—and it was a good brand. Sage had always bought the best when he was buying. He tipped the bottle to Jackie's lips and administered the gin carefully. A dose of medicine. Jackie reached up, but Sage held the bottle tightly, pulling it away as Jackie swallowed.

"Thanks." Jackie wiped his mouth with the back of a shaky hand. "The rest of that's just gonna go to waste, Sage."

"Yeah, well . . ." Sage lifted a shoulder as he capped the bottle. "Better to waste the gin than get wasted ourselves." He slipped the bottle back into his pocket and gripped Jackie's shoulder again. "Right, buddy?" Jackie nodded dumbly. "You'll stop shaking in a minute."

"For a while, at least."

"Yes," Sage said quietly. "For a while."

The keys rattled in the lock again, and both men looked up. "Time to face the music, Jackie."

Sage helped Jackie to his feet. The handcuffs were always the worst part. The clicking sound pinched his heart.

"Think he'll be okay for an hour or so?" the officer asked Sage.

"He won't make it through any lectures from the judge."

"You've heard 'em all, anyway," said the policeman with a laugh. "Haven't you, Jackie?"

Jackie cast a soulful look over his shoulder. "I'm sorry, Sage. I met up with a couple guys I haven't seen in a while. Just wanted to hang out." He gave a tremulous sigh. "Six months down the tubes now, huh?"

"You'll start over." Sage nodded toward the open door. "First things first, Jackie. We'll be waiting for you."

"I was doin' good, though, wasn't I?"

"You were doing great."

Jackie squared his shoulders and crossed the threshold with his escort. "See? I was doin' great."

"You weren't doing so great when they picked you up last night," the officer had to remind him.

Sage was glad to walk out of the cell. He put his hand over his breast pocket as he watched the man in uniform lead Jackie down the hall. He could feel the heat of the liquid burning his hand through the glass and the cotton cloth. No matter how vehemently he denied it, the old longing nagged at the weaker part of his brain. He gave the men's room door a hard shove and strode to the sink to pour the rest of the stuff out. He never carried a bottle with a broken seal, and he never tossed a loaded bottle, not even the single-shot model. He rinsed it out before he dropped it in the trash. If he'd left any corners, it was only water, which couldn't hurt anybody. Sage was thorough. He had to be. He was responsible for his own actions, and he had the weaker part of his brain to consider.

Chapter 1

SUN-BRONZED AND bare to the waist, the man wielding the jack-hammer was an arresting sight. His flesh vibrated as though charged by the power he held in his grip. A red bandanna kept the sweat out of his eyes, but his body was beaded with it, and the moisture glistened like the mica in a granite road cut in the South Dakota sun. Small beads gathered in the valley mid-chest, forming a rivulet that made a quick run to the sleek plane of his abdomen and disappeared into his jeans.

Megan's gaze skittered over the power tool framed by the man's flexed-knee stance. Its bit gouged without mercy at the face of bedrock that had been gauged, sampled, and declared by Megan McBride to be in the way of progress. She wondered how this man felt about changing the face of the earth. After all, he was an Indian—Native American, she amended mentally—and traditionally they resented the kinds of changes she was in the business of making. Perhaps it didn't offend him too much. He was doing his job and doing it well. If he had any sense that he was being watched, he gave no indication of it as he concentrated on his work.

"Sage Parker."

Megan jumped at the words shouted close to her ear. She turned a questioning look at the older man who stood behind her shoulder. Didn't Bob think she knew the names of the men on her crew by now? "Good man," Bob said. "Let's go back to the trailer where we can talk."

The noise level wouldn't be much better in the mobile office, but at least it would be possible to talk there. The machine-gun rattle of the jackhammer became distant as they made their way down a steep grade, turning their feet sideways to keep from sliding. Bob Krueger was a gentleman of the old school, prepared to offer Megan a hand despite the fact that her young body handled this activity far more gracefully than his older one did, but her guarded glance put the brakes on his impulse. She was the engineer in charge of a road construction project with an all-male crew. She was mindful of watching her step.

She noted the progress of the big yellow earthmovers. The operators monitored one another, each challenging himself to move more dirt than the other. It was a form of competition that kept an otherwise tedious job interesting. They would blast through more rock before the day was out, and if all went well, they would remain on schedule.

"How're you getting along with Taylor?" Bob offered the question after they'd closed the trailer door and shut the worst of the dust outside.

Megan eyed her foreman's desk. He wasn't much of a recordkeeper, and the desk showed little sign of organized use.

"So far, so good," she said. "But, in *his* mind, I think the project is yours, and I'm just a messenger."

Bob sat on the corner of Megan's desk, clear of all but two file folders and a clipboard. She was careful to protect her work from the fine dust that was always in the air on a construction site.

"For all intents and purposes, this *is* your project, Megan. Has Taylor challenged your authority in any way?" Bob asked. He was a veteran of the Highway Department and a man with enough experience to know that skill was the measure of a good highway engineer.

"Not yet," Megan said as she pulled out a file drawer. "But I think he'd like to. Whenever we talk, I get the feeling there's one more thing he wants to say, but he decides he hasn't quite got me figured out well enough to risk it."

"Are you ready with a response?"

She withdrew a folder and gave the older man a smile. "How long have you known me, Bob?"

"Since you started with the highway department. What was it? Five—six years ago?"

"Eight, if you count my summers on the survey crew." She raised an eyebrow as she slid the drawer shut. "I'll admit I didn't always have a ready response in those days, but since then I've regularly updated my repertoire."

"Loaded with classics, I'm sure."

Megan laughed. "Whatever brings the most respect. With these guys, that's likely to be honky-tonk rather than classical."

Bob chuckled as Megan handed him the folder. He flipped it open. "Anyone else causing you any problems?" She was his protégé, and he wanted this project to go well almost as much as she did.

"Not really. Not . . . seriously." Bob glanced up from the first page of her report and waited for a follow-up. She folded her arms and leaned back against the edge of the desk. "A couple of the men seem to have trouble getting themselves to work sometimes."

"Transportation problems?"

She lifted her shoulder. "They've offered that as an excuse once or twice."

"Are they pals with Taylor or something?"

Megan chortled. "Hardly."

"It doesn't matter. A lot of guys are looking for work, Megan. Don't put up with any—"

"Taylor would like to fire them." With a look, she told him how uncomfortable she was with the problem. "We had very few applications from Native Americans, and I don't want to fire the ones we've got. They're good workers, but there are two men, one in particular . . ."

"Not Parker, I hope."

Megan shook her head quickly. "No, Parker's completely reliable."

Bob nodded and smiled. "Parker's the best man on your crew. I'd hate to hear he wasn't making it to work."

Visions of the man flashed through Megan's mind. Parker could handle almost any job on the site, from heavy equipment to explosives. In her business, she saw brawny, sweaty men all the time. It was Sage Parker's versatility that caught her attention, not his virility. Reliability, versatility—attributes that mattered. His good looks were part of the vision, sure—visions were *visual*—but the part of the vision that mattered was the work that was getting done.

"So why don't you see if he can help you with the others?"

Megan frowned. "Who? Parker?"

"If you're not ready to fire these guys, you might get some ideas on how to handle them from Parker. I hear he's got some kind of recovery program going on the reservation."

"Recovery program?" She pronounced the words as though they were part of a foreign tongue.

"For alcoholism."

"Nobody said these men had a drinking problem, and I haven't seen any reason to . . ." She folded her arms. "I'm not jumping to any conclusions."

"Of course you're not," Bob said calmly. "Neither am I. I'm suggesting you let Parker in on your concern and see what he's got to say. I've worked with him off and on over the years. He's put down a lot of miles."

"You don't think he'd . . . take offense?"

"You're the boss here, Megan. And you're the only woman." Bob nodded toward the door and offered a conspiratorial grin. "For the most part these guys are worried about offending *you*."

WHENEVER KARL Taylor went to the office, there were bets taken. One of these days he was bound to make the same kind of remark to McBride's face as he made behind her back, and one of them was going to come flying out the door. Some said the lady would flee in tears. Others thought she'd kick Taylor out on his ass. Either way, Sage enjoyed the suspense right along with the rest of the crew. They were disappointed once again when Taylor emerged at quitting time and closed the door behind him.

"Hey, it's time to knock off for the day!" he announced. "What's everybody standing around here for? How about a stop at the Red Rooster?"

Sage only half-listened as he buttoned his shirt, calculating the distance between his sweaty body and his shower. He tossed his leather gloves on the pickup seat and dug into his pocket for keys. He smiled when he noticed the way the stiffened gloves had landed, with the fingers curled and clawing at the air. Great for a movie, he thought. *Ravaging Gloves.*

"Hey, Sage."

Sage turned his head toward the hand on his shoulder and looked up at Scott Allen's friendly, sunburned face. "Come on over to the Rooster with us. Let's you and me play some pool."

"Some other time, man. I've got horses standing around a dry stock tank right about now."

"Gotta take some time off once in a while." Scott gave Sage a parting pat on the shoulder. "You work too hard, buddy."

"Making up for lost time," was the reply Sage regularly gave to that comment, but he knew few people really understood what it meant.

"Parker!" Taylor's voice brought Sage around again, this time more slowly. He needed the extra seconds to call up his patience. "Boss lady wants to see you before you take off." Taylor snatched off his cap and wiped his forehead with his sleeve. He chuckled as he put it back on and adjusted the bill. "Ain't that a crock? My wife's the only 'boss lady' I ever expected to answer to, and there's no way in hell she'd take on a job like this."

"Thought you said your wife used to flag," Scott said.

"Back when she was husband hunting. Now she's home raising kids."

Sage stuffed his shirttails into his jeans and slammed his pickup door. He'd heard enough of Taylor's wisdom on women. He wanted to tell the ruddy-faced foreman that spouting that kind of crap on this particular job was a sure sign of his insecurity, but Sage needed the work. The fact that the engineer on the project was a woman didn't bother him. Being summoned to the boss's office was another matter.

"Hey, Sage, why don't you stop in for something cold to drink?" another man asked as he walked by.

"I already asked him, Randy. He's gotta get home."

Sage offered the two young men a smile and lifted a forefinger as he walked past their pickup. "You have one for me, Randy. Just one."

"The legend lives on," Scott teased. "You entered up in the bronc riding this weekend, Sage? I'd like to have a chance to beat you out, just once."

Sage laughed. "You wish. The legend lives on because I know when to quit. You guys take it easy."

Sage lifted the bandanna from his head, raked his fingers through his hair, wadded the cloth and stuck it in his back pocket. The metal steps wobbled under his work boots as he took a deep breath and reached for the doorknob. He'd turned this summons over in his mind several times, and he couldn't come up with a reason for it. He'd been doing his job. He'd done every task Taylor had tossed at him, and he'd never been late for work. But experience told him that being called to the office generally meant he was about to be reprimanded, and he'd never handled that well.

When McBride looked up from the chart on her desk and smiled, his first thought was, *Don't do that, lady. It makes you look too damn cute.*

On second thought, hadn't he outgrown that first thought?

"Taylor said you wanted to see me."

"Yes. I know it's time to go home, and I promise not to keep you long." She rose from her chair and moved to the front of the desk.

Sage stood about as close to her now as he'd ever been, and it occurred to him that he hadn't noticed how small she was. She wore her honey-blond hair cropped short in back and styled longer on top. He didn't see any makeup, and the clarity in those deep blue eyes made him uneasy. It wasn't a look he could deal with. There was nothing hazy or frosty or even provocative about it. Her eyes were simply bright and clear.

"Bob Krueger was here today. He's pleased with our progress." She folded her arms and leaned back against the desk. There was nothing feminine about her khaki jumpsuit—except maybe the way she had the collar turned up in the back—or her lace-up work boots, besides the fact that they were the smallest pair he'd ever seen. Sage shoved his hands into his pockets and waited for her to come to the point. "He had high praise for you."

But? "I've worked on a few of Bob's projects."

"So he said. You seem to be trained for every job on the site."

"I've had a lot of experience in highway construction."

"Are you an engineer, too?"

He returned her level gaze. "I've had some vocational training, but I've never been to college." He jerked his chin toward a cabinet. "That's all in your files. Somebody decided I was qualified for this job, and they hired me."

"I think you're *over*qualified, Sage. You should have applied for foreman."

Sage scowled. What was this all about, anyway? "We've got a foreman on this project, and you're the engineer. My paycheck's the same whether I set charges or operate a blade."

"I just want you to know the opportunity's there the next time you apply. Bob thinks very highly of you."

Sage drew his hands out of his pockets slowly as he struggled to fit the pieces of this conversation together. That clarity he'd seen in her eyes might have been misleading.

"Am I being fired from *this* project, or what?"

"Of course not. I just wanted to pass Bob's compliment on to the person who should hear it, and then . . ." She raised her eyebrows in a kind of confession. "I wanted to ask for a favor."

"A favor?"

She braced her hands on the desk at either side of her hips. The suit she wore gave no hint of the shape of those hips, but the crisp cotton fabric had stretched across her thighs when she leaned back. It wasn't the first time he'd caught himself wondering about those thighs.

"Advice, really," she said. "I don't know what to do about Jackie Flying Elk. He hasn't been to work for two days, and Karl wants to fire him."

Sage drew a long breath and released it slowly. He had to remind himself that, yes, Jackie was also a concern of his. He'd taken four hours' leave on Jackie's account. But his concern wasn't the same as his *business*, and the man was responsible for his own job. This woman had called him in here to talk about one of her employees just because he was Lakota.

She paused for about two seconds, but Sage made no comment. "Jackie is very good at his job, and I don't want to fire him."

She waited another two seconds. Was he supposed to thank her?

"I'd like to give him another chance. He's got to get back here tomorrow or have a good excuse, Sage. I can't—"

"Why are you telling me this?"

"Well . . ." She glanced down at her knees. She knew it was a good question, and he wondered how long it would take her to come up with a straight answer. "I can't find a phone number for him."

"He doesn't have a phone. I can tell you where he lives." Not the response she was looking for. The look told him he hadn't been wrong about those eyes. They hid nothing.

"I thought maybe you could talk to him. You're friends, aren't you?"

"Of course. Jackie Flying Elk, Gary Little Bird, Lawrence Archambault. Who else have you got? We're all buddies. I even get along pretty good with some of the white guys on the crew."

The woman pushed her fingers through her hair and cast a glance at the ceiling. Now he'd done it.

"I'm going about this all wrong." She braced her hands against the desk again. "I was hoping you'd talk to Jackie. Tell him to come back to work tomorrow. I don't know what else to do."

Sage shrugged. "If Jackie's run out of chances, you do what you have to." And he wouldn't be making any suggestions.

"I'm trying to be fair." Cornered, McBride bristled like a cat, but there would be no hissing. She collected herself almost instantly, and her all-biz tone never wavered. "I've wondered. . . . It's possible that Jackie has a drinking problem, and if he does—"

"It's also possible that *I* have a drinking problem." And probable that she'd heard all about it.

"If you do, it doesn't interfere with your work." Her fur was up again. "In Jackie's case, it will mean the loss of his job. He's definitely letting it get out of hand if it's . . . if it's what I think it is."

"You're very perceptive, Miss McBride. It does sound like Jackie might have a problem." He might as well take what pleasure he could from this conversation. She was every bit as uncomfortable now as he'd been when he'd first come through the door. "I can't solve it for him."

"All I'm asking you to do," she said carefully, "is *talk* to him. Tell him to be here at eight tomorrow morning."

"Jackie won't make it to work tomorrow, and no amount of talk is going to change that."

Megan's shoulders sagged, and she looked as though he'd just surprised her with an unexpected checkmate. "Why not?"

"Because he's sick, Miss McBride."

"Why didn't you tell me that in the first place? If he's sick—"

"He *was* drunk. Now he's sick. It takes a while to dry out."

She would have kept the desk between them, but his answer surprised her. All she wanted to hear was, *sure, I can talk to him.* Just that. But he was standing there telling her things that made her uneasy, and there was no emotion whatever in his dark eyes. If she had her desk and her charts and her aerial photographs spread out between them, she would feel stronger. She thought of Jackie, who worked like a beaver and kept the crew laughing at his jokes. "Is he in jail?"

"He's in a detoxification unit."

"Could we call that a hospital?"

"You can call it whatever you want. They have some medical people on call." He glanced away. "Shouldn't've said anything."

"Would they be able to give me any indication of how long—"

"Look, you're not gonna know what they can tell you unless you call and ask." He lifted one corner of his mouth in a humorless smile. "You don't have to risk actually setting foot on Big Thunder soil, Miss McBride. The detox unit has a phone."

"I have been to the reservation," she said patiently. "Please understand that Jackie's problem bears no reflection on the Native American members of our crew. Anyone who misses work without calling in gets a warning, a reprimand, and then—"

"He gets canned. If you have a policy, why aren't you sticking to it?"

Megan came away from the desk and took a stance that said she might be willing to square off with this man in defense of the poor man she'd hoped he would defend. "I believe the circumstances might be mitigating," she said.

"In what way?"

"He . . ." Pick something, she told herself. "You said yourself Jackie doesn't have a phone."

"So I did."

"And you said he was sick."

He'd said it once. His level stare said he hadn't changed his mind.

"Illness is a valid excuse for missing work."

"So there you have it." Half smiling, he raised his brow. "Your problem is solved."

"But for how long?"

"Good question." Sage had been standing over a jackhammer most of the day. He decided Taylor owed him a seat, so he sat on the foreman's desk. "What are you going to do about Gary Little Bird?"

"He's not as bad. He's only missed one day without calling in. He got a warning."

"You must have forgiven the day he came to work an hour late."

"He had car trouble."

"Did he?" He folded his arms across his chest. "Did you know that before this weekend, Jackie hadn't had a drink in six months?"

"But he's—"

"Missed work. I know. Because he drives an Indian car." He lifted one shoulder. "Or should I say *Native American*? Probably came out of Detroit. We buy American made, American used. Before the summer's over, my pickup will be sitting along the road halfway between my place and here, and I'll be tinkering under the hood for most of the morning. It's heated up on me twice in the last week."

"If that happens—"

"You'll dock me. That's the policy." He stood up and tucked his thumbs in the pockets of his jeans. "Look, Miss McBride, I'm sure you mean well. You know, by rights it's Taylor who runs the crew. I'll do what I can for Jackie, but that doesn't include taking care of him on the job. I suggest you make that call and pump them for answers."

On impulse, Megan offered a handshake.

"Thank you for your time, Sage. I've learned a great deal, and I hope you didn't feel like I was being . . ." Her hand disappeared in his. She knew because she looked. He didn't squeeze, didn't shake, merely closed his big hand around her small one. It felt so good that she lost her train of thought and had to miss one or two beats before she could wind the meeting up on the appropriate high note. "Bob Krueger *did* say you were the best man I had on this crew. I thought you should know that."

Sage nodded, released her hand, and left without another word.

HIS FAMILY HAD lived on the western side of Big Thunder Indian Reservation for at least five generations. Before that, they had been part of the nomadic Lakota people, also known as west river Sioux. They were not related to the Comanche Parkers, but he was often asked if the famous Quanah Parker had been an ancestor. So far as he knew, he had no famous ancestors. His great-grandmother had married a mixed-blood named Parker, who had given her his name and his child and then wandered away.

Sage turned his battered blue pickup at the approach to his part of Parker land and drove between the two huge posts that had been set there in better days. The crossbar had fallen some time ago. Sage had set a goal for himself. When he owned a hundred head of cattle outright, he would put up another crossbar and hang a sign. With a hundred head, he could call his place a ranch again.

His piece of prairie bordered some of the most scenic land east of the Black Hills—the South Dakota Badlands. The government had once ceded all this land to the Lakota, including the Black Hills, but gold had been discovered, and the Hills had been seized once white occupation had become an accomplished fact. The Lakota were assigned to various Dakota Territory reservations, which shrank in size over the years. Sage's people had been given a site within teasing reach of the sacred Hills. The Badlands had been a farcical substitute.

Later, the government decided that the Badlands were unique in their own way, and Badlands National Park was created. It had the look of terrain from a science fiction film. Tourists remarked that it certainly was stark, beautiful, *bad* land, and they traveled on to the Black Hills to see the faces of the presidents. Sage leased government land, the land that had once been part of Big Thunder but was now called "public domain," and his stock grazed it. Even through his darkest days, he had managed to salvage his claim to the land.

He'd lost his home, but he was feeling no pain by the time he'd stepped aside and watched a truck haul it away. The pain came later. Not much later, but much pain. Now, he was replacing the double-wide he'd shared with his family with a house, and he was building it himself, board by board.

He parked the pickup near the barn and peered between the corral rails. There stood the five horses for whom the roar of the blue pickup was a call to dinner. Sage was glad to see them, too. He remembered the day six years ago when he'd sold the last of his horses. It had been like selling his soul. His uncle Vern bought the last two, and he'd given Sage a terrible look of pity as he'd led them away. Sage never wanted to see that look again, and he'd vowed to feed his horses at least as well as he fed himself.

He balanced himself on the top of the corral, anchoring his boot heels on the second rail. At his back, the five horses ground their oats with teeth that were as efficient as any millstone. It made good music, a rich, rhythmical sound. His father had measured his own success by the number of horses he'd owned. Sage lifted his head toward the eastern horizon and watched his cows amble over the hill in single file, following the well-worn path their predecessors had made for them. He kept them close while the calves were new, and the stock tank was their watering hole for now. Later he would move them out to the hills for better grazing.

Here was more wealth, Sage told himself. Fourteen cows, and all but one had calved successfully. The dry cow would be sold and replaced. Not many ranchers would consider fourteen cows a measure of wealth, but few had learned as Sage had. The cows were hard-earned. They were living testament to his effort to rebuild his life. The house, even in its skeletal state, was a beginning. It stood on the spot where the old house had been. Not the big trailer house the bank had financed when he'd started out. Not the little three-room job the government had built for his parents when *they* were starting out, the one everybody had called a "six-fifty" when more land had been taken in return for houses built for six-hundred and fifty dollars each. No, Sage's new house would stand where the cabin his grandparents had occupied when he was a young child once stood.

He was putting it there because he needed to recall that time. He needed to reconnect himself with those good memories. During the summer when they'd built the log house, the family had lived in a tent that stood near the grove of cottonwoods. Only the cottonwoods hadn't been there then. They'd made a baseball diamond where the corral now stood, and his family had been its own team. His father's cousin's family, the rival team, had lived four miles away. Those had indeed been good times, and it was worth digging back through all the baggage of what his life had been in the interim to recall them.

He might have pitched a tent for himself for the summer, but he wouldn't finish the house before winter. The little silver turtle of a trailer he lived in served his needs adequately. It provided enough hot water for the quick shower he'd been looking forward to, along with a refrigerator large enough to preserve the hamburger he was about to cook and a bed that held—as long as he slept corner to corner—all but his feet. He worked hard enough during the day so that the size of the bed didn't matter when he finally fell into it at night. Nor did the fact that he slept alone bother him. At least he wasn't hurting anyone. Not anymore.

He eyed the trailer and thought of Megan McBride. She worked in a little trailer, but he was sure she didn't live in one. In the last few weeks, he'd permitted himself one foolish indulgence. From a safe distance, he'd watched McBride at work. It hadn't troubled him that a woman was engineering the construction project. In his culture, women took charge as a matter of course, though they spoiled their men in the way of women everywhere. It *had* disturbed him when he realized he'd begun to fantasize about her, but he continued to indulge himself. He enjoyed watching her assert her authority on the job. She was smart. She knew hot mix from cold, at least in terms of asphalt. She knew the lay of the land and the shape of the plan. He wondered about the shape of the legs she hid under her jumpsuits. He wondered how strong they were, how agile, how smooth. He'd bet on those heavy work boots housing slender ankles and small, feminine toes.

There were other women in his life—those he met with at least twice a week in the recovery group he'd christened Medicine Wheel. The difference was that Megan McBride was unattainable, which made it safe to think about her. Safe, maybe, but unwise. He'd come to grips with that fact earlier that day when she'd turned the tables on him. *She'd* watched *him* work. She'd observed his skill, the progress he was making, the way his piece of work fit into the scheme of the project. Those things she'd seen through the eyes of an engineer. But she'd lingered, and he'd felt the scrutiny of a woman's eyes. A man knew when a woman was taking a good look at his chest. When he was doing a man's work, his form was at its best. *Take a good look, woman. Look your fill.*

Later, she'd asked him to discuss problems that were human and not mechanical, and another barrier had been ripped away. He saw through her. She was a caretaker, a do-gooder, pure and simple. That was the characteristic that drew them to one another, and the one he had to avoid.

Still, he wondered what she had seen when she'd looked at him through a woman's eyes.

Chapter 2

SOUTH DAKOTA'S chain of jewels was the Black Hills. Megan loved her job because it took her outdoors, and this was her favorite part of a state that boasted a wonderful variety of terrain. She had worked her science in all corners of it. Nearly flat farmland stretched over the eastern portion of the state. Heading west, the land began to pucker into rolling hills and buttes that were harbingers of what one would find nearly two hundred miles from the wide Missouri, the river bisecting the state from north to south. But the hint did little to prepare the traveler for that first glimpse of the Hills, which appeared in the distance as a blue-black uprising against a sky that had thoroughly dominated the vista over hundreds of South Dakota miles.

Megan's project involved paving a stretch of gravel running east-west in the southern portion of the Hills. To the east was the Big Thunder Sioux Indian Reservation. The town of Hot Springs was to the southwest. The tourists' hills—with granite sculptures, gold mines and little towns still rowdy enough to be called Western—stood to the north. Beneath this land lay a maze of caverns, an underground world built by subterranean water and as yet largely unexplored. This tourist's dream could become a highway engineer's nightmare. The initial survey and sample work for this project was proving unreliable.

Karl Taylor straightened slowly as he looked up from the charts spread across his "boss lady's" desk. Megan stood on the opposite side, arms folded, waiting for a response. "So how much deeper you think you're gonna go?" he finally asked.

His tone made it clear that he intended to object to her answer, whatever it was. He'd obviously been waiting for a good place to draw the line, and this would be it. Like the South Dakota buttes, his regularly scheduled objections to her decisions had been harbingers of an inevitable uprising.

"I'm projecting ten feet, but it might be more."

"Ten *feet?* That's a major change in the plans."

"I realize that."

The door opened, and both of them turned as Sage Parker stepped in and closed it behind him. Taylor lifted an accusing eyebrow at Megan and planted his fist on either his waist or his hip. His body was as lacking in contour as his mouth was in restraint.

"I sent for Parker because he's running the scraper," Megan said.

"So what? I'm running Parker, along with the rest of the crew."

"*I'm* running the *project*. This stretch has turned out to be a slough." Megan tapped the topographical map with a closely trimmed fingernail. "We'll dig out the clay even if we have to go down fifteen or twenty feet, and we'll backfill it. I also want to raise the grade so we get better—"

"Raise the grade? You're talking major changes, McBride. Look at this, Parker." Like an eager woodpecker, Taylor's finger drummed at a spot on the map. "She's talking ten, twenty feet down here, which means bringing in more heavy equipment."

The Scene was one Sage would have preferred to walk out on. Taylor was the construction foreman, and McBride was the engineer. It was up to them to have this out and then let him know how to set up his equipment. He would move as much dirt as he was told to move. Against his own better judgment, he stepped closer to the desk and glanced at the fingerprint Taylor had made on the map. He didn't need a picture. He'd been out there digging in it.

"This is a big job, McBride," Taylor said. "And you're making it bigger. Have you checked with Krueger?"

"He's out on a site." McBride thrust her hands into the pockets of her jumpsuit. "The changes are necessary," she said quietly. "There's no question."

"There's plenty of question." Taylor gave the map a final tap with his knuckles and turned to Sage. "Wouldn't you say, Parker?"

Sage eyed Taylor's red, round face, then McBride's, which was smooth and tanned that golden shade that only a true blonde seemed to be able to achieve. He figured this threesome could line up two ways in Taylor's so-called mind: two whites and one Indian, in which case the discussion was between them, or two men and one woman. For some reason, Taylor had chosen the latter. Did he think Sage would feel honored?

Sage smiled to himself as he glanced down at the map again. "I've paved over this stuff before, Taylor. You have, too. In another year, you'll have more potholes than blacktop, and you'll have to resurface."

"So we resurface," Taylor said. "That's not our problem right now. The problem is, the specs don't call for all this digging and backfilling. I say get Krueger out here and see what he says before we make any decisions."

"*We* don't have a decision to make. It's my design," McBride insisted. "It needs to be changed, and I'm changing it."

"Fine." Taylor reached out and snatched the pencil that was perched above Megan's ear. He grinned as he handed it to her. "You go right ahead and change your *design*. Let me know if Krueger approves it." He turned to Sage and nodded toward the door. "Shut the equipment down, Parker. We're knocking off for the day."

Her eyes turned icy, and her jaw became rigid. Sage felt the heat of her humiliation. Out of respect, he did not permit himself to pity her. He told her with a brief look that her self-control had not gone unnoticed. Her glance was just as quick and no less communicative. In good time, she would make her point without losing her temper. It was not her knowledge at issue; it was her authority.

BOB KRUEGER UPHELD her decision, and the digging proceeded. Krueger warned Taylor against giving Megan any problems, and Taylor cheerfully accepted both the warning and the order to proceed with the changes. Both had come from a man. If a man wanted to drag this job out, Taylor had no objections.

Megan had hoped to see the digging completed before the first inevitable June downpour, but two days later, she knew it wasn't to be. Between the subterranean water and the deluge from the sky, the crew was up to its knees in water, and they were again two men short. Taylor's cheer was short-lived.

"I tell you what," Taylor shouted over the roar of a compressor used to power the water pumps. "If those two Indians aren't back on the job tomorrow, I'm gonna ship 'em both off to an equal opportunity cannery."

Megan glanced at Sage, who was busy arranging a compressor hose and had no visible reaction to Taylor's remark. She hoped he hadn't heard it. "Gary called in," she told Taylor. "He couldn't get out to the highway, and he said Jackie's road is pure gumbo."

"Yeah, well, *we're* here." He gestured widely at the men sitting in their cars and pickups. "These guys are here."

The sky was gunmetal gray, and the hilltops were lost in the thickness of it. Megan adjusted her yellow slicker collar as another runnel of rainwater slithered down the back of her neck. "This isn't going to break today," she said. "We just need someone to stay and man the pumps."

"Parker!"

Parker. As always, it was Parker. She watched Taylor shout orders into Sage's face. Water dripped from the brim of Sage's orange hardhat as he offered a calm reply. Taylor slogged over to a blue pickup, and Megan heard him tell Randy Whiteman to relieve Sage on the pumps at two o'clock that afternoon.

Heading for his own pickup, Taylor backpedaled a few steps as he announced to Megan, "I'm outta here. If this lets up, I'll see you tomorrow." He turned on his heel, slipped, flailed wildly, and narrowly missed planting his butt in the mud. "Damn moon shit," he muttered as he took more care trekking across the slick organic goop that was a road builder's worst enemy.

Tires spun and threw gravel in their wake as, one by one, the crew members' vehicles took to the road. The unimproved cutoff was closed to through traffic, forcing other drivers to use the longer paved route, a twenty-mile jog to the south. On a day like this, Megan figured the paved route was preferable, although the plan she was formulating for herself would take her over a long stretch of gravel road within the hour.

The *thunk* of a closing door drew her head around. Sage had taken shelter in his old blue pickup. She'd intended to offer him the office. Rain tapped on her hard hat. Mud sucked at her work boots as she made her way to the passenger side and rapped at the window. The other door opened, and he did a chin-up over the roof of the cab.

"Come around this side," she was told. "That door doesn't open."

She could hear the seesaw moan of a steel guitar playing on the radio, but he flicked it off when she reached his side. He pushed the door open, and she stuck her head inside. Water dripped from her hat onto his jeans.

"Would you like to use the office?" she asked.

His face was inches from hers. "I need to stay close to the pump in case it clogs up."

"May I speak with you for a moment?"

"Come on in." He slid over.

"I'll get your seat wet."

He laughed and nodded at the puddle she was making under the steering wheel. "You'll get *your* seat wet." He grabbed a faded blue towel from the dashboard and wiped the driver's seat. "You wanna give me your slicker? Mine's over here on the floor."

Sage took another swipe with the towel just before Megan's butt claimed the seat. She pulled the door shut, dropped her hat to the floor, and tossed her head, flinging droplets like a lawn sprinkler. He blotted his face with the towel.

"Oh. I'm sorry."

"Let's face it." He smiled and tossed her the towel. "We're wet. Should I turn on some heat?"

"Not for me. I'm fine." She gave her nape a brisk rub with the terry-cloth. "Do you mind doing this?"

"What?"

"Staying to man the pumps."

"It's better than losing a day's pay."

She turned to find him watching her. His hair dangled across his forehead and curved over his damp collar like black fringe. The chambray and denim covering his shoulders and his thighs were soaked, and she imagined his socks were as wet as hers. "I'm glad it's your choice," she said. "Everybody else seems to have specialized, while you're always doing something different. I wondered if Taylor was assigning you whatever nobody else wanted to do."

"Taylor might have a bad mouth on him, but he knows his dirt." Sage raked his fingers through his hair in a vain attempt to push it back from his forehead. "I've got a lot of experience, and he doesn't mind making use of it. Neither do I."

The rain pattered against the roof of the pickup. Megan peered through the windshield at the big yellow bulldozer sitting idle only a few yards away. "Still, nobody likes to sit around all day in wet clothes."

"Then maybe somebody oughta go home and change." He smiled when she turned to him again. "I've been ranching most of my life," he said. "I spend a lot of time in wet clothes."

"And I've got a stop to make before I can go back to Hot Springs, so I'll be wet a while longer, too."

She was dancing around her purpose for being in his pickup, but she'd get there eventually. She was the boss, didn't really need an ally, but it would be good to have one on site. And Parker was the one she wanted.

"Want some coffee?" He leaned toward her and reached under her legs, smiling at the wary look she gave him. "It's under the seat."

"Coffee would be great." She tried to stem the shiver that crept along her spine, but it won out, spreading in ripples to all her extremities.

Sage tossed the Thermos bottle into his left hand and reached for the keys with his right. "Hit the accelerator," he said as he turned on the ignition. "A little heat wouldn't hurt, either."

"I guess not. I hate it when my socks get wet."

"So do I." He spun the cap on the Thermos and stuck it between his knees while he unscrewed the stopper. "Take them off and let them dry out." He glanced past the rising steam at the gauges behind the steering wheel. "I've got enough gas to keep the heat on for a while."

"But you have to be able to get home. How far is it?"

"From here to my place? About thirty-five miles. Just across the line." He handed her the coffee he'd poured. "We'll have to share. I don't have an extra cup."

Megan held the cup close to her nose and inhaled the rich aroma of strong, black coffee. The steam warmed her face as she sipped. "Mmm," she murmured between sips. "Perfect. What line?"

"The one between Indian Country and everyplace else. But I make *cowboy* coffee."

"I like strong coffee. On a day like this, you could set up a stand."

He chuckled. "I don't see too many prospective customers."

"Which leads you to wonder why I'm still here." Without meeting his eyes, she handed him the cup.

"The thought crossed my mind." He tasted the coffee from what was now their shared cup and grimaced. "This isn't my best. I had to hurry it up this morning. Had to fix a gate the horses knocked down."

"And you still made it to work on time." She turned toward him and rested her elbow on the steering wheel. "Taylor was gunning for Gary and Jackie again this morning."

"I heard."

"Word got around quickly, I'm sure." She drew a deep breath and sighed. "I don't want you to take offense at the things he says, Sage."

"Why?"

"Well, because you're doing such a good job. Taylor has such a—"

"No, I mean what's with *you* not wanting *me* to take offense? If I take offense, it'll be between me and Taylor. Why does that concern you?"

"Because Taylor's a bigot, and the project could suffer from his attitude. If he keeps this up and we lose all our Indians. I mean, our Native—"

Sage's laughter cut her short. "Lose all our Indians?" He shook his head, still snickering. "Ah, that's a good one. Anything like losing all our marbles? You're gonna lose yours just trying to figure out what to call us."

"Native Americans." She folded her arms and lifted her chin. "I *meant* to say Native Americans. I know that's what you prefer to be called."

"Who told you that?" He eyed her over the rim of the cup as he sipped the hot coffee.

"I think I read that the preferred term is currently—" She looked at him across the narrow distance between them. There was something steamy about his very presence. She'd read that Indians considered it rude to look directly into a person's face, but he was frankly assessing hers. His amusement lingered as a bright sheen in his dark eyes. "I seem to be saying the wrong things again," she said quietly. "What do you prefer to be called?"

"Sage."

She smiled as he handed her the cup. "It's an unusual name."

"Lots of Parkers around, but you won't run across too many Sages." He lifted one shoulder. "We've got some Native Americans at Big Thunder. And we've got some Indians who aren't up on the current term. Columbus called us Indians, but he'd pretty much lost his marbles by then. Or his compass, or some damn thing. And America was named for some Italian guy."

"How about Sioux, then?"

"That's the French version of what the Chippewa called us, and it was sort of like being called a snake in the grass. The old ones say we're Lakota, which has nothing to do with being from a certain place or being there first. It means 'allies.'" He raised an eyebrow. "Are you lookin' to be an ally of the allies?"

"I certainly don't want to be an enemy." She sipped the coffee and added, "I want to be fair."

"And if the Office of Equal Opportunity Employment is sending anyone out from Washington these days, you want them to see minorities working on this project." He laughed. "They'll see *you*. A woman at the helm must be worth at least half a dozen Indians working as flagmen."

"Indians?"

"Or maybe three Native Americans on 'dozers."

"Sage—"

"Or one damn-near civilized Sioux carrying a clipboard and driving a highway department pickup. That could be very impressive."

She passed him the coffee and held up her other hand in surrender. "Truce, Sage. Please. Complying with OEO regs is somebody else's worry. I'm really trying to be fair. I know jobs are scarce on the reservation, and I'll call you whatever you suggest if you'll just tell me what I can do to persuade Jackie and Gary to stick with us and get to work on time every day."

Sage rested the cup on his knee and looked at her as though he was considering setting aside some doubt. "What do you want to be called?"

She tipped her head to one side, frowning, weighing her options.

"Like you, I'm kind of at a loss," he said. "What do you suggest I call you? Boss lady or Miss McBride?"

"Megan," she said.

"Okay, Megan, here's the deal. If Taylor tries to make this a racial thing, he'll get trouble. I'll report it. If a guy's not getting to work, you deal with *him*, and you don't generalize the issue to include the rest of us. That's just good supervision."

"I think Taylor has it in for the Indians on the crew."

"You might be right." He offered the cup again. "Want another hit?" She shook her head, so he drained it himself. "I think he's got it in for you," he added, gesturing with the empty cup.

"I can handle that."

"And I can handle the other if it comes my way." The cup clattered against the top of the Thermos. He screwed it down tight. "Look, Megan, you've got good instincts, but they're misdirected. Jackie has some growing up to do, and he's determined to do it the hard way. Gary . . ." He gave a careless shrug. "Well, Gary'll hold up his end pretty well and cover for himself when he doesn't. You're giving them equal opportunity. You don't have to wipe their noses and pack their lunches for them."

"That isn't what I had in mind. I'm just trying to be—"

"Fair. I know. If the guys from OEO come around, I'll be sure and tell them how you went out of your way to be fair." He glanced out the side window. "You were dead right about digging this stuff out," he told her. "It's a real deep pocket of pure moon . . . slime."

She smiled, wondering whether he had chosen his words carefully in deference to her gender or her position. She decided it didn't matter. It was a sign of respect either way, and she appreciated it. Early on in her career, she'd taken a stab at talking like one of the guys, and she'd sounded silly. One of *the guys* had done her the favor of telling her that she said the word *shit* funny, like it left an unfamiliar taste in her mouth.

Not his exact words, but what he'd said had cured her.

"I *am* good at what I do. And so are you."

"This is what I do to pay the bills," he told her as he slid the Thermos bottle back under the seat. "What I really do is ranch, and I can be good at that, too, when I put my heart into it."

"Are you . . . do you have a family?"

"Yeah." He sat up slowly and looked her straight in the eye. "I've got two kids. They live with my. . . . They live with their mother in Omaha. We're divorced." A moment passed before the look in his eyes softened, and she wondered what he'd anticipated. Or safeguarded. His wistful smile hinted that her silence was golden. "What about you? Ever been married?"

She gave her head a quick shake. "No. Never."

"Close?"

"Once. Sort of." Squaring her shoulders, she glanced away. "I've worked hard to get where I am. I haven't had time for much else."

"You know what?" A fine mist of perspiration gave his face a soft luster. "This conversation is getting pretty damn personal. We're fogging up the windows here."

They were vapor-locked together in the cab of his pickup, surrounded by a silver-gray curtain. It gave her a warm, cozy feeling.

"Warm enough yet?"

She looked at him, surprised. Did it show? "I do need to get going."

He turned off the ignition and pulled the keys. "You never did dry your socks out."

She laughed easily. "I think I can live with wet feet."

"Maybe I can help you out." He unlocked the glove compartment and produced a pair of white tube socks, neatly folded into a military roll. He turned to hand them to her, caught that little frown of hers, and glanced back into the open compartment. She'd seen the airplane bottle. He was packing a shot of whiskey. "I don't drink on the job, if that's what you're thinking." He closed the compartment, turned his head slowly, and gave her a hard look. It wasn't necessary to tell her anything else. The bottle was sealed. "I don't drink at all anymore."

"So that's . . ."

It was none of her business. "It's for medicinal purposes."

"Cough medicine?"

He didn't laugh. Something in the tone of her voice said she'd heard that one before.

Who hadn't?

"It isn't for me. Not even on a day like this." He reached for her hand. Shock flashed in her eyes when he touched her, and he knew it had to do with the bottle and the fact that she didn't quite believe him. Still, she didn't pull away. He laid the roll of socks in her hand and closed her fingers around them. "I want you to keep your feet warm, Megan. My job may depend on your continued good health."

"What about you?"

"I'll be slogging through this mud until Randy comes on at two. What good will one pair of socks do me?"

"Thank you." She reminded him of a kid trying out shoplifting for the first time the way she stuffed his socks into her jumpsuit pocket.

"One thing I've got plenty of is socks. Now . . ." He handed her the top slicker, then picked up his own. "Since I can't see out this window, I'd better go check on the pumps."

"Thank you for the coffee, too." She crunched the raincoat into the space between herself and the door and pulled it around her shoulders. "This conversation has really been helpful."

"Uh-uh, Megan. Watch the sarcasm."

"I mean it," she protested. "You've given me a lot to think about."

He gave her a sidelong glance as he snapped his slicker up the front. "Then let me add one more thought for the day," he said.

"What's that?"

"Projects don't suffer from bigotry. People do." He pushed his hair back and trapped it under his hard hat. "The Indians aren't yours to lose. And we aren't yours to save, either."

"Did I sound that pompous?" She bent to retrieve her hat from the floor.

"Yeah. You did." He grinned and jerked his chin toward the door behind her. "After you, Megan. This baby's only got one exit."

Sage shut the compressor off and waded through six inches of water toward a pump that wasn't doing its job. Water filled his boots and crept up the legs of his jeans. He took a break from cussing out the machine and watched the highway department pickup barrel down the gravel road. She was headed east, toward the sign that said, Welcome To Big Thunder Sioux Indian Reservation. Maybe she'd stop at the Red Rooster. Some of the boys who were knocking off for the day were no doubt knocking a few back. They'd gladly buy her a round.

Why the hell had he given that woman his extra pair of socks?

Maybe because she wanted him to call her *Megan.*

AS LONG AS THEY'D had to shut down for the day, Megan had decided to visit the agency town of Big Thunder. In the rain, it looked more bedraggled than she'd anticipated. Rows of tract houses, nearly identical except for the assortment of bland pastel colors, stood in various states of disrepair. Funding from the Department of Housing and Urban Development must be harder to come by these days. In her search for the Bureau of Indian Affairs office building, Megan passed the Indian Health Service Clinic and the tribal offices.

Her front tire hit a pothole and splashed a cascade of water on the words THUNDER NO. 1 spray-painted in red on the sidewalk. She didn't follow high school sports, but everybody knew the boys' basketball team had brought home a state championship this year. They'd been the underdog, edged out much bigger schools—big news in South Dakota, a state long on square miles and short on people to fill them.

But the square mileage was good for Megan's business. No matter their numbers, people had to go places, and they let the Highway Department know if they were running into potholes.

She'd have to give Pete a little grief about the one that had probably just thrown her front end out of alignment. She'd taken some engineering classes from Pete Petersen, who was in charge of the BIA Roads Department at Big Thunder. He recognized her immediately when she walked into his office, and he offered her more coffee and all the time she wanted.

"I hear you've got Sage Parker on your project," Pete said after the initial amenities and personal news had been exchanged. "He's spent a few seasons working for me. Good man. Damn good man, long as he stays sober. He's not one of the ones you're concerned about, is he?"

"Not at all." Megan flexed her foot and glanced past her crossed knees at the toe of her work boot. Damn good man was damn right. Thanks to Sage Parker, she was wearing dry socks. "I don't think there's a piece of equipment on the site he can't handle, and he's there every day, just like clockwork."

"He was a heavy equipment operator when he was in the Army years back. Kind of a local hero in his day, too. Hell of a bull rider. Had a pretty little wife. 'Course, everybody around here wants to ranch, and he did that, too. Sage had it all." The springs in Pete's desk chair squeaked as he leaned back and folded his hands over his droopy paunch. "Guess every one of us has at least one lesson to learn the hard way."

"What happened?" Megan asked.

"Sage always was a hard worker. But he was young and hard-headed, used to drink hard and party hearty. You'd hear about his exploits, you'd think . . ." Pete shook his head slowly and tapped his thumbs together. "When the bubble burst, Sage came down harder than most. He had a lot to lose, and he lost it all. First time he went up to Fort Meade for treatment for alcoholism, they had to drag him kicking and screaming. They say he checked himself into a different program the second time around."

"I understand he's running a recovery program of his own now."

"Kind of a post-treatment program, I guess. They talk about traditional values and reviving the community. He calls it the Medicine Wheel." Pete sat up quickly. The springy chair swatted him in the back as he planted his elbows on the desk. "Yep," he drawled. "Some people around here think Sage Parker walks on water. Others want to see his program slide right down the tubes."

"Why?"

His humorless smile gave his answer a chilling edge. "Business. On and off the reservation both. You got your liquor sales, your pawn brokers, your loan sharking. Those people are making money."

"Off other people's misery," Megan reflected.

"That's right. That's the way of the world, I'm afraid. One man gets well, and he goes out tilting at windmills. The bloodsuckers start gunning for him." Pete slapped his palm against the desktop and smiled. "Damn, I hope he knocks a few of them flat on their asses. There's some kind of a public hearing going on in the tribal office at four o'clock. Could be interesting." He checked his watch. "If they're running on Indian time, it should be getting started about now. It's four-thirty.

"There's been some talk about pushing the council to do something about liquor sales around here. It's all screwed up, the way the laws and the licenses and the courts operate, squeezing these people in some crazy kind of a vise." He gave a dry chuckle and shook his head. "Vise? Vice? Either way, you get yourself trapped. You oughta take a walk over there, give a listen. Might be an eye-opener for you, Megan." He glanced at the clock on the wall. "In fact, I'll walk over with you."

Chapter 3

THE MEETING AT the tribal office building was already in progress. Pete and Megan shook the water from their raincoats and made their way toward the double doors. He shouldered a path through the lingerers, and Megan followed closely behind him.

A man standing near the door directed them to two folding chairs. Megan noticed that people preferred to stand against the walls and gather near the door rather than fill the folding chairs set up for spectators. She was happy to take a seat, where she could keep a low profile. No one stared, but she was feeling some curiosity vibes. Was it egocentricity, or plain paranoia? She was used to being outnumbered gender-wise, and she'd been in rooms full of people she didn't know, but coming off the talk she'd had with Sage, this felt different. She was different. Not *in* the minority, but she *was* the minority.

Wasn't she? Was this how it felt?

She was with Pete, and he wasn't Native American, but he worked here. She pushed her damp hair back behind her ears and slouched self-consciously, wondering whether her presence was an intrusion. She almost wanted to stand up and explain herself.

Almost.

Her interest soon overtook her discomfort. Pete tipped his balding head toward her and identified the people sitting behind the table at the front of the room—the tribal chairman, vice chairman, and secretary. Members of the tribal council sat at the two tables that formed the sides of a square. The fourth table was for petitioners and spokespersons. A young woman was speaking into the witness's microphone, and a child continually reached for her from the lap of a man wearing a black cowboy hat. Megan leaned sideways for a better view. Sage Parker. She'd never seen anything on his head but a hard hat. The cowboy hat suited him better.

He shifted the toddler from one knee to the other and bounced him occasionally. The youngster attempted a quick slide over Sage's thigh, but a protective arm brought him up short and settled him back in place.

Megan caught a glimpse of the little boy's black-eyed scowl as Sage pulled the small blue and white striped T-shirt down over his round little belly. Sage, too, appeared to listen with one ear, and he handled the baby as naturally as he did a jackhammer.

Megan leaned toward Pete and whispered, "Who's the speaker?"

"That's Jackie Flying Elk's wife, Regina. She's a beauty, isn't she?"

For some reason, she hadn't imagined Jackie with a beautiful wife. With the number of heads in her way, Megan couldn't see much besides the woman's long, satiny fall of black hair, and that was enough to trigger a pang of envy. Megan's short hair was comfortable, practical, and perfectly suited to her line of work, but secretly she coveted long hair, and Regina's was worth coveting. The child on Sage's lap thought so, too, and he nearly managed to snatch a handful of it before Sage caught him. He brought the little hand to his mouth and playfully nibbled the child's fat fingers. It was a side of the man Megan had not imagined, and it gave her a warm feeling just to watch. Mingled with the warmth was something else, something strangely akin to the envy of a woman who had something Megan might want.

"Is that her child?" Megan whispered.

"Which one?" Pete craned his neck for a glimpse past a dozen rows of intervening heads. "Oh, yeah, there's Sage. Figured he'd be here." He shrugged. "Probably Regina's. Sage's kids are older. Besides, the wife took them somewhere out of state. From what I hear, she won't let him near them."

The boy on Sage's lap wasn't the only young child in the room. The voices of several others, along with the continual shuffle of people moving in and out of the room, caused an undercurrent that didn't seem to disturb anyone but Megan. She was annoyed with herself when she realized that Regina was concluding her remarks, and Megan had lost track of the argument. But her response to a question from one of the councilmen struck a familiar chord. Yes, Regina was aware that prohibition on the reservation had put a lot of money into the pockets of bootleggers, but it was a drop in the bucket compared to what Taylor was raking in.

Taylor?

"That's the guy they're trying to close down." Pete's nod turned Megan's attention to a big man sitting near the exit at the front of the room. A little wheat-colored hair, a lot of wild eyebrow, ruddy face, beach ball belly—put a beard on him and he could be Santa Claus. "Floyd Taylor runs a grocery store in town here. He offers credit—most people here don't have credit cards or even checking accounts—even cash advances, almost like a payday loan kind of a thing. But his store is on the reservation, and he needs a business permit from the tribe. Didn't used to, but things are changing around here. Even some of the incorporated towns—they're like little islands, people call them 'white towns'— they're tightening up on liquor licenses, cooperating more with the council. But off the reservation, just the other side of the Nebraska state line, Taylor owns two package stores. He does pretty much what he wants to down there."

"He's not related to Karl Taylor, is he?"

"Floyd's his older brother. They've got three more built just like them."

If Floyd was anything like Karl, Megan already knew where her sympathies lay in this issue. She'd never joined the crew at the Red Rooster, their favorite off-reservation happy hour spot, because she had no interest in finding out what kind of conversation Karl Taylor might make after a few beers.

Floyd Taylor raised his hand like a schoolboy as he came to his feet and took a couple of steps toward the tables. "Mr. Chairman? I'd like to ask Mrs. Flying Elk a question, if I could." No one objected as the big blond with the gravelly voice turned toward the witness table.

"He gets to ask questions?" Megan whispered.

Pete shrugged.

"Now, we're all grown-ups here, most of us, and a grown-up has to make a living the best way he knows how." Taylor hitched up his pants. "Here in the town of Big Thunder, I just run a grocery store. In the off-rez towns around here, I own other businesses. Licensed businesses. All well-behaved grown-ups are welcome." He looked at Regina. "I'd just like to know if I'm to blame for the way your husband drinks, Mrs. Flying Elk. Are you saying it's my fault he ended up back in detox again?"

Regina's voice was strong and clear. "No, Mr. Taylor. I'm not saying it's your fault."

"It just seems to me that's what this is all about, this hearing. I'm a businessman. I abide by the laws, both tribal and state, and I do business with whoever comes in the door, unless he's under age." Taylor gave an inclusive gesture. "I see a lot of familiar faces in this room, and, hell, you all know me. Old Uncle Floyd. You come to me when you need gas money, when you've got a sick kid, or when you just run a little short at the end of the month, and I don't turn you down." His open-handed gesture was directed at Regina. "Everybody's family at Floyd's Foods, you know that. I can't sell alcohol at Floyd's. You don't want to go making any trouble for me. I never twist anybody's arm, Mrs. Flying Elk. Your husband's a big boy, and he makes his own decisions."

"I know that," Regina said. "My husband is not the issue."

"Then what is?"

"Didn't you hear one word of what I said, Mr. Taylor?"

"Mrs. Flying Elk," the chairman said through his microphone, "is there anything you want to add to your statement at this time?"

"I've said all I have to say." She pushed her chair back and leaned forward to add, "Anyone who has no ears won't hear me anyway. Thank you, Mr. Chairman."

Regina moved to the chair next to Sage's and took the child from his lap. Two more speakers took the chair behind the witness table and offered prepared statements, but impromptu testimony from the floor was permitted, as well. Characteristic of each speech were the final words, "That's all I have to say." Much of the testimony gave personal witness to the far-reaching effects of alcohol within the community and ended with a plea for the people, as a whole, to reject its use. Megan heard the courage in each speaker's voice as heartrending stories were offered publicly, but she knew that none of this would convict Floyd Taylor of anything in a court of law. Technically, the reservation was dry, but there were "white towns" within the bounds of the reservation, and across the state line the town of White Clay existed solely for the sale of alcohol. Taylor did business no matter what the circumstance.

On the other side, people claimed that they should all have the right to choose for themselves. "If they're gonna drink, they're gonna drink," one man said. "We've got enough bootleggers around here now, selling to minors. It's like Prohibition days. Well, it *is* Prohibition days. Banning it just makes it worse."

Finally, Sage came to the microphone. The room grew quieter, and there was a sense of expectation as he arranged several manila folders on the table. Megan wondered how he'd managed to work until two, stop to change into his red Western shirt and a pair of jeans that were certainly newer and drier than the ones he'd been wearing earlier, and get here for this meeting. He'd obviously defied all speed limits.

His introductory remarks reviewed his reasons for pushing the tribal council to petition the state against the renewal of Floyd Taylor's liquor licenses. From a file of police reports, he cited numerous complaints against Taylor for bootlegging on the reservation, for service to customers who were clearly intoxicated, and for serving or selling to minors. In some cases, Taylor had blamed someone else or paid a nominal fine. In others, no one would testify against him, or the testimony of a few had been refuted by a greater number, and the issue had died quietly.

"Mr. Taylor is not responsible for one man's relapse," Sage argued, "but he is responsible to this community to uphold its laws. As a rule, his establishments defy the spirit of our laws. The sale of alcohol is illegal on this side of the line, but it's okay on that side of the line. Mr. Taylor takes advantage on both sides. This reservation's been dry for almost a hundred years." He glanced in the direction of the last speaker. "And maybe you're right. Maybe prohibition only serves to line some people's pockets. You want to sell liquor on the reservation, fine. Issue our own license. Hold sellers responsible for the way they do business in our community. But right now, demand that the state do the same. To me, it's about the health of the people, not the sale of a product. And we all know that *Uncle Floyd* doesn't give a damn about our people who suffer, about our kids who suffer because their parents—"

"Other people's kids aren't my responsibility," Taylor injected.

"When you continue to serve their parents long after neither one can stand up, whose responsibility are the kids who get left in the car, Taylor?"

"What difference does it make?" Taylor slouched back in his chair and waved the matter away with one hand. "Somebody calls the police, and the whole thing is taken care of without any trouble. I'm not looking for any trouble."

"Which is why you don't trouble too many customers about their age," Sage grumbled.

"Hey, look, I do my best. They show some kind of ID, I can't always be sure it shows how old they really are." A slow grin crossed Floyd Taylor's face. "You know damn well you got by a time or two, Sage. 'Course, that was when my dad was running the place, and the law wasn't as tough then. Speaking of which . . ." He braced his hands on his knees and thrust his ruddy face forward. "I can think of a few times when it was *your* kids out in the car."

There was a moment of heavy silence before Sage's voice came over the microphone again. "I'm paying the price for that, Taylor. My children no longer live with me."

Megan felt tightness in her chest as she drew her next breath. A shared sense of despair pervaded the room. Those with children drew them closer, and most of the others hung their heads.

"Mr. Chairman." Attention turned to the councilman who had broken the silence. "I move we table this matter. We need time to look over the information Mr. Parker has presented to us before we approach the State of South Dakota with a complaint from the council."

The motion was passed, and the meeting was quickly adjourned. Megan stood and watched Sage deliver his folders to the chairman. Then he turned, and they connected immediately. He froze as though he'd lost his bearings. She smiled and waited for him to come over and speak to her. But he acknowledged her with a nod and turned to the people who had been sitting near him.

All righty, then.

She took her raincoat from the back of the chair and offered Pete a handshake. "Thanks for your time, Pete. This was interesting. How long do you think the debate will continue?"

"I don't know. Taylor wants it settled. The council's power has increased over the years. They might be able to keep him from doing the kind of business that's made him a wealthy man."

"It sounds like he shouldn't *be* in business," she said as she and Pete moved with the crowd toward the door. "Not around here, anyway."

"There are a lot of sides to this issue."

"And prohibition is kind of a been-there-done-that proposition. I guess I wasn't really aware . . ."

"People think they know about the alcohol problem on the reservation, but they don't know Indian Country," Pete said.

Megan lifted one shoulder. "The know Prohibition didn't work very well for the rest of the country."

"Some people accuse Sage's group of favoring prohibition."

"I didn't get that impression." They'd reached the lobby, and Megan was putting on her raincoat. "I hope this lets up soon. I'm battling ground water as well as rain."

"Project's getting interesting, huh?" Pete pulled a floppy canvas hat down over his brow. "You were the first woman ever enrolled in any of my classes. Not that I've done that much teaching, but you did come as a surprise." He offered a proud-teacher smile. "You'll do fine."

Megan dashed down the sidewalk and hopped across the rivulet of water washing past the curb. Within the shelter of her pickup, she shucked her raincoat and stuffed it under the front seat. She was combing her fingers through her damp hair when the door on the passenger side swung open and Sage slid into the seat. Water dripped from the brim of his hat, and his denim jacket was soaked. He tossed the hat on the seat between them and angled toward her. "You drove a long way to satisfy your curiosity."

The guarded look in his eyes was unsettling, and she found herself searching for excuses. "Pete Petersen was a teacher of mine. I came to ask for some advice. I didn't know about the hearing, but when he suggested we drop in, I thought I could learn more about . . ."

"And did you?"

"Yes, I did. I learned a great deal."

He was staring right through her, and she felt as if her forehead had become a message display board posting her every thought, every opinion, every recommendation nobody had asked for. She fussed with her hair again, pulled a few locks toward her eyebrows and watched dollops of water splash on the windshield from an overhanging cottonwood tree.

"Even if we lose this one in the end, it's worth the effort," he said quietly. Megan wondered whether he was confiding in her or simply coming to terms with the odds. "It's another chance to bring it out in the open and get the people to take a look."

"With all those complaints, it's kind of shocking they haven't closed Floyd Taylor down before this."

"Shocking?" He sighed. "Was that the only part that shocked you?"

"I wasn't really shocked." She watched a small, waferlike cottonwood seed slide down the glass. "I don't live in a vacuum. I read. I watch the news, the History Channel, educational TV. And I've been here before, Sage. I didn't really know anybody, but I—"

"You know Petersen."

"Okay, so his office was the only place I could go to without an appointment."

"An appointment? Damn." He chuckled. "An *appointment*."

"You know what I mean. I've been to Big Thunder. Driven through for . . . I don't remember exactly why. Joy riding, maybe."

"Did you stop anywhere? Get out of the car?"

"I didn't have any reason to."

"How about getting a burger at the café, or gas, or maybe reading the plaque on the veterans' monument?"

She shook her head.

"Didn't need any of those things, huh? But today you were looking for—"

"*Advice*. I said I wanted advice. I asked you, but you seemed . . ." She looked him in the eye and said quietly, "I didn't know you'd be there. I'm glad I went, but it wasn't to hear you speak. Not that I wouldn't have if I'd known, but I didn't—"

"How'd I sound?"

"Good!" *Too eager.* But thank God he'd switched gears. "Really interesting, very—"

"Nervous?"

"Not at all."

"I was scared shitless."

"It didn't show."

"Good thing I didn't turn around and see my boss in the audience. Would've been the straw that broke the cowboy's . . ." He smiled. "I did okay?" She matched his smile. "Put that in my next evaluation. Good communication skills. Even if he won't help me keep our Indians in line."

Their straight-face completion lasted only a couple of seconds. He won. But they both had a good laugh.

"Okay," he said finally. "So you wanted advice from your teacher. Why go to a council meeting?"

"To *learn*, Sage. It's important to be sensitive to the fact that an employee is a human being and to deal with him as a person rather than a machine." She knew it sounded like something out of a book, but the book was what she knew. "In order to do that, I have to—"

"Sensitive." He smiled at the windshield. "I like that." After a moment, he turned to her, and his eyes mellowed. "Do you realize how soft that makes you sound?"

"A man like Karl Taylor might mistake sensitivity for weakness." Her eyes narrowed. "I didn't think you would."

"I didn't say weak. I said soft." He propped his elbow on the back of the seat and rested his temple against his knuckles. "A lot of people are willing to drive extra miles to avoid passing through a reservation, especially this one. They're sure we lie in wait to slash their tires and siphon their gas." He raised one dark eyebrow. "Since you're here, I guess I can't call you weak."

"I'm not soft, either." She folded her arms across her breasts.

There was little cheer in the smile he gave her. "And the tires on this truck aren't yours. So what do you think all this sensitivity leads to?"

"Fairness," she said.

"Oh, yeah." He snapped his fingers. "I remember now. You're the one who's determined to be fair."

"I want to deal fairly with everyone, and I don't think that necessarily means dealing with all people in exactly the same way. I'm here to learn more about—"

"You being the dealer makes it pretty nice. You get to deal out second chances whenever you're feeling particularly sensitive." He eyed her with a challenge. "Do I get one?"

"I don't know," she answered quietly. She'd seen him expose himself before the crowd. He hadn't asked for sympathy then. What was he looking for now? "I think you're asking the wrong person."

She'd struck the right chord. He closed his eyes and used his fingertips to smooth the creases from his brow. "Sometimes I think I owe the whole world an apology, and I don't like the feeling." He lowered his hand and offered a tentative smile, made genuine this time by the soft luster in his eyes. "I was just taking a guilt trip and looking for a traveling companion."

"I'm sorry about your children, Sage."

"Uh-uh." He jabbed his chest with his thumb. "I'm the one who's sorry. What Taylor said about my neglect, that part was true." His sigh was a long, hollow sound. He settled back against the seat, and together they watched two drenched figures hurry past the hood of the pickup. "I can go to these meetings and say all the things that need to be said, and they can say, 'Who the hell do you think you are? We all know you.' And maybe somebody like Taylor speaks up to remind me. Like I need reminding."

"Two people so far have told me who you are," Megan said. Her heart had ballooned with sympathy at the sound of his sigh, but she was determined to deflate the feeling to a size and shape that might be more acceptable to him. "Bob Krueger and Pete Petersen both said you were the best man on my crew. They said—"

"They said I'm a hell of a good worker when I'm sober, and they'd heard I've really got it together now."

"They *know* you've got it together. It's been several years, hasn't it?"

"Four. I've got an anniversary coming up." He chuckled. "I never remembered my wedding anniversary, but I remember the day I quit drinking. I remember the hour."

"And you've started a recovery group," she said. "Is it like Alcoholics Anonymous?"

"Yeah, pretty much." He nodded. "But it never was a one-man show. It has to be a group effort. And a community effort? That would be powerful."

"Nobody approved of the tactics Taylor used, the things he said."

She was taking a bit of liberty considering she was acquainted with exactly two people at the meeting.

Sage lifted one shoulder. "The man's fighting for his livelihood. He'll use all the ammunition available to him, and I spent a lot of years building that munitions dump."

He turned to her again and saw the expectation in her eyes. He was confiding in her. She liked that. She was an outside pair of ears, and he wanted to talk. "Some of the old ones remember Prohibition, and they think we're trying to bring it back."

"That was a long time ago."

"Not for us," he said. "It wasn't until the 1950s that selling liquor to Indians became legal at all in this country, and even then, each tribe had to opt in. Mine didn't." Her surprise must have been written all over her face because he elbowed her and gave a rich, deep chuckle. "You didn't know that, did you? Most people don't. Before 1953, the people went to bootleggers instead of bars. Then they sat in their cars or went out behind the privy and slugged it down. That's the way we drink, like we're afraid a hand's going to reach out of the dark and take it away from us. So we haven't cultivated too many social drinking skills."

"You're certainly not alone in that."

"Maybe not, but I sure wish the old whiskey drummers and the bootleggers had brought along those classy traditions. You know, the etiquette—the towel over the arm and checking out the cork." He smiled, and his brown eyes brightened. "Aren't you impressed by a guy who knows how to order wine?"

"I haven't given it much thought."

"I have. Just lately, since I started trying to put the pieces together. I want to know, why us?" He braced his hand against the dashboard. "We have beautiful old traditions, but not one of them has anything to do with having a drink before dinner. Hell, Muscatel comes with a screw cap, and who can tell anything about its 'bouquet' when you're passing the bottle with a bunch of guys behind the outhouse?"

Her laughter sputtered in her throat, and it was useless to try to hold it in. The image he'd conjured for her was wonderfully absurd. The heavy weight of her sympathy was lifted as they laughed together.

"Does Muscatel have a bouquet?" she wondered.

"They used to call it 'Mustn't Tell.' I guess 'Mustn't Smell' fits, too."

"Oh, Lord." Her laughter wound down, and she shook her head. "This isn't something we should be laughing about."

"Why not? You know how much Indians love to laugh? Hell, shit happens. You can't let it kill your sense of humor." He grinned. "You can take yours to the bank, but mine's goin' with me to the grave."

The notion seemed strange to her. Serious matters were to be met with complete gravity, and she had to admit, she didn't know how much Indian people liked to laugh. "What's the difference between Prohibition and what you're trying to do?"

He ticked the points off without a moment's hesitation, because he knew them well. "I don't want *them* to tell *us* we can or can't drink. I want *us* to decide we won't. I want us to say *no*, individually and collectively. I want Taylor and his kind to be out of business simply because we don't want what he's got to sell. Every one of us suffers from it."

"Obviously not everyone agrees."

"Not yet, but we're growing in number." His conviction brightened his dark eyes. "Wet or dry, we get to decide. We take charge, do it in our own way. Traditionally, our decisions were made by consensus, which is hard to get. You have to keep talking, keep reminding people."

"At the meeting, everyone had a chance to say his piece."

"That's right," he said with a quick nod. He lifted one finger to punctuate his promise. "You get a circle of Indian people together, and you'll hear some speeches. We love to make speeches, and we have a style all our own."

"Was it an intrusion?" she asked. "My being there today, I mean."

"No, it wasn't. I guess I got a little defensive." His eyes were bright, and his smile spread slowly. The damp hair that fell across his forehead gave him an unexpectedly boyish look. "I wasn't expecting my boss to be part of the audience."

"And I didn't come to spy on you." She returned his smile. "I wouldn't do that to someone who loaned me dry socks."

Sage knew he had to be crazy. For the second time in one day, he was sitting in a pickup with this woman while a curtain of rain dropped around them, interfering with his fragile connection with reality. And he was grinning about it.

TWO WEEKS LATER, Megan recalled every word that had passed between them in that pickup as she considered her problem with Karl Taylor. Sage hadn't said that she *was* soft. He'd said the importance she placed on sensitivity made her *sound* soft. She hadn't been offended. He hadn't been offensive. But Taylor *had* offended her—once too often—

and Bob Krueger had agreed to take him off the project.

Megan slid her report into a manila envelope and sealed it carefully. Her complaint would become part of Taylor's personnel file, and he would be reprimanded. Off the record, there would be those who would reiterate the notion that this was a man's job, and any woman who demanded the right to be out here with a road crew might as well expect some sexual hassle. The notion was obsolete, but it was alive. But it wouldn't be kicking her. She peered through her office window and watched Bob Krueger pull up in a highway department car. Bob wasn't there to give Taylor the news. Megan had done that herself, and since he hadn't shown up for work that morning, she assumed he'd gone to the State Highway Department office in Pierre. Bob was there to pick up her written complaint and to discuss replacing Taylor.

And to listen. Bob was the consummate listener. Megan had already reported her complaint over the phone. She needed to repeat it face-to-face. She'd played it cool, but she needed to vent her frustration. What she didn't need to do was wave her arms about and let her voice climb as she spoke, which wouldn't happen if she felt completely confident. She wouldn't be bullied or manhandled, but she was still trying to convince herself that she'd been absolutely fair. Totally unbiased.

Truth be told, she really did not like that man.

"So there were no witnesses." Bob leaned across her desk and stubbed his cigarette out in the jar lid she'd supplied.

Megan turned to the window and drew a calming breath as she watched an earthmover crawl up a hill. "There was no one else around."

"And this was the first time Taylor tried anything like this?"

Megan sighed. "It was the first clearly overt gesture. A couple of times, he made a point to cut off my space, to make me walk around him. He made a stupid remark once, and I told him he was way out of line."

"But this time he actually cornered you."

She nodded toward the metal cabinets and patiently repeated, "Against the files."

"And told you . . ."

"That my skin looked so soft it made his palms itch. It's in the report, word for word."

"And you told him . . ."

"To get the hell out of my way."

"Which he did." Bob leaned back in his chair. "I'm not defending these guys, Megan, but this kind of thing has happened before. By my count, this is the third time."

She folded her arms tightly and turned from the window. "And it may not be the last. It's not a man's world anymore, Bob. I don't come equipped with a black belt in karate. I don't have to. I know the law."

"Taylor does, too. I knew you weren't a good match, but I wanted his experience." Bob dismissed his mistake with a wave of the hand. Time to move on. "After the winter we just had, we've got too damn many projects going this summer. I've got everybody working. You said you've got a replacement in mind?"

Megan nodded. "Parker."

"That's what I thought. He's the logical choice." Bob shook his head slowly. "He won't do it, Megan. I've offered it to him before."

"*This* job?"

"Not this project, but others." With a smile, Bob recalled, "He doesn't want to give orders, he says. He just wants to work."

Megan turned toward the window again. Sage was the right man for the job. The fact that she liked him wasn't a crime. The crew liked him, too. He was *likable*. He was also capable, which was why she had chosen him. "I'm going to offer him the position anyway," she said firmly. "With his experience and his skills, *he* knows he's the logical choice. It would be unfair not to offer it to him."

WHEN SAGE SAW the dark green car parked next to the office, he knew his lunch break was shot. Megan had sent for him, Krueger was there, and he'd heard about Taylor. It wasn't hard to put one and one and one together and foresee the "great opportunity" on the horizon. He mounted the wobbly metal steps to the trailer, slapped some of the dust off the seat of his jeans and buttoned a couple of shirt buttons, leaving two still open. Hell, it was too hot to dress for the occasion.

"You wanted to see me?" Sage glanced from the man seated near the desk to the woman standing behind it. He wasn't sure whose idea this was, but he figured he could handle both of them if they tried to tag-team him.

"We've had to pull Taylor off this project," Bob announced. "You probably heard."

"Yeah, I heard." He'd been hearing it all morning from the guys who'd been with Taylor at the Red Rooster the night before. And all morning long, he'd resisted the temptation to storm the office and demand to know what that jackass had said to her, what he'd *really* done.

He had to remind himself that he was part of her construction crew, not her goddamn champion. She'd obviously taken care of the situation on her own. It was none of his business what Taylor had said or done.

"I want you to take over as construction supervisor," she said simply.

"I don't want the job." *Period.*

Or not.

Megan moved to the front of the desk and stood as rigidly as he did. "You should have had it to begin with. With all your skills, it's time you moved ahead in this business."

"Who says I want to move ahead?" He smiled slightly when her eyes gave her away. He knew that look. *What's wrong with you, Parker? I'm handing you a gift horse.* And he was coming back at her with a new concept. "I need a job, Miss McBride. I need to put food on my table, gas in my bulk tank, and pay my child support. I don't need a foreman's headaches."

"Some foremen *cause* headaches," Megan pointed out. "Properly handled, this job—"

"Sage." Bob came to his feet slowly. "I know you've turned us down before. I also know you're trying to rebuild that ranch of yours." He adjusted his pants, rested his hands at his hips and smiled. "You'll damn near double your pay with this job, son. *Double* it. You'll be that much closer to getting that place back on its feet."

Sage had anticipated this argument, too. It was the one point the idea had in its favor. He'd never gotten along very well with money, but it was hard to get along without it. And it was impossible to build much of a cattle operation without it. He turned away and shoved his hands in his back pockets. "A foreman doesn't make an engineer's decisions," he reflected. "And an engineer lets the foreman handle the crew." He turned and gave Megan a pointed look. "You don't seem to want to work it that way, though."

"Taylor was letting his racial prejudices influence his decisions. Nothing works very well *that* way."

"What makes you think it'll work my way? You and me, we might be worse news yet."

Megan smiled and offered him a ring of keys. "I think it's worth a try."

Chapter 4

THEY'D STOPPED asking him to join them at the Rooster after work, but Sage could always tell who'd been there for last call when the crew came in the next morning. With Scott, it meant sunglasses. Randy loaded up on coffee, no matter how hot the weather was. Gary wasn't talking to anyone this morning. And Jackie was a no-show again. Detox hadn't done him much good.

Sage squinted into the sun as he approached the trio. Randy drained his Thermos cup while Gary leaned on a shovel handle and scowled at the approach of authority.

"You guys taking another break?"

"It's hot," Scott grumbled. "We're thirsty."

Sage nodded. "Rough night, huh?"

Faces were stony, lips sealed. Gary propped his foot on the shoulder of the shovel blade.

"You can either give me the time back at noon or after five," Sage said quietly. "You guys haven't done a damn thing all morning."

"This job's going to your head, Sage." Randy turned on the affable if wan smile, which generally allowed him to say almost anything without causing offense. "You know, Taylor had a mean mouth on him, but, times like this, he'd usually cut us some slack."

"You're not working for Taylor anymore." Sage looked at Gary, who appeared to be ignoring the conversation. "Did you see Jackie last night?"

Gary lifted his shoulder and wiped his face against his sleeve.

Sage glanced back at Randy, then at Scott. "Listen, I don't give a damn what you guys do on your own time, but when you come to work, you be ready to put in an eight-hour day."

He watched the three men in his rear-view mirror as he pulled away slowly in his pickup. They'd gone grudgingly back to laying the gravel and clay base for the blacktop soon to come. Gary was pissed because he'd been taken off the gravel truck. Randy was pouting because Sage hadn't tapped him on the shoulder and told him everything was okay, and Scott was feeling sorry for himself because his head hurt. Sage knew how that went. At the moment, he didn't much like his three-week-old job. He floored the accelerator. A cloud of dust veiled the reflections in the mirror.

One truth he'd discovered about himself was that he didn't much like being disliked. In his drinking days, he'd been in his glory when people were cheering for him or slapping him on the back and calling him "friend." In his drinking days, he would have told those three to take it easy today, and he'd have relished the acceptance he would have gotten in return. But, hell, he didn't need that shit anymore. That was yesterday. Today, he had a job to do, and if he did it well, he'd get some worthwhile satisfaction out of it. He didn't have to please the crew, and they didn't have to like him. They had to respect him. So he had to give them something worth respecting.

Jackie's car was parked near the office. Sage muttered another curse, gripped the steering wheel, and arced it to park the pickup alongside the car. Jackie was asleep with his mouth hanging open and his neck arched over the top of the seat. Sage tapped on the roof. Jackie jerked his head up and looked around.

"Hey, Sage." He squeezed one eye shut and squinted through the other. "Sorry I'm late. Thought I'd check the office first, then follow your tracks."

Sage squatted on his boot heels next to the car door, putting his eyes on a level with Jackie's. "You been home yet?"

"Sure." Jackie grinned. "Sure, I been home. I'm okay, Sage. The alarm clock didn't work is all."

Jackie's breath smelled like sewer water. "Guess you forgot to brush your teeth, huh?"

It's too late, Jackie. Spare us both. Don't lie to me.

"Yeah. I was in a hurry." The smile faded, and Jackie played his trump, the one reference that might gain him sympathy from a guy who'd been there. "The ol' lady'll throw me out if I lose this job. She's countin' on fixing an old house up into a store. Smart woman. Deserves a better man, and that's what I'm gonna be." He grinned again. "So whatcha got for me today? Gravel or oil?"

"Your last paycheck. I'm sorry, Jackie." Sage straightened slowly and patted the roof of the car a couple of times the way he would the man's shoulder if it had been handier. "Go on back to sleep. I don't want you on the road again 'til you've slept it off." He turned and headed for the office, where he saw movement in the window.

"Hey, Sage, I'm okay. I swear it!"

Sage stopped and turned back toward the car. "Let me know when you're ready for treatment, Jackie. I'll drive you there myself."

Megan was waiting for him. He avoided her eyes as he reached for the clipboard on his desk.

"Are you sure he's been drinking?"

He looked up. His eyes hardened when he saw that innocent expression. She wanted him to be prosecutor, judge, and jury while she played the bleeding-heart advocate. "Did you talk to him?"

"Yes, I did. He came to the office as soon as he got here."

He turned to the list on his clipboard and added some figures. She wasn't stupid. She was as sure as he was.

"You fired him?"

Was that an accusation or an observation?

"I read the policy." He glanced up. His eyeballs felt like rocks. "I didn't write it. My job was to read it and follow it."

"I think if you gave him something—the promise of a job, maybe—he might opt for treatment. There's a provision for that in the policy."

The clipboard clattered when he tossed it on the desk. "I know about the provision." And he resented her for pointing it out like she had some kind of special grace she could turn over like a baton, and now he was supposed to hand off to Jackie. *His* friend, Jackie. Hell, he'd done what he had to do. Grace didn't come with the territory. "Jackie knows about it, too, and he knows how to ask. He's been there before."

"Maybe he can't ask."

"Then maybe he's not ready."

"He needs help, Sage."

They heard the roar of an engine, and they both turned toward the window. Sage took two steps closer in time to watch Jackie pull away in a hail of gravel. "Goddamnit. I told him to wait."

"For what?" Megan asked.

"I told him to go back to sleep for a while."

She folded her arms and injected a note of sarcasm into her voice. "You fired him, and then you expected him to curl up and go to sleep on our doorstep?"

"*Our* doorstep?" He whirled from the window and jabbed a finger into the air. "This is *your* doorstep. Mine's thirty-five miles east of here." And if Jackie showed up on *his* doorstep, Sage would give him his bed and make his own in the cab of his pickup.

She pointed toward the window. "You can't fire a man and not expect him to go off hurt and angry like that."

"How many men have you fired?" He shouted the question and allowed two seconds for an answer. Her blue eyes flashed her message of defiance. "That's what I thought. Look, if you're out to save drunks, you oughta get yourself into another line of work." He jerked his head in the direction she'd indicated. "Go after him. Go on, coax him. Persuade him to get treatment again."

"What would be wrong with that?" Megan clenched her fists in the shelter of her armpits and loosed a stinging dart. "How many times have *you* needed treatment, Mr. Parker?"

His voice was steely and cold. "None of your damn business."

She pressed her lips together, turned them into a tight seam, and he almost smiled. He imagined her biting her wayward tongue. "You're right," she said softly. "That wasn't—"

"First you hired me to blast rock and dig out a road, and all I had to worry about was moving dirt. Now you've got me moving people. I don't enjoy moving people, Miss McBride." Anger dissolved as the realization dawned in his brain. "But I can do it. And since the job's mine, I *will* do it."

He moved toward the door and turned with one quiet comment. "You can't save drunks, Megan. It can't be done that way. But you come to a Medicine Wheel meeting sometime, and you can watch how they can save themselves a day, maybe an hour, maybe just a minute at a time."

He climbed into his truck and headed downhill from the office toward the site where more earthwork had been started. Halfway down the hill, the pickup lunged toward the shoulder, and Sage fought with the shuddering steering wheel with one hand while he downshifted with the other. The pickup lurched, listed to the right, and stopped. Sage glanced at the old hood ornament and the empty air beyond, where the gravel gave way to a fifty-foot drop-off. His left hand was cramped from the strain of holding the wheel. His right trembled. He pushed the door open and stumbled out.

"What happened?"

Sage looked up as he stepped back from the pickup. Megan was running toward him, and the words *to the rescue* flitted across his mind as he turned back to the crippled vehicle. "What happened?" He hitched his hands on his hips. "The damn wheel fell off, obviously."

"I know," she panted. With a wave of her hand, she told him, "It's back there. I mean, what *happened?* How did it just—"

"How the hell do I know?" He stalked past her, hoping she hadn't noticed the way he was shaking. Maybe it didn't show on the outside. Cold anger, sure, let her see that, but not fear.

"Good Lord, you almost went off the—"

"I know!"

The hubcap lay twenty feet from the tire, but he didn't see any lug nuts anywhere. A piece of paper was stuffed into the rim, and the rim itself wasn't even bent. The whole damn thing had just *flown off.*

Not without help, he decided as he jammed the paper into his pocket before Megan reached him with her next question.

"What was that?"

"Nothing." He came to his feet and glanced away as she stepped up to him. "Just a piece of trash."

"Trash?"

"Trash. Road trash." He looked up at the top of the hill and mentally measured the distance he'd driven before the tire fell off. It wasn't much. "You wanna help me find those lug nuts?"

"Lug nuts?"

"Is there something wrong with the way I pronounce these words? *Trash,*" he said with exaggerated care. "And *lug nuts.*" He started up the rise.

She followed, muttering. "I don't understand why you're picking up trash at a time like this."

"Seems as good a time as any. Litter just brings tears to my eyes."

"Sage, I think someone may have tampered with your pickup."

"Really." His little joke had just sailed right over her head. They'd never get along socially. He liked his humor dry as a bone. He knelt to retrieve a shiny lug nut.

"You don't think it could have been Jackie, do you?" She angled to the left. "Here's another one."

"He didn't have time."

"Did you see anyone else around?"

"I was too busy arguing with you. How many have you got?"

"Two."

"One more."

"You know, you're entitled to the use of a department vehicle now."

"I'd rather drive my own." He spied another metallic glint in the dirt and picked up his pace.

"Why?"

"It's got character." And it didn't have South Dakota Highway Department emblazoned on the side. Randy's suggestion that the job had gone to his head had hit a nerve. He didn't want to wear any badges. He didn't even like having a desk. All he'd need was a sign on his pickup and they'd all hate him.

"You don't think it was someone who resented your getting this job, do you?"

"Hell, I don't know!" He rose from the ground with the last of the lug nuts. He looked up, saw her standing there, saw the concern in her eyes, and felt like a piece of road trash himself. "Look, I'm sorry." With a jerk of his chin, he indicated the pickup. From the higher vantage point they could see just how close he'd come to careening over the edge. "Scared the hell out of me." He wanted to kick himself as soon as he'd said it, but there it was.

"Me, too."

He gave a nervous laugh. *Her, too?*

Well, why not? Who'd want to see somebody drive his pickup off a cliff? It didn't have to mean anything personal.

"It must've been a prank." She lifted her arm slowly and opened her hand. His fingertips tingled, dragging lightly over the center of her palm as he claimed first one lug nut, then the other. "They probably thought it would just fall right off."

"Probably." He looked into her eyes, lowered his gaze to her lips. They were full and naturally pink, and he had the worst urge to touch them with the same two fingers that had flirted with her palm.

"I don't think anyone wanted to h-hurt you." The sweet sound of the catch in her breath made his mouth go dry. "I think it was just a prank. Don't you?"

"Please don't ask me questions when you know I don't have any answers," he said quietly. "I hate that." And he hated the fact that he was clenching his fists against the urge to touch her. The lug nuts cut into his hand.

"I think it was just a prank," she said again.

"I think I'd better see if I can get the damn tire back on the pickup." *Before you read whatever part of me is thinking at the moment.* He figured his close brush with death must have triggered his sudden, hard, urgent lust for . . . life.

"Do you have enough tools?" she called after him as he ambled back down the hill.

It felt good to laugh. He stood the tire on edge and started it rolling. "I sure have," he sang out. "All I'll ever need."

Once he had the pickup on the road again, he pulled the crumpled paper from his pocket and smoothed it out in the center of the steering wheel. "Accidents happen," the penciled note warned. "Don't interfere with free enterprise. It's the American way."

RED CALF, SOUTH DAKOTA, was a hole in the Badlands' wall. Megan drove past Floyd's Tavern on the off-reservation side of town, allowing herself a quick glance at the single car parked in front to assure herself that there were no crying children inside. She told herself she wouldn't trust any meat from Floyd's Foods, the clapboard building that stood next door. The windows on both structures were covered with bars. She wondered who was being locked out. Ghosts? The town looked pretty dead.

A phone call to Pete Petersen and a little research on Pete's part had turned up the information she'd needed to attend a Medicine Wheel meeting. Sage had invited her—challenged her, really—and something in the back of her mind wouldn't let the idea fade away. There was nothing wrong with caring, but she wanted to care from an enlightened point of view. She'd come to Red Calf to be enlightened.

The size of the Red Calf Community Center said something about the size of the Indian side of the community. A hundred people might have been able to crowd inside if most of them were small. The sign taped to the door said the Medicine Wheel meeting was in progress and anyone was welcome to attend. According to the sign, Megan was half an hour late. Pete had told her 8:00 p.m. She dreaded walking in late, but she opened the door and stepped inside.

A single bright, bare bulb in the ceiling illuminated a small circle of people, who turned in their folding chairs at the sound of the door. Megan searched for a familiar face and felt a rush of relief when she found one.

"Welcome." Maybe it was his surprise at seeing her that had Sage rising from his chair as though a revered elder had just walked in. "Take my seat. It's all warmed up."

"I'm sorry to interrupt." She took a tentative step toward the chair. "I thought . . . I was told the meeting started at eight."

Sage flipped another chair open and pushed it into the circle, telling her again with a glance at the chair he'd vacated that she should sit down.

"You must have seen one of the posters. We need to change those. They should just say *join us Thursday night*."

"Yeah," one of the men said. "We'll just talk among ourselves 'til you get here." He laughed.

"I'm really just—"

"Bernard's kidding you," Sage said. "And it's okay to laugh with him. You might as well, 'cause he's not gonna quit doing it. We get here when we can and leave when we're finished. And you don't have to tell us anything. You've joined us. You're part of the circle. As the night passes, you're welcome to share what you will. We don't give last names, and what's said here stays here."

"Would I be breaking a confidence if I explained our—" Her hand fluttered between them. "How I know you?"

"Like I said, share what you will." He gave a tight smile that said *might as well lay all your disclaimers out first.*

"I'm Megan. I'm a highway engineer," Megan said quietly, trying not to sound as though she fancied herself some kind of a guest speaker. "We're working on a road project just west of here. Sage—" She smiled, first at him and then at Bernard. Kidding, after all, was a connection. "Sage has just been promoted to construction supervisor."

No one smiled back. Not even Bernard.

"I know this is like an AA group—so I've been told—and but I've never been to AA, so, so, um, because I don't have a problem with alcohol or anything, you know . . ." She lifted one shoulder. "Not a *personal* problem, anyway."

"How very fortunate for you."

She looked quickly at Sage. He returned a sober look, but she could tell he was struggling with it. The look in his eyes said she amused the hell out of him. While she was squirming. Which wasn't funny. "I just mean I don't drink . . . much."

"Neither do I." One corner of his mouth twitched.

"I know that. I understand that." She looked at the ceiling, casting about for help. "I'm going about this all wrong."

"You don't have to protect yourself here, Megan. That's the beauty of the circle. We're all equal. The meetings are open, and there's no right or wrong way to tell us what's bothering you."

"Nothing," Megan said quickly. Maybe this wasn't such a good idea. "Nothing's really bothering me. I came to learn. I mean, you suggested that I come to a meeting sometime, so here I am. I want to understand so I can maybe . . . help. Well, not *help* exactly, but maybe do my job

49

better."

"Your engineering job?" an older woman sitting across from Megan asked. "I'll tell you what bothers me about these blacktop roads. Tourists. People who want to drive around in our backyards and then drive off to tell their friends about what it's like in Red Calf. We don't need so much blacktop. When I was a girl, we had mostly gravel."

"What tourists?" Bernard put in. "There's no tourists bothering you, Gertie. Hell, when you were a girl, we didn't have roads."

"We did have roads." Gertie's tone suggested no more emotion than her wrinkled brown face betrayed. "We had all the roads we needed."

Tommy chuckled. "Because they hadn't invented cars yet."

Megan didn't know whether to chuckle with the chucklers or sympathize with Gertie by keeping a straight face. At least she, *thought* it was straight. Hard to tell with the light she noticed dancing in the old woman's eyes.

She glanced at Sage, but he was staring at the floor. "I'm not here because of curiosity," she said quietly. "A couple of the men on the crew, *our*—" Again she gestured to indicate that she and Sage were in this together. "Our crew. Members of your community, I believe—well, they have a problem with drinking. That is, they *seem* to have a problem with drinking."

"A problem that interferes with their work?" Sage asked without looking up.

"Yes." She looked around the room again as her self-consciousness began to take a backseat to her cause. "We had to fire one of the men, and I hated to see that happen. He was a good worker before he started drinking again, and I'm sure he needed his job."

"Anybody else here need his job?" Sage asked, and there was a round of chuckling. "Most of these people don't have jobs, Megan. There aren't too many jobs around."

"I know. That's why I'm concerned when I have to fire someone." She looked around quickly again. No one was looking at her. No one seemed to be listening, and she felt driven to regain their attention. "It seems like such a waste when a man is good at his job, and then, just because of alcohol, he's—"

"You're talking about my husband."

Megan turned toward the voice and recognized the woman from the council meeting, the one with the beautiful long hair. "I'm sorry," Megan said. "I didn't mean—"

"Sage fired him, not you."

Megan's back stiffened. "Sage has his job to do, too."

"Jackie stopped coming to Medicine Wheel," Regina said. "He stopped going to work every day, and he deserved to be fired. Now he's stopped coming home at night."

"I'm sorry," Megan said again.

"Being sorry for him only makes him worse," Regina said. "Don't be sorry for him. He can get drunk on pity the same as he gets drunk on wine."

"But if he had his job, surely—"

"What we're telling you, Megan, is that the job was a small part of Jackie's loss," Sage said. "He has to get his soul back before he can work again."

He looked at her now, and in his eyes she saw his acceptance of her presence, of her concern, of her fumbling attempt to understand. "Is there anything I can do?" she asked.

"You can pray," said the older woman who had spoken before. "For yourself, and for the rest of us, to whatever god you believe in."

That wasn't what Megan had in mind. It had nothing to do with Jackie's job or with hers. She looked to Sage for a better answer. "I think awareness is important," she explained. "For an employer, a supervisor. There must be something we can do to make it easier adjust to, um . . ." *Words, words. What are the words?* "You know, the whole one-day-at-a-time routine. Routine is a good thing, isn't it?"

"Sometimes," Sage said. "Awareness is a good thing. So be aware that you can make it easy for a drunk to go on doing what he's doing routinely. You can never make it easy for him to change his ways."

"If somebody goes in for treatment, try to hold his job for him," said one man. "When I got out, I didn't have much to go back to. But I had this group." His mouth opened in a gap-toothed grin. "I'll have a job when Regina and Tootsie open their store."

"We've bought a house for it now," Regina announced. There was a low murmur of approval. "The White Shields' house. They're moving to Big Thunder."

Conversation turned to plans for bringing grocery prices down in Red Calf. Floyd's was the only store, and, because the town was so isolated, he charged outrageously for food.

"Jackie borrowed money from Uncle Floyd again, and Floyd tried to get me to pay it," Regina complained. "You should see the interest he's got tacked on."

"That's Jackie's debt," Sage reminded her. "You worry about opening up that store."

"I'll help you paint it."

"We'll need to knock out some walls."

"You guys can live upstairs."

"I know where you can get one of those big freezers for next to nothing."

"Don't listen to Gertie." Bernard nodded at Megan. "You keep rollin' out that blacktop."

IT HAD GONE WELL. Sage lay across his bed from corner to corner and stared at the ceiling that curved three feet above his head as he played the meeting over in his mind. Jackie's relapse was a loss, but these things happened. The group members put it in perspective as they planned their course. Get rid of *Uncle* Floyd, and build a new store. Individual recovery would lead to community recovery. Ollie Walks Long had gone to treatment. The group would have his house fixed up for him when he got back. They would clean it up and paint it, put new screens on the windows. It was important to have a decent place to live. Not fancy, but decent. You had to start someplace, and that was a good place to start. Jackie would come back, Sage decided, and they would help him start again, too.

He reached across the bed and groped for the switch on the little oscillating fan that whirred in the darkness next to him. He turned it up as high as it would go and promised himself that one day he would sleep in an air-conditioned bedroom again. He propped his head on his elbow and turned his face toward the hot breeze. Hell, just a bedroom would be nice. The back end of a fifteen-foot trailer could hardly be called a bedroom. He'd had a bedroom once, with an air conditioner in the window, but there had been too many times when that room had heated up even with the air on full blast. God, how the two of them had argued.

He remembered how pretty she'd been when she was seventeen. Riva Maxon. All he remembered about her from those days was that she had long blond hair, and she could do one hell of a spread-eagle at the end of a cheer. He'd gone to an Indian boarding school in Nebraska, and she'd gone to public school. She hadn't cheered for his team, but he'd soon had her cheering for him. She'd planned to go to college, but he'd changed her plans. He rodeoed in the summer, and she'd followed the circuit and learned all about cowboys. She'd had quite a teacher.

He was driven then, and he'd pushed hard—for thrills, for quick intensity, for sex on demand. To this day, he didn't know what devil it was that had eaten at him so voraciously from the inside out. He had never been able to get enough of anything. He'd always wanted more. Drinking made him powerful and glib, made the women fun and easy, made the risks and the close calls seem like the best part of living. For a time, he'd led a charmed life. He'd gotten by. He'd smashed the front fender, but he hadn't wrecked the car. He'd caught hell for flirting, but he hadn't gotten caught cheating. He'd paid most of his bills. But he hadn't catapulted himself high enough. Each time he'd come down, he seemed to find himself one rung lower, and he'd needed a closer call, a greater thrill, a bigger bottle to get himself back up there again.

Just the memory made him sweat. He edged closer to the fan and tried to replace those dark images with something else. Something that made him feel good.

Megan.

Clean, fresh hair that left the soft down on the back of her neck exposed. Clear-eyed innocence and courage. It had taken courage to do what she'd done tonight. At one point, he'd thought she was going to bolt, but she'd stayed. She was a bona fide caretaker, sure as hell, but there was hope for her. She'd been willing to listen. And when she'd sat down in that chair and turned her face up to him, she'd made his insides turn to slush.

He commended himself for remembering that look on her face above all else. He'd spent hours wondering about her legs, and he'd finally gotten a look at them. They were nice, but it was her face that stuck fast in his thoughts. He couldn't remember when he'd given a woman's face such a big piece of his mind.

Yes, he could. He did. He remembered Riva's face when it was pretty and unguarded, but he also remembered when it wasn't pretty anymore. He remembered how she'd looked with her eyes narrowed and her lips thin and white as she spat obscenities at him. He wondered how he'd looked when they'd matched each other curse for curse. Nothing like the loving man he'd promised to be. Had he ever loved her? Was he capable of giving love? If he'd ever loved anyone, he didn't remember what it felt like.

No, that wasn't true. He loved his children. God, he wanted to believe he'd always loved his two children. But he'd hurt them. He'd catered to himself and his addiction at their expense.

Sage rolled onto his back and studied the metal seams in the ceiling again. He didn't want to hurt anyone else. He didn't want to turn anyone else ugly. His pain was his, and he felt it every day. He didn't anesthetize himself anymore. Losing his children would always hurt, but he didn't bottle it up anymore. He admitted it. He'd hurt them, and he lived with that truth. *Awareness is a good thing.* He would do what he could for the others who lived with the same kind of pain, and he would do his damnedest not to cause any more.

Brenda and Tommy. She was twelve now, and he was nine. It had been six years since Riva had left him and taken the kids with her. She'd remarried, and she wanted him to pay his child support and stay out of their lives. His letters were usually returned unopened, but not all of them, so maybe some had slipped through. He just wanted the kids to know he cared. That was all. He didn't want to screw anything up for them, but it didn't hurt to care. Smiling to himself, he wiped the sweat off his chest with the corner of the sheet.

It doesn't hurt to care. That sounded like something Megan might say. Probably *had* said. He believed she did care about Jackie and Gary. Maybe even him. Well, if she let herself get too deeply involved, she would soon find out how much it hurt to care.

Damn, he wished they would answer his letters. With a groan, he turned his face toward the wall.

If they would just send me a picture.

Chapter 5

TERRY HAYNES wasn't satisfied with his assignment. Out of the corner of his eye, Sage had watched Haynes use his boot heel to dig a hole in the soft ridge of clay base that the blade had left along the edge of the new road. Sage flipped the metal cover over his clipboard and waited while the rest of the crew headed for the equipment. He figured he and Haynes were about due.

"I want the overtime on the oiler," Haynes announced, his colorless eyes aglow with the bravado he'd been working himself up to during Sage's brief talk with the crew.

"You worked overtime last week," Sage reminded him quietly. There wasn't much Sage liked about Haynes. He was sloppy, both in his personal habits and his work. Sage didn't like the tobacco stains on the wiry young man's scraggly blond mustache, nor the little bits of tobacco between his teeth, nor his off-color sense of humor. Moreover, he didn't like the way the man handled the oiler. Sage had suggested, instructed, and reprimanded, but Haynes knew it all. "I'm turning the oiler over to Archambault and putting you on the ground for a while."

Haynes shoved his hands in his back pockets and spat brown juice into the grass. "I'm going to file a complaint."

"That's your right." Sage turned to walk away.

"I don't much care for the way you take care of your Indian friends first, Parker."

Sage mentally counted through the single digits as he turned back slowly. "I don't much care for the way you run the oiler. I told you how I wanted it done, and you chose not to listen."

"I don't know who the hell you think you are, Parker." Haynes shifted his weight from one foot to the other and stuck out his chin, adding emphasis to the snoose bulge beneath his lower lip. "You go from labor to foreman overnight. What do you know about oiling? How many jobs you been on? They got some kinda Indian preference with state jobs now?"

In his head, Sage saw his fist connect with Haynes's mouth, splattering blood and brown slime all over that seedy mustache. He gripped the clipboard tightly in his right hand. "You're on the ground, or you're on your way back to wherever you come from, Haynes."

"You got an in with Krueger. Everybody knows that. And McBride—"

"File your complaint." Sage turned on his heel, his gut churning as he headed toward a big yellow bulldozer, the only piece of equipment that wasn't moving at the moment. The roar of powerful diesel engines filled his ears, and he fastened his mind on the noise. He associated the sound with ripping out, packing down, knocking flat, and he needed to get his hands on the controls of that 'dozer. He needed to substitute the work for ripping Haynes's teeth out of his mouth and packing them down his throat.

MEGAN HAD SPENT the first part of the week in Pierre at the highway department office. It was good to get back to her apartment for a few days. Staying in a Hot Springs motel for the better part of the summer was part of the highway engineer's territory, and she didn't mind it. She wasn't a homebody. Sometimes she wondered why she even needed her own apartment, but the answer to that question came quickly. The other choice was having a home base with her parents.

It was late afternoon when she climbed the steps to the office. She'd toured the site, and she planned to pick up some charts and head for Hot Springs. The project was going well. Krueger was pleased with the progress they were making, and he was especially pleased with her positive report on Sage's job performance. He'd long believed in Sage's potential, and he liked being right about people.

Sage pulled up in front of the office soon after she did. She smiled when she heard the old blue pickup's engine refuse to die even after he'd shut it off. She wondered if he did his own tune-ups, and if he did, how he found the time. She knew he was burning the candle at both ends these days.

Black dirt ringed his eyes where his sunglasses had been. Megan tried not to giggle, but he looked like a raccoon. He tossed the glasses on the desk and pulled the blue bandanna off his head. He ruffled his hair with impatient hands, but the deep crease was going nowhere. "What's so funny?"

"It's good to see you." Oh, she was smiling, all right.

"How's life in the big city?"

"Not as exciting as it is out here." she said, smiling. "It all looks good."

"What looks good? Your road?"

"My road." She liked the idea, and she gave a quick laugh. "It's taking shape. This time next year, there'll be traffic on it."

Sage unrolled the bandanna and wiped his face, smearing away the raccoon. The man Megan faced now might have been a soldier camouflaged for a fight, waiting for sundown. Her smile dissolved. His face was calm, but she could feel his mood. It was heated.

"Look, Megan—" He stuffed the bandanna in his back pocket and sat on the edge of his desk. "I want out of this job. I want my old job back."

Her face dropped. "Why?"

"I'm not a good fit. I'm a rancher who works construction to make ends meet. I don't like ordering people around."

Megan pushed the charts aside and sat on her desk, facing him. "There's always an adjustment period, Sage. The crew is coming around. They're beginning to see you as their supervisor instead of one of the guys. And you're doing a good job. I know it's a change, and maybe you're right. Maybe I can't make the change any easier, but this personnel change has already made *my* life easier. Bob says—"

"I don't care what Bob says." He worked to control his tone, to keep it even. Forget about Bob, he wanted her to listen to *him* now, hear what he had to tell her. "I'm sorry, but I can't do this anymore. I don't *want* to do this anymore."

"Why not?"

He gauged the look in her eyes, looking for her to forget about what she was going to come back with and just listen. "I've got a temper," he confessed quietly. "When somebody mouths off to me, I get knots in my gut. I don't want to lose it, Megan." He met her gaze, and it made his eyes sting. He glanced away. "I've got my temper under control now, and I don't want to lose it."

"Did something happen today?"

"You might say that."

But she wasn't going to say anything. She was listening. No presumption, no anticipating the worst. He owed her no drama.

He drew a deep breath. Ordinarily, he would let the incident with Haynes go, but he was just too damned tired. He knew his limits. He hadn't talked to anybody the rest of the day. He couldn't talk to Randy or

Gary or any of the rest of the crew. It wouldn't be right. He'd done his job, and all that was left was writing it up. But he wanted to tell somebody, just to get it out, and unloading on Megan didn't feel right, either. But she was all he had.

"I took Haynes off the oiler, and he didn't take it too well."

"How did you handle it?" she asked.

"I handled it okay." He frowned a bit as he reconsidered. "I handled it better than okay, but that ain't the point. Give me a horse or a cow, I'll show you all kinds of patience. You ever try to handle a damn jackass?"

"Show me a woman who hasn't."

"I gotta do all the showing?" He couldn't help smiling a little. "Figures. Do tell, Miss McBride."

"Somebody has to, and you've been chosen. You're getting paid to tell people what to do." She stepped closer, stopped only a foot from his desk. "I'm asking you not to quit, Sage. Show them what you can do."

He saw the fire in her eyes, and he tipped his head back and gave a quick laugh. "Show who?" he demanded. "The crew? The highway department? Who?" He came to his feet, and she followed him with her eyes, lifting her chin as he rose above her. "I'm not out to prove what a 'good Indian' I can be. I'm not out to be a 'super success story.'"

"That isn't what I meant," she said evenly.

"You know, you have a lot of trouble with saying things you don't mean. Who am I supposed to make this big effort for? You?"

"Yourself. Your . . . your . . ." She gestured helplessly.

"Don't say 'my people,' or you'll blow what's left of my patience all to hell." She looked at him through widening eyes and closed her mouth. "Wise move." He turned toward the window. He needed space. "I know I help fill a minority quota. I can live with that, because I also know I can move as much damn dirt as any man. Beyond that, I don't have any point to prove."

"I'm filling a quota, too," Megan told him quietly. "I was given this project because the department had been accused of sex discrimination."

He turned just enough so he could see her face. "Who made the accusation?"

"I did. When I asked for this project, Bob Krueger went out on a limb for me."

"So we're both tokens." With a nod, he turned to the window again. "And that scrawny little buzzard is up there leaping from one limb to the next. I suppose you're anxious for me to pan out as foreman for his sake."

"Bob took a stand. I don't see how we can allow ourselves to fail him."

"Fail *him*?" Sage faced her and shook his head. "Uh-uh, lady, don't lay that one on me. You wanted to prove a point, and you did it. You're a woman, you're an engineer, you spoke up, and you got the job. Good for Bob."

"That's not fair."

"I didn't take this job because Bob Krueger was dying to stick his neck out for me."

"Of course not."

"I took it because it pays better."

"So you took the bull by the horns." Megan took a step closer. "It was a good move for you, Sage. You know it was. Don't—"

"Have you ever taken a bull by the horns?" The wide-legged stance she took as she folded her arms and glared in response to his question made him laugh again. "Not literally, right? I have, and let me tell you, it gives you a rush of power. Just like the one *you* get from trying to fix things for people."

"What are you talking about? I'm not trying to fix anything. I re-commended you for this job because . . . because, like it or not, you were right for it."

"Did you go up to Pierre and let them all know what a great choice you'd made?"

"No."

"How the Indian boy you handpicked was making good?"

"You're hardly a boy."

"Yeah, but I was handpicked to carry your banner, wasn't I?" She stood her ground as he edged closer, the volume of his voice on the rise. "Wasn't I, Megan? How many causes can one little wisp of a woman push for, anyway?"

They stared at each another for a moment, both wondering how much of what they'd hurled at each another was truth and how much was pure frustration.

Finally, Megan turned and walked away. "I'd rather you wouldn't quit, but if you're determined to do it, do it in writing."

He closed the door quietly.

IF THE TIRE WAS going to go or the pickup was destined to overheat, Sage figured this was the time for it to happen. Careening down the gravel hill, he took pleasure in plowing up a billowing wake of dust. He felt as though the top of his head was about to blow. The lady was using him, sure as hell. He'd tried to level with her, and she'd given him some guidance counselor's pep talk. She'd sooner talk than hear something that didn't fit into her master plan.

He felt cut off. He wasn't part of the family. He wasn't part of the crowd. He wasn't even part of the crew anymore. The one person on the job that he should have been able to talk to had told him everything was just terrific. This was the way it was supposed to be, according to her. He would get used to it, just the way he'd gotten used to the other ties that had been cut. Used to it, hell! Adjust? He would have liked nothing better than to adjust her high and mighty little nose a few pegs lower.

He was pushing too hard. The pickup fishtailed, and he caught himself enjoying the moment of peril before he managed to align the front end with the back again. No, he was *being* pushed, he told himself, and he needed to push back. Purely on impulse, he reached for the glove compartment. His hand froze when he felt the heat of the metal button under his finger. The glove compartment was locked, and the keys were in the ignition. He kept that little bottle sealed and locked up tight.

God help him, he was reaching for an anesthetic on an impulse from the past. *That's all over*, he reminded himself. Four years past. He felt clammy, nearly sick. Staring hard at the road, he passed his fingers over his forehead, and they came away wet.

Slow down. Breathe deeply, slow down, keep driving, and let these minutes tick by one at a time.

Chapter 6

HE HAD THE weekend to cool off. Sage put road construction on the back burner that Saturday morning and busied his hands and his heart with other labor. It might have been *her* road, but this house was his. He'd resisted shortcuts and detours, and he was doing it right this time. The only parts he hadn't been able to handle himself so far were drawing the blueprints, pouring the basement, and raising the roof beams. Though the design was his, he'd paid a friend to do the prints. He'd hired a cement contractor, and Medicine Wheel members had helped him raise the wall frames and the heavy ceiling beams that would be exposed when the house was finished.

He'd chosen the site carefully. It was the ground where a cabin once stood, where the seeds of his life had been planted. His taproot was there. Taproots grew deep in prairie sod. In times of drought, they grew even deeper and clung tenaciously to the heart of the earth. Sage knew his was here, in this spot his family had chosen. The structures they'd built in the interim had been without foundation, and they'd disappeared. The cabin was gone, too, but it had left him with distant memories and good stories. He wasn't sure how much of his childhood memory was really his own and how much came from stories, but it felt fundamental and untarnished, and he was determined to reconnect himself with that taproot. Without it, he'd withered in times of drought.

Sage admired his work as he organized his tools. The studs and rafters cast long shadows in the slanted rays of the morning sun. He could finally see structure. It was beginning to look like a real house. He'd been living all cramped up long enough. He was giving himself good-sized rooms. Three bedrooms. He was thinking positively. Eventually, one of his letters would be answered, and Brenda and Tommy would each have a room when they came to visit after school got out for the summer. It was a dream he cherished. He wondered whether Brenda still loved horses as much as she had when she was a little girl, and whether Tommy ever sucked his thumb anymore. Every time his mother had plucked it out of his mouth, the dark-eyed little boy had waited until she'd turned her back, and then he'd shoved it right back in.

Sage tied his carpenter's apron over his belt and told himself to get to work. A man could drive himself crazy wondering about some things. He climbed the ladder to the roof. He had a subfloor, and all the wall frames and partitions were in place. Once he finished this part, he could say he had a roof over his head. By winter, he hoped to have the shell finished and the shingling done. If he could afford to put in a wood-burning stove, he could work inside during the winter. He was collecting a paycheck now that might cover those things. But only if he continued as foreman. More responsibility, more grief, more money. It was a trade-off he knew he could handle. He'd tried some dead-end alternatives. The view from a dead end was head-up-the-ass dismal.

From the top of his roof, he could see the edge of the world. To the north, the rows of cottonwoods, silver-leafed Russian olives, and thick wild plum bushes provided shelter from the winter wind. The Great Plains rolled to the south like a dun-colored blanket, with green and yellow beadwork applied deep within the nap. Flat-topped buttes ringed the horizon, and the sky was gloriously high, wide and blue.

Time didn't figure into this job. Sage liked that. He hummed to himself as he worked. The resounding, rhythmic tap of his hammer was his accompaniment, and the song was one he'd learned recently from a medicine man. It was a song to sweat by, the old man had told him, and Sage was doing just that. His body was purging itself. Yesterday's anger was dissipating. Basking bare-chested in the morning sun, he gave voice to his sense of relief.

A bright yellow highway department pickup slowed at the approach to his rutted driveway. Sage willed the quick tie-up in the pit of his stomach to go away as he braced himself on one knee and stretched his torso. He watched the vehicle draw near.

What is she doing here?

MEGAN STEPPED around a stack of plywood and squinted at a rafter that pointed the way to the sun. "Sage? Are you up there?"

His head rose over the ridge of the roof and caused an eclipse. His face was shadowed, and the sun's rays seemed to crown him. "Morning," he said. "Taking the scenic route?"

"Not exactly." Maybe. Sage Parker made a pretty nice picture. She stepped closer to the ladder. "I came to see you. Could you use a short break?"

"I was just on my way down."

She watched him negotiate the ladder. He wore vintage high-top basketball shoes and well-worn jeans. His hair gleamed blue-black in the sun. "I won't keep you long," she promised.

"That's too bad." He skipped the last three rungs and hopped to the ground. "I'd just about decided I wanted to be kept." He wiped the sweat from his brow with the back of his wrist and gave her a slow smile. "On the job. Building McBride's road."

"Really?" It was the one piece of news she hadn't anticipated. "I guess I can put away my speech, then."

"You came prepared with a speech?" Still smiling, he hooked his thumbs in his belt. "I've gotta hear this."

"I'll just skip to the last line. I'm sorry for anything I said yesterday that sounded patronizing."

"Patronizing?" He glanced overhead, gave mock consideration, and then nodded. "Yeah, that's a good word for it."

"The truth is, I need a good foreman on this project, and you're good. You don't let anyone slide by. The crew respects you, and that includes Haynes. They all know you're not asking them to do anything you haven't done yourself. That's why you're right for this job. No other reason."

"All that was part of the last line?"

She smiled. "So I backtracked a little. The apology seemed a little naked."

"I'm sorry I flew off the handle. The truth is, I was mad." He shrugged. "I got over it."

"Haynes is a hothead. He's probably over it by now, too."

Sage laughed. "I've been called a hothead myself."

"But you've got it under control now," she reminded him.

"I'm working on it." He untied his carpenter's apron and laid it on top of his toolbox. "How about some coffee?"

"I really don't mean to keep you from your work." She looked up at the skeletal structure. "And this looks like quite a project. You're building this all by yourself?"

"I've had a little help." He moved to the stack of plywood sheets. "Just let me rack up another load of lumber, and then I'll show you around."

The plywood rack leaning against the roof looked like another ladder, but it had two wedges nailed halfway up, which held a supply of plywood and put it within reach of a man on the roof. Megan watched him lift a sheet into place. "That's ingenious."

"It's an extra pair of hands." When he'd filled the rack, he motioned for her to follow him through the opening that would become the front door. "Give me a woman's opinion of the floor plan."

Megan stepped across the threshold. "I'm better equipped to give you an opinion on the design of your driveway."

"You wanna help me rearrange the ruts?"

"There's one place that angles a little too far to the left." She indicated a sharp curve with her hand as she passed under the header of an interior doorway.

"It lacks good engineering," he said absently.

"So what's this?" She waved a hand at the rafters. "The gym?"

"The kitchen. Dining area over here. Nice view of the road, so you can see who's coming and throw some coffee on. Exposed beams. Patio door. The deck comes later." He drew pictures in the air. "Everything but the view and the beams will come later, bit by bit, once I have a roof over my head. But I see it all finished." He touched his temple with his forefinger. "Right here. That's what keeps me going."

Two could play this game. She imagined a redwood deck on the tree-lined side of the house. "When did you start?"

"Three years ago." He laughed at her look of surprise. "It might be a lifelong project. I don't have any credit."

"You mean you're doing this without a loan?"

"I've had loans. I got behind on my payments, and the creditors sold everything on the place that was portable, even the house. It didn't cover what I owed, but they divvied up the money and went away satisfied." He leaned on a future windowsill and looked through future glass. She followed his lead and watched as the breeze made the tall grass ripple. "My land—the part that I actually own—is in trust, so they didn't try to mess with it."

"You mean because your ranch is part of the reservation?"

He nodded. "It's my land, but the trustee relationship between the federal government and the tribe makes it pretty complicated to use Indian land as collateral. So—" He leaned against the windowsill and faced her with a smile that surprised her. "I lost the leased land, too, but I've got some of that back now. I lost everything but the land I actually had title to."

"It was precious to you," she concluded solemnly. "Part of your heritage."

"We call the earth Grandmother."

She nodded. This was what she wanted to hear, the kind of beliefs he held, the kind that him the man he was. She had only read about Lakota beliefs. She wouldn't presume. She would listen and learn. But she had to wonder about the way he was watching her, the laughter gathering in his eyes, his twitching mouth, that barely-contained grin.

He gave a dry chuckle. "There was a time when I would have sold Grandmother in her wheelchair for another ticket on the merry-go-round," he told her. "But there were federal restrictions that wouldn't let me go quite that far."

Really?

It was hard to imagine the man in front of her being the man he'd described. He was exaggerating. He was being dramatic. Sarcastic.

She was dead-on sincere, and he was laughing at her.

"If you weren't close to the land, then why all this?" Her gesture encompassed the house and all that surrounded it. "You're obviously sinking every penny you make back into this place."

"Almost," he agreed. "I'm a rancher. Rebuilding my life means rebuilding this place. When I was drinking, booze was the buffer between me and everything I cared about. I wasn't really close to anything. Of the things I cared about, the land is what I have left. It's where I have to start." He smiled. "Everything else had legs."

He moved away from the windowsill and jerked his chin toward the rest of the house. "C'mon. We haven't finished the tour. Bedroom . . . bathroom . . . bedroom . . . *my* bedroom. Get this!" He walked through a wall and gestured with a flourish. "Room for a king-size bed." She questioned his excitement with a look, and he laughed as he pointed between the wall studs at the tiny trailer on the other side of the driveway. "That's what I'm sleeping in now."

"Okay, that's too small for you. But are you sure about a king? I'd go with queen-size in this space."

He took another look and shook his head. "I see a king."

She leaned her shoulder against the door frame and folded her arms. "What about stock? You can't buy cattle without credit."

"Who says?" Pride glistened in his eyes as he rested his hands on his hips. "I've got fourteen stock cows and five horses now. And they're mine, free and clear. I'll sell the calves in the fall and buy bred heifers." His enthusiasm was unvarnished, like a boy dreaming of taking flight. "Hey, I've got plenty of time. I'm only thirty-four. When I was twenty-four, I thought time was running out on me. Now I've got all the time in the world. By next spring, I might have twenty cows and all the outside walls up, but if I only have eighteen cows and a roof—" he shrugged "—I'll still be doing what I want to do. You like horses?"

"I love horses."

He gave the familiar chin-jerk toward the corral. Then he stepped between two wall studs and dropped to the ground. When Megan got to the edge of the subfloor he was waiting, offering his hand to help her down.

It wasn't that far. She was perfectly capable. But she guarded the protest on the tip of her tongue. Their eyes met, and she read the message. The offer of his hand was a chance to touch, and the choice was hers. She took it. It felt strong and hot, like reaching to warm her hand at the fire and getting licked without getting burned. Her feet hit the ground, she looked up, and the smile in his eyes held her still for another moment, her hand in his. He nodded toward the corral, gave her hand a gentle squeeze, and they walked together.

A stout sorrel gelding stood in one corner of the corral, with a brown and white pinto mare and her colt in another. The colt stole the show. His springy white mane and sassy flag of a tail were set off by well-defined patches of dark brown. He pranced circles around his mother as Sage stepped onto one rail, swung his leg over the top of the fence and sat down. Megan clambered up one rail at a time.

"I was stretching it a little. I've got four horses and a colt, but he's one hell of a colt."

"He's beautiful. I think he counts as a horse."

"The first thing I did was repair the corrals and put up the pole barn. I used to have a prefab metal barn, but it was auctioned off. I used wood this time. It's warmer in the winter and cooler in the summer."

He could bore the pants off his rare visitors describing his plans, but she seemed interested. She was listening to him, anyway. She hadn't stopped to borrow something or return it, wasn't asking to cut his prairie hay on shares. Sure, she'd come because she wanted something from him, wanted *him*, but he'd already decided to keep his new job, so she had him. And she was still here.

"Maybe it's a little like building a road," he said. "I need to see it take shape. I'm watching it rise from the dust, kind of like me—my own resurrection. I'd been sober for about a year when I came back out here and dug the first posthole. I'd been avoiding the place, but I learned something that day about making a start."

He remembered the day, and the tears he'd shed as he'd rammed the posthole digger into the ground, making a mark. Taking a step. He scanned the east end of the corral and found his benchmark. "One post. That was all I had. I came back the next day, and it was still there, so I knew I'd actually done it. I'd taken that first step."

"One post," she echoed, and then she smiled at him. "From the ground up. I admire your courage."

He looked at her and found that the complete sincerity in her eyes embarrassed him. "Courage, hell," he tossed off as he jumped down from the corral. "No more than it takes anybody else to put one foot in front of the other. I only had one direction left to go, and that was up." He cocked his head to one side as he looked up at her. "I promised coffee, didn't I? How about some lunch?"

In three steps, Megan was down on the ground beside him. "I really didn't mean to keep you from your work."

"I have to eat sometime." He made a point of surveying the way her slim figure suited blue jeans and pink top. No sleeves. Nice arms. First time he'd seen them, shoulder to fingertips. He winked at her. "You do, too. You can have coffee and a sandwich with me, or drive into Red Calf for beer and pizza at Floyd's."

"Which is closed."

"Damn, that's right!" He snapped his fingers. "A bunch of troublemakers shut him down in Red Calf, at least for the time being. Guess it's sandwiches or sandwiches."

She returned his smile. "Sandwiches, then."

He hesitated at the foot of the small wooden step under the door to the tiny trailer where he was about to entertain his boss.

Come to think of it, he'd just winked at his boss. *Damn.*

"There's not much room," he said. "And not much ventilation. It gets pretty hot and, uh, pretty cramped."

"Hey, I live in an apartment, just big enough to store the clothes I never wear and the TV I never have time to watch." She laid a hand on his arm, looked up at him and winked. *Winked.* So they were even. "I'm not even much of a cook, but I can spread mayonnaise."

"Maybe I can find something cold to drink. Should we eat in the dining room?" With a quick grin, he nodded toward the new house.

"Oh, yes, let's."

The trailer was, as promised, hot and cramped. Sage set the sandwich makings on the counter, and Megan put them together while he found two cans of Coke in the fridge and dug up a bag of potato chips to go with their meal. It felt good to get back outside, where the air was moving and space was unlimited. They sat cross-legged on the plywood subfloor, ate sandwiches, and talked about the house. Which room would he finish first? What kind of floors would he have? What kind of heat?

"Three bedrooms is a lot for one person. Is there a chance your family might come back to you?"

He shook his head. "My family belongs to somebody else now. My wife remarried, and she doesn't want any interference from me."

"If you're paying child support, you could probably insist on some—"

He waved the suggestion away. "I'm not going to insist on anything. I'm hoping they'll give me a chance to redeem myself, but they have some pretty bad memories, and I can understand . . ."

"Were you . . . did you ever . . . physically . . ." She was staring at him, wide-eyed, *damn*. Worse, she couldn't spit the word out.

"Hurt anybody? No doubt. Hit anybody? No. I don't think so." He shook his head slightly. "Pretty sure I would've heard about it." He started to take a drink, changed his mind, lifted his gaze, and gave her an unguarded look. His eyes stung. "I started having blackouts. I'd wake up with a godawful hangover and realize I'd lost a day somewhere. I had no idea where I'd been, or what I'd done."

"That's scary."

"Damn right it's scary. You have to try to get people to tell you what you did without letting them know you don't remember. I had a black eye once, and I never found out who gave it to me." A corner of his mouth twitched. "I think it was my brother." He drew a deep breath and glanced toward the highway. "Once I found out I'd driven my daughter to school, and I didn't remember doing it." He looked at Megan. "I was dead drunk, and I was out on the road with that kid in the car."

It was her turn to glance away, but she fought the impulse, and the words just tumbled out. "My father drinks too much, too."

The startled look in her eyes said it all. It wasn't so much a matter of whom she was telling, but the very fact that she was telling that surprised her. She'd betrayed the family secret. He wanted to feel chosen, but he couldn't let himself go there. The time had come, and he was a handy sounding board. "Maybe that's why you have this concern for—"

"He's not an alcoholic." The claim tumbled out quickly. Automatically, like a line from a role she'd been assigned. "I guess I would say he's more a . . . a problem drinker."

"A problem drinker?" He gave a sympathetic smile. "What's that?"

"Well, he's never lost his job over it or anything. He doesn't fight, and he doesn't, you know, do anything really *bad*." She stared at the hole in the top of the pop can and lifted her shoulders in a helpless shrug. "He just drinks too much sometimes. *Most* of the time."

He was watching her become, for the moment, the little girl she'd once been, the one who'd been told not to talk about her father's drinking. "It bothers you to see him drink?" he asked gently.

"I don't have to be around it anymore." She smiled quickly, swept her hair back from her forehead and squared her shoulders. She was a woman again. "I do think my mother should do something about him, though. He's getting too old to behave so foolishly."

"I wish my wife had done something about me, too." He chuckled, shaking his head at the beauty of the notion. "It would have been a hell of a lot less work for me if she'd just taken the bull by the horns—" he gave Megan a lopsided grin along with the expression "—and made me quit drinking. Bull-headed as hell. Maybe she could have sewn my mouth shut or something."

"Well, it's just . . . it's just so . . ." She wasn't going to laugh. He watched her swallow the temptation. She crushed the empty Coke can with the heels of her hands. "It's good that you've done it for yourself. I admire you for it. You've started the recovery group, and you're building this place from scratch." She lifted her hands to indicate the work that surrounded them. "I just think it's wonderful."

She sounded a little like that school counselor giving him a pep talk again, but he knew that was to be expected. She'd put all her eggs into her professional basket. There she was sure, sharp, determined to achieve. In her personal life, she wore blinders.

"What do you hear about Karl Taylor?" he asked as he jiggled his pop can and judged he had about two more swallows left.

"I saw him when I was in Pierre. I ran into him in the parking lot at the highway department."

"Did he say anything to you?"

"Some dumb comment about equal opportunity."

"Mine?"

"You might say that." She gave him the single arched slybrow.

"Yeah, I did." He smiled. "Now, what did Taylor say?"

"That maybe I was giving you equal opportunity at the trap I'd baited for him."

"Did you punch his lights out?"

"I ignored him. There's nothing a gasbag like that hates more." She rolled her eyes. "Like I would actually be interested in Taylor. *Ugh.*"

"You know that Floyd is Karl's brother," Sage said, and she nodded. "I think one of them might have had something to do with setting my tire up to fall off."

Her eyes widened. "Really?"

"Really," he echoed with a nod. "And if I'm right, then I think you need to be careful, too."

"Karl's been with the department for twenty years, at least. He's not going to jeopardize his job by trying to get back at me."

"No?" He shook his head. "I wouldn't bet on it, Megan. I'd stay clear of him."

"I'm sure Karl Taylor and I will be happy to stay clear of each other." She smiled. "I'm so glad you've decided to stay on as foreman, Sage. You've already made my job easier."

"Oh yeah?" She nodded. "Well, how about you making *my* job a little easier?" He stood up, and she followed suit, looking at him curiously. "Can you handle a hammer?" He headed for the tool box.

"Of course."

"How about heights?"

"No problem."

"Then if you're going to hang around here on my day off—" He tossed a hammer in the air, caught it by the head and offered her the handle. "—I'm gonna put you to work."

She took the tool in her hand. "You mean I get to be on the crew?"

"You get to be the *whole* crew, since I seem to be stuck with the foreman's job."

"We'll see if I can stand working for you. Lead the way."

"You've gotta wear one of these." He handed her a canvas carpenter's apron advertising Schultz Lumber, then reached for his leather one.

She laughed. "For this I spent four years in college?"

"And we'll be using these," he told her as he dipped into a box of eight-penny nails and dropped a handful into one of his apron pocket. "So fill up your pockets. This project is on a tight budget, so if you bend too many nails—" She dropped a couple from the handful she was loading into her apron and glanced up quickly. He returned the sassy wink she'd surprised him with earlier. "I'll keep you after five and make you straighten them out."

"Tyrant." She knelt to pick up the lost nails.

"You bet. That's why I'm so perfect for my job." He gestured toward the ladder. "You go up first, and I'll hold the ladder steady."

He watched her step carefully from the ladder to the plywood sheathing that was already nailed in place. She turned, found her balance on the pitched roof and looked out over the prairie. "You sure you're okay up there?" he asked.

"I'm fine." She shaded her face with her hand. "What a gorgeous view!"

The breeze lifted her honey-colored hair back from her face, and she reminded him of a fine-carved figure on the bow of a sailing vessel.

"I'll say."

Chapter 7

I GUESS REGINA finally reported Jackie missing."

Sage pushed the button under his thumb, but he hesitated in pulling open the pickup door. He turned a puzzled look toward Gary Little Bird. "I thought he'd run off to North Dakota."

"That's what Regina thought. He's got relatives up there, and that's where he always goes. But she got hold of them, and they said he never showed up there."

Sage left the door ajar. It was quitting time, and crewmembers were heading for their vehicles. Megan's was parked next to his, and out of the corner of his eye, he noted that Gary's news had caught her attention.

"It's been at least a week since he's been home," Sage reflected. "Nobody's seen him?"

"Well, the cops did some checking, and I guess Roger Makes War and Henry Treetop finally admitted they were with him Monday night."

Sage braced his hand on the top of the cab and peered at Gary. "That's four days. Nobody's seen him since?"

Gary shook his head. "First they said they'd taken him home after a party and let him off near his house. Now they admit they're not exactly sure where they put him out of the car. He said something about going to work and told them to let him off." Gary shrugged. "They pulled over, and he got out. That was the last they saw of him."

"What time was that?"

Gary offered a feeble laugh. "Hell, Sage, they don't know. They were all pretty wasted. They figure sometime after midnight."

"And he said he was coming to work?" Megan asked as she joined the two men. "Poor Jackie."

Sage directed a sigh skyward. "Yeah," he said disgustedly. "Poor Jackie."

"Well, listen, I'd better be taking off." Gary shoved his hands in his pockets and took a couple of steps backward. "I'll let you know if I hear anything else." He grinned at Megan. "My brother's a dispatcher at the police station, so I get all the news."

"Coming to work in the middle of the night," Megan mused as Gary walked away. "I wonder how far—"

"God*damn.*" Sage closed his eyes as the memory of a smell burst open in his brain. He jerked on the pickup door and hopped in.

"Sage, what is it?"

Megan fastened both hands on the door handle, and he gave her a hard look through the half-open window. "Stay here. I'll be right back, so just stay here."

It had been somewhere between the construction site and the highway. The pickup plowed furrows into the gravel as Sage pushed the accelerator ever closer to the floor and tried to remember where he'd stopped to fix that flat on his way to work . . . when? Had it been Wednesday morning? How far from the highway? The memory of the odor became sharper, and he began to feel queasy all over again. It wasn't only the smell. It was the strange feeling he'd had that the odor was beckoning him somehow. He'd ignored all but the fact that the stench was sickening, and he'd hurried to change the tire and move on.

He braked suddenly. There was nothing notable about the spot—no landmark to distinguish it from the rest of the four-strand barbed wire separating miles of grassy prairie from miles of gravel road. But something appealed to him to stop there, and he knew instinctively what it was. Deep in his gut, he connected with it again. Wiser men than he would have cautioned him to resist this kind of eerie summons, but resisting wasn't possible this time. He left the pickup door standing open and cleared the roadside ditch with one long leap.

He ignored the approach of another vehicle as he negotiated the barbed wire, stretching two strands above his head and holding two down under his boot. The stench was still in the air. Putrefying flesh. It should have been an animal, the carcass of something meant to live and die out there in the middle of nowhere. Sage knew it wasn't. He dreaded what he would find, but he ran unerringly toward it. Two ravens sprang from the grass, black wings aflutter as they pumped hard to gain height quickly.

Sage slowed his approach. A snatch of blue lay in the grass ahead. His thudding heartbeat encroached on the vast quiet. The shroud of crisp prairie grass crunched beneath Sage's boots. He stood before the gaping face of death and heard its bleak cry echo in his head.

"Christ," he whispered. He tipped his head back and watched the white wisp of a cloud slip by.

The soft swish of grass drew him around. *Megan.* His heart tripped into overdrive. She shouldn't see this. No one should. The one good thing he could do now was to spare her. He ran like a man possessed and caught her, trapping her arms between them. She looked up at him, and her eyes posed the unspeakable question

"It's him," he said.

"Jackie?"

He nodded. The color drained from her face, but still, she leaned to peer past him. He held fast. "It's bad. You can't go over there. He's dead, and it's . . . it's really bad."

"But . . ." Her face crumpled. "You mean he's been there all this time?" He nodded solemnly, and she had no words. There were only the small sounds. "Oh . . . oh . . ."

He put his arm around her and turned their backs to Jackie's resting place, their faces to the fresh breeze. He couldn't allow her to see what he had seen. Sage was there to protect them both. Megan and Jackie. The living could share their grief, but the dead had a right to some privacy. The least he could do was spare Jackie's torn and bloated remains the final indignity of being viewed.

"How did you know?" she asked, her voice toneless.

"I had a flat tire the other morning. I could smell death, but I figured it was an animal."

"But then today . . ."

"Today, I knew." *Today, I heard him call me.*

"How? I mean . . . all by himself out here?" Megan slipped her arm around his waist. "Did he fall?"

Her gesture was a comfort to him. "He could have passed out and died of exposure."

"But it's summer," she protested. "It hasn't rained this week, and it's not that cold at night."

"It can still happen," he said. "Any number of things could have happened. Something inside, like heart failure or alcohol poisoning. He could have gone into shock. He could have choked on his own vomit."

"Oh, God."

"He's dead. That's it. That's all."

"But what about those two men who left him out here in the middle of nowhere?"

"I don't know." He shook his head and sighed heavily. "I don't know. All I know is, my friend found the other way to get off the merry-go-round."

"The other way?"

74

"You quit drinking and step off or keep it up and let the booze take you down." Sage took her shoulders in his hands. She winced, and he discovered a tear in her sleeve and blood on his hand. "You got hung up on the barbed wire?"

She lifted her face with a blank stare.

"You're bleeding."

She looked at his hand and then scrunched her shoulder, frowning. He pulled the torn edges of fabric apart to expose the patch of skin oozing healthy red blood. *Life.* Their friend Jackie had bled the last of his.

"It's nothing." She gave her head a quick little shake. "Nothing. Just a scratch."

"You'll need a tetanus shot. That stuff's probably rusty."

"I think I'm caught up, but I'll check. It doesn't hurt." They both looked up at once. Her eyes glistened. "We can't leave him."

"I'll stay with him." The body had been ravaged, but Sage would protect what was left. "You call Law and Order. I mean the tribal police, not the county. I don't care about jurisdiction. Tell them we know it's him."

Megan tightened her grip on him and nodded.

"And don't tell anybody else." He had her full attention, eye to eye and heart to heart, and he hated to send her away. "We'll take care of him."

TWO DAYS AFTER Jackie's body had been discovered, another tribal council hearing was on the schedule. Megan went to the council chambers on her own this time. The chair next to Sage was empty. He looked up when she took it, and he greeted her with a nod. She touched his hand and then turned her attention to the activity in the room. The councilmen were getting coffee and shuffling through papers, and there were people milling around, moving chairs, talking privately.

"Have they started yet?"

"Sort of," he said softly. "We're between issues at the moment."

"Will you be speaking?"

Sage nodded, eyes on the chairman, who was examining some papers.

Jackie's wife sat only a few chairs away. "How's Regina doing?" Megan whispered.

"Okay, I guess." Sage leaned forward and rested his elbows on his knees, a manila folder dangling from his hand. He had a presentation to give. Clearly, he didn't need any distractions.

Megan settled back to wait and watch. Listen and learn, she told herself. But not to other people's conversations. When you tune in, that's eavesdropping, *so quit it.*

"They said the autopsy was inconclusive," a man behind her was saying. "They said it was like examining two-week-old hamburger."

"No ears, that one," a woman's voice said. "Last time he was in detox, the doctor told him his liver was gonna get him sooner or later."

"Rotten hamburger, rotten liver—what's the difference? When your time comes, what's left is just coyote bait anyway."

"Eeez, what a thing to say. He was only thirty-five."

"I'm out of cigarettes." The complaint was punctuated with a smoker's cough. "Ask Boo Boo if he's got any."

"We'll be eating potato salad over you pretty soon if you don't quit mooching smokes. Listen to you."

The woman leaned past Megan and tapped someone who was sitting just down from Sage. Megan glanced up, curious to see who Boo Boo was, and realized Sage was watching her. She felt her face grow warm. Instant guilt-burn.

He smiled. "You go to a wake, you fill up on potato salad." He laid a hand on her arm and inclined his chin toward the side door. Megan followed the direction of his gaze.

Floyd Taylor had slipped into the room, accompanied by his brother, Karl. Side by side, the two reminded Megan of the pair of bulldog bookends that sat on her father's desk and defied anyone to tamper with his papers. Karl was none too subtle about sizing up the assembly, and Megan felt his cold stare the moment he picked her out of the crowd.

The meeting resumed. The chairman expressed his condolences to Regina and invited her to be first to speak on the next item on the agenda. Regina stood tall, her strong voice cracking only once as she read the statement she'd prepared. She said it was too late for her husband, but she didn't want alcoholism to kill his children. She wanted to see tighter control over the sale of alcohol. "Whatever it takes," she said. "Off-reservation sale or on, alcohol is alcohol, and it kills us Indians. *Kills* us."

When Sage came to the microphone, he asked whether the councilmen had had time to study the information he'd presented to them at the last hearing. There were a couple of nods, a couple of voices, all affirmative. But there were a few who didn't seem to hear the question.

"Once again, I've come before this council to speak about the welfare of the people you represent. You have suspended Floyd Taylor's permit temporarily, and that's a start. If you've read those reports, then you know in your gut that the way Mr. Taylor conducts business in and around the Big Thunder Nation jeopardizes our health."

Floyd came to his feet. "I object to that kind of talk, Mr. Chairman." He pointed a beefy finger at Sage. "And I could get you for slander, Parker. You've got no business accusing me." He addressed the chairman again. "You come to Floyd's Foods, I sell you meat and potatoes, and I let you buy on credit. Toward the end of the month, people need a little help, and I let them sign for their groceries. Where it's legal, I sell alcoholic beverages. It's just another product. A customer buys a bottle, I don't tell him how to use it."

"I'm not finished, Taylor," Sage said.

"You accused me, Parker." Taylor pointed at Sage and then swung back to the council. "I'm not gonna tell you how to govern here—you know best—but you've got no call to shut me down. There's a hundred ways to get drunk. In my store, we sell vanilla extract, rubbing alcohol—hell, it's none of my business how a customer wants to use it. And how about cough medicine? Tell the clinic to stop giving out cough medicine. If people want to get drunk—"

"Sit down, Mr. Taylor," the chairman ordered in a calm voice. "Mr. Parker has the floor."

"We're going to bury a man tomorrow," Sage continued without sparing Taylor another glance. "This was a man who wanted to quit drinking, *tried hard* to quit drinking. We all watched him. Some of us encouraged him, and some of us laughed and told him he'd never make it. He didn't. So when we put him in the ground tomorrow, we can think to ourselves that this is the way it is, and nothing's ever going to change. Or, like Regina, we can keep reminding ourselves that this is not what we want for our children. We can make this decision for ourselves."

He lowered his voice and stirred the silence. "I want us to formally petition the state to revoke Mr. Taylor's liquor licenses. There's plenty of evidence to support our claims. They *will* investigate. Maybe they'll give him a warning. Maybe a suspension, give him time to clean up his act. We keep the pressure on." He turned and glared at Taylor. "And we stop doing business with him where we have the final say. And my final say is, no more business permits for *Uncle* Floyd."

After the applause, the discussion continued, but it was largely redundant and uninspiring after the impact of Sage's presentation. Once again, the issue was tabled.

"Tabled!" Megan snapped as they stood to leave. "What kind of a decision is that?"

"It's a reprieve," Sage said quietly. "We don't have enough votes, but we're being given a little more time, thanks to Jackie."

"I want to speak to his wife." Megan searched the crowd and spotted the beautiful fall of black hair. She made her way to Regina's side and offered her hand as she'd seen the others do. It was not so much a handshake as a pressing of one palm against another. Megan expressed her sorrow, and Regina nodded with sad dignity.

"Have they brought him home yet?" Sage asked.

"They're taking him to the church basement," she said. "He should be there soon."

"I'll drive you over." He turned to Megan. "The funeral's tomorrow morning. I won't get to work until about one."

She nodded and pulled back from the conversation, watching the crowd split and move past them on either side. She knew she'd done what she could; she'd given moral support at the meeting, and she'd expressed condolences to Jackie's widow. It was time she left Sage to share Regina's grief. Her peripheral vision blurred as she fastened her attention on them.

When they moved toward the door, she followed, giving them space. She was an outsider, but somehow she couldn't bring herself to make a graceful exit. She had known Jackie, too, and she'd been concerned about him. She had been there when Sage had discovered his body. She felt she had a part in this, although she wasn't sure what her part was. Not the gawker. Not the suspicious stranger. She cared about what was going on here, and she wanted it known.

She wanted Sage to turn to her and draw her in.

She chided herself mentally for her selfishness. Regina had lost her husband, and Sage had lost a friend. Megan shared no real part in their grief. They hardly noticed when she moved away and headed toward her pickup.

At the last moment Sage turned, smiled and said, "Thanks for coming."

THE SMALL WHITE frame church was packed with mourners. A man standing near the door offered Megan one of the folding chairs arranged behind the pews and handed her a hymnal. She opened the book and found hymns in the Lakota language.

Sage was one of the six solemn-faced pallbearers. They were all dressed differently, none in a dark suit. One wore a plaid Western shirt buttoned tightly around his neck and adorned with a beaded bolo tie. Another wore a white shirt with a leather vest, and a third was dressed in a dated beige suit. This was the first time Megan had seen Sage dressed up, and, although his blue sport jacket and tan slacks might not have been deemed appropriate for the occasion in other circles, she saw that fashion was not the measure of anything here. One dressed in his best, whatever it might be, and came to say goodbye.

As she watched Sage perform his duties and then take a seat in the front row, Megan was struck unexpectedly by the sheer beauty of the man. It wasn't just the rich contrast between his white shirt and his brown skin, or the shiny fullness of his black hair, but it was the way he moved, the way he carried himself. He did nothing to call attention to himself, and yet he commanded it. There was a kind of serenity in his face that inspired serenity in the heart of one who watched him. There was solace in knowing he had survived his own suffering and had found peace.

The service alternated English with Lakota, and it spoke of Jackie's death as part of life. Megan recognized the tunes of familiar hymns, but it was as though each note were being pulled through a sieve by mournful voices in a language that tore at the soul without any translation. By the time she pulled her pickup into line at the end of the cortege, she was more aching heart than considering mind, and she was drawn up the hill for the finish.

There was no hearse. The casket, draped in a red, white, and blue star quilt, was unloaded from the back of a pickup. The six men carried it through a gate marked by two tall, white poles. Megan waited inside her pickup, watching the crowd file along the perimeter of the woven wire fence. Old women wore dark sweaters and tri-cornered scarves to keep the warm wind off their gray heads. Children let the tips of their fingers bounce along the woven wire squares as they followed along to the gravesite.

Megan climbed down from the pickup and brushed at the wrinkles in her navy blue skirt. Overhead, the clouds were thick and gray and rushing quickly across the sky. She took her place at the end of the line and followed unobtrusively. She walked past graves marked simply, some with wooden crosses, some with small white frames of wood.

There were a few headstones and a few faded plastic floral tributes. For the most part, this was prairie. It was buffalo grass, prickly pear cactus, and purple South Dakota coneflowers. And it was the dust foretold in graveside prayer.

There were no blankets of fake grass to profane the earth that would receive Jackie's body. The casket was lowered by strong hands and sturdy ropes. It settled, and six rope ends followed, thudding as they hit the blanket. As the mourners sang another hymn, Sage left the grave-side and came to stand beside Megan. He must have seen the tears welling in her eyes, because he took her hand. Gratefully, she hung on tight, for life was as dear at that moment as it had ever been.

When the last note of the hymn had drifted out over the grass, another sound took its place. It was Regina's keening—the high-pitched song of grief that only a woman's voice could carry and only a woman's heartbreak could produce. Her sorrow echoed in the hills while Sage and the other pall bearers filled the grave. And the earth took her husband back to her womb.

"WHY DID YOU come?" Sage asked. They sat together in her pickup and watched the others drive away.

"I was with you when you found him." She glanced over her shoulder at the fresh mound of earth behind the fence. "I wanted to see him put to rest."

"Grief is one thing. Pity's another." She turned back to him. Something glinted in his dark eyes. Not tears or even mist, but something about pain. A reflection, maybe. Or a warning. "You know that, don't you?"

"I've never witnessed the kind of grief I heard today. I'd thought maybe . . ." She glanced away again. ". . . maybe people were disgusted with him, the way they talked . . . maybe because of the way he died."

"Were you disgusted with him?"

She shook her head quickly and looked down at her hands. Tears burned in her throat again. "It must have been a terrible way to die. Alone like that."

"What makes you think anyone else would come to this hill today with feelings of disgust?"

She heard no malice in his voice and saw none in his eyes, but his question sounded accusing. She wanted to accuse him in return. "It just seemed like the man was floundering for all the world to see, and no one

80

wanted to . . ." She shook her head.

"To take care of him?"

His voice was soft, but she saw the challenge in his eyes. She sought the words to meet it. "Some people need to be taken care of . . . sometimes."

"Children do," he said. "But if you treat a man like a child, he's tempted to behave like a child."

"Indian people have been treated shamefully," she agreed. "I know that. I don't want to be part of that. I want to be open-minded and fair, and I want to try to make things right in whatever small way—"

"Make things right?" He chuckled. "How is one little white lady going to make things right?"

"In my own small way," she repeated, emphasizing each word. "I cared about Jackie."

"Do you care about the rest of the crew the same way?"

"Yes," she said firmly, and then, "I think so. They haven't put me to the test. He didn't want to miss work, Sage. He didn't *want* to be late. He would apologize and explain, and all the while you knew he'd embarrassed himself again, dug a deeper hole for himself. And when he was doing well, he was such a good worker, and so willing to—"

"Megan." He touched her shoulder and waited until she looked into his eyes. "A man can drown in pity, and you're pouring it out by the bucketful."

She stared for a moment. "Is that all it is? Pity?"

"It sure sounds like it. Can you tell me you respected Jackie? One rational, independent adult to another, did you think of him that way?" She looked down at her hands and gave her head a quick shake. "You felt sorry for him, and you thought you knew how to fix things."

She shook her head. Her throat burned. "I didn't mean to drown anyone. I got close enough to see his boot, lying there in the grass." She closed her eyes, and there it was again. "The color of his shirt, I saw that, too, and I knew it was him, but I wanted to see for myself. Maybe it really wasn't, maybe . . ." She drew a steadying breath. "I don't feel sorry. I just feel very sad."

"Grief isn't pity," he said gently, and he slid his arm behind her neck and squeezed her shoulder. She tipped her head to the side, resting her forehead on his arm. "Pity seems . . . what was that good word you used before? Patronizing? Pity seems patronizing. Grief is honest and natural at a time like this. And what I see in you now is grief."

Chapter 8

THIS IS WHERE we've got problems." Sage pointed to the map on Megan's desk. "This is pretty soft stuff."

"The old roadbed has a quarter mile of washboard there," Megan said as she moved around the desk to get a right-side-up look at the spot he was indicating. "The culvert should go in here."

"Yeah, but the hill's there. I'm working down here, and that clay just doesn't quit."

"Maybe one culvert won't do it." She opened a plastic sandwich bag and peered at the contents. "How far down are you?"

"I've scraped off a couple of feet. You're going to end up with a real dip if you don't make some adjustments there."

"I need to get down there this afternoon. Now . . ." She waved the plastic bag under his nose. "I'll trade you half a tuna sandwich for almost anything else."

He pushed the map aside and leaned his hip against the desk. "How about canned chopped meat?" he offered. She looked doubtful. "Liverwurst? What about tongue?" Even as his eyes danced, he wondered what he thought he was doing, teasing her. He knew he'd allowed too much friendliness to seep into this relationship, knew he was enjoying it way too much.

"Which is it?" she asked, her eyes warming to his.

"Which would you like?"

They let the question stand between them for a moment before he reached across the desk and dragged his black lunchbox closer. He produced a plastic-wrapped sandwich and handed it to her. "Summer sausage on rye. Be my guest."

"Just half." She tried to exchange half of hers for it, but he shook his head.

"I'll pass on the fish."

"I can't let you go hungry." She pushed his sandwich back at him.

He edged away as it occurred to him there were all kinds of hunger. "I've got another one." He proved it to her, then nodded at her cooler.

"If you've got anything cold to drink in there, I'll trade for a share of that. All I've got is hot coffee."

"On a day like this?" She hiked herself up to sit on the desk, flipped back the lid of her cooler and brought out a bottle of lemon-flavored mineral water. "I've got another one."

Sage watched her unscrew the cap on the bottle before she handed it to him. They'd just discussed a hitch in the project like two professional equals, and now she was opening a bottle of water for him and worrying about whether he was going to get enough to eat. In recent weeks, he'd become comfortable with their working relationship. If the crew had been taking bets on anything when he went into the office the way they had when Taylor had been working with her, Sage figured they'd given it up. Heads no longer turned at the sight of the two of them together, and he figured they were now seen as a team. Engineer and construction foreman. But when they took a break, he wanted to tease her about little things, like something she ate or wore or said, and he wanted to smile at her in a way that had nothing to do with any road project. He took the bottle from her hand, and his fingers brushed over hers. His eyes met hers, and all he saw was a woman he wanted.

The flavored water slid over his tongue like fire-fighting foam. Just what he needed. Tart bubbles. A mouthful of grin-kill.

He scowled at the bottle. "You actually *pay* for this stuff?"

"The first taste is always the worst," she said with a smile. "Once you get used to it, it's like the champagne of bottled water."

"Champagne?" He studied the label before he tried it again. He grimaced. "Yeah, you'd have to acquire the taste for it."

She uncapped another bottle. "It's really good when the weather's hot. Quenches your thirst better than sweet, sticky pop."

He admired the delicate curve of her neck as she lifted her chin and tipped the bottle to her lips. There was no denying the heat. It might reach a hundred degrees before the day was out, but Megan wouldn't wilt. She would bloom. Her face glowed with a soft sheen. Nothing sticky, he thought, but maybe sweet. He imagined touching his lips to her forehead and then licking them. He liked his sugar with a little salt.

"I can't resist sweets," he said. She lowered the bottle and blotted her upper lip with the back of her hand. He smiled. "I'm worse than a kid."

"Mmm, but when it's this hot—" She took the sandwich he'd given her in both hands and studied it. "A cold beer would be good with this."

"Sure would." She gave him the surprised look of someone who'd just stepped on his toe. He laughed. "You'll get no argument from me on that point. I've always been a great fan of cold beer on hot days."

"A fan," she said quickly. "That's what we need in here. Better yet, a bathtub. Wouldn't that be a fine way to spend the lunch hour? Soak in the tub, dry off in front of the fan. You'd be a new person, refreshed and ready to take on more dirt."

"You'd walk out the door smellin' like a rose."

"No, something fruity." She lifted the water bottle. "Maybe lemon."

"And you'd find the whole crew hanging around the windows." He took a drink. On that note, he needed to wet his whistle, keep the wolf at bay. "Ever tried a sweat bath?"

"You mean, like a sauna?"

"Couldn't say. I've never sauna-ed. I'm thinking Lakota style." He gauged her interest by the look in her eyes. It was there. He had her at *Lakota style*. "It's better than an ordinary bath. You sweat. You get rid of all the excesses and the need to indulge in excesses. You cleanse yourself from the inside out, and *then* you rinse off all the crap. Nothing wrong with a little dirt. It's what's polluting you on the inside that you wanna wash away."

"Purification? Like a religious thing?"

"Like a religious thing." It was probably her use of the word *thing* that made him hold back, keeping it light. "A tribute to Grandmother, sort of like buying her flowers or something."

"How often do you do this?"

"As often as I need to." He lifted an eyebrow. "How often do you sauna?"

"I don't. But I bathe pretty often. Not the same, huh?" She smiled, and he shook his head. "Do you do this as a group?"

"Not usually. Not unless—"

"I mean as part of the Medicine Wheel program."

Aha. He could see her mind conjuring up a picture. She was thinking coed. He studied her for a moment, taking the time to make her squirm a little before he shook his head. "Men and women don't sweat together. At least, not in a Lakota sweat lodge. Now you go to some kind of New Age retreat, who knows? You pay your money, you take your chances."

She shifted her perch on the desktop. He smiled.

"So you have two lodges." She drew the idea of separation in the air. "The men in one, and the women . . ."

"Traditionally, yeah, with a holy man or an elder woman, someone who knows the way. It's a personal experience, not a party." Suddenly, he realized he knew little about her personal life, her traditions, her circle of friends, her idea of a party. He spread his hands. "It's more like—"

"Like going to church?"

"Not exactly." It occurred to him it wasn't like anything else, which was probably why he did it. *Inipi* was at once confining and liberating.

"More like meditation or maybe yoga?" she persisted.

"What's yoga like?"

"I'm not sure. There's an early morning yoga show on TV, and I keep trying to get into it because everybody looks so comfortable in their own skin, like they've discovered the meaning of life, and they move so gracefully." She tipped her body to the side and sketched an arc with one arm. "And I'm a klutz. I always overdo, and I ache all over the next day."

"*Ohan.*" He chuckled. "I know the feeling."

"So they tell you to take a hot bath, a nice long soak. I got out of the tub once and fainted dead away. The water was boiling hot, and I was overdone."

"Then you might wanna stay away from—"

"How hot does it get in your sweat lodge? Does anyone ever faint?"

He was stuck on the image of her stepping out of a steamy tub and crumpling to the floor, all wet, all pink, and all nude. But sitting right in front of him was a woman who was all eyes and ears because he was just so damn fascinating.

Focus, Parker.

He cleared his throat and started drawing her a picture with his hands. "The lodge is a willow frame covered with tarps. You have four doors—places where you can open a flap—that are part of the ceremony. You take four little breaks, and you open a different door each time. Four directions, four doors, four intervals. But you can go out whenever you need to, especially if you feel like you might faint. There's no clock, no rule book, no script or anything."

"So I can't read up on it?"

"Sure, you can." He smiled. "Let me know if you find out we're doing it wrong."

"I'll even bring in the book." She worked on her sandwich for a moment, finally gave him her sparkly-eyed, just-kidding look. "You speak Lakota?"

"A little, but not by the book."

"What did you say? *Ohan.*"

"Did I say that?" She nodded. He chuckled. Maybe he spoke more Lakota than he realized.

And if it came out without thinking, maybe she was getting under his skin. "You say the last part kind of . . . *ohan*. I guess use your tongue to force it halfway through your nose." She tried again, and he grinned. "Better."

"By the man, not the book." She crumpled her napkin and scored three feet from the basket. "I've got a lot of time at night for reading. Not much to do in Hot Springs."

"They've got some natural hot baths there. Have you ever tried Evans Plunge?"

She shrugged. "Once."

"It used to be a sacred place. Now it's just a tourist attraction."

"Now it's recreational. And crowded. Not very relaxing." She took an apple from her lunchbox, offered Sage the first bite. "Nothing personal about the experience." They looked at each other, faces straight, completely serious.

Then they broke out in bright-eyed smiles, and he waved temptation away.

IT HAD BEEN AN unusual lunch hour. One of a kind. A personal experience. Had it lasted an hour? He wasn't counting the minutes, wasn't watching the clock. He'd had her livin' on Lakota time, his version of the tune he was humming as he climbed into the seat of the big yellow earthmover and brought it to life with the flick of a key.

A personal experience like the one they'd just shared was meant to lead to another one. He could have suggested a movie. He could have suggested they see it together, and she might have said she didn't think anything good was playing, and he could have said they'd have to rent an oldie and take it to his place. Or hers. The thought had crossed his mind many times—his place or hers—but he'd dismissed it because it made no sense. First off, Megan outranked him on the road crew, and second, he didn't know how to socialize.

His wife had wanted what her family and friends called a "social life," and he'd never really understood what that was. Whatever it was, it always involved drinking, which was okay by him. It took a couple of quick shots to get the party going, even with his own friends. With hers, it took a few. But when he'd started to have a little too much fun, she'd tried to rein him in. How was he supposed to party with a bit in his mouth? Pretty soon, she'd accused him of ruining that social life she'd wanted so bad. He'd thought he'd been doing what he was supposed to do. Making it bad. Hell, he'd always been the life of the party. The baddest guy around. Which wasn't saying much. Nobody ever made much of an impression on him when they were "socializing," at least not that he remembered. The people and their relationships and his relationship to them all ran together in a hazy blur.

Now he went to Medicine Wheel, and he worked. He had friends in both places. Relationships were clear to him. On the job, there were fellow workers. In Medicine Wheel, there were people who cared about his recovery as much as he cared about theirs. But this idea of a social life was still vague. He wondered if there was a sober way to manage it. What would it be like to be with a woman and be stone-cold sober? Why did the words "stone" and "cold" seem to slip in front of "sober" so automatically? The cold part of it scared him. He'd given it a try a couple of times when he'd first sobered up, and cold was the only way he could describe it.

Megan was different. He thought about her in a way he remembered thinking of no one else. It wasn't in terms of his own needs. He liked to remember the talks they'd had about roadbeds and ranching, about solving problems with ground water and prairie dogs. He was haunted by the trickle of perspiration he'd seen slip down her temple, and he imagined brushing it away. Nothing more. Just to be granted the privilege of touching her face without asking, without explaining.

He wanted to be close to her, felt good simply standing beside her, but when he thought about it the way he was doing now, it scared him. She kept coming into his life through different doors, and he had to admit—to himself, at least—that he wanted her to keep coming back. He wanted her to open his private doors and let him open hers. He wanted her to trust him as long as he was trustworthy, accept him as long as he was acceptable. Hell, he wanted her to be able to *like* him. That, in a nutshell, was his fear. Maybe with the doors open, there was really nothing about the man behind the curtain for a woman to like.

After quitting time, he found Megan's pickup still parked beside the office trailer. He had half hoped she was gone for the day. The engineer and foreman had worked out all their personal problems. They had a problem with the contour of the grade, maybe, but no problem between the engineer and the foreman. It was after quitting time, and the foreman should've been heading home. If she'd already left, the question of seeing her for a few more minutes, talking with her about anything he could come up with, would have been settled. Instead of heading home, he'd decided to drive back to the office just to satisfy himself she was no longer there.

But she was.

No choice, he had to satisfy himself some other way. A quick look and a few words would do it.

One for the road.

"Hey, you're still here?" He pulled the door shut with a sweaty palm.

Megan looked up from the calculations on the legal pad on her desk and smiled. She looked relaxed, but there was an innocent pencil getting a firm rubdown between her thumb and forefinger. "I'm just about finished. I'm surprised *you're* still here."

He sat on the edge of the desk and twisted his head to get a look at her figures. They all ran together. His mouth was dry. "You got it all solved now?"

"I think so. I think we pretty much worked it out this afternoon. A little more elevation and another culvert." He nodded, and she tossed her pencil on top of her figures. "Is the roof finished yet?"

"The roof?"

She disappeared behind the desk and came back up with her lunch cooler.

"Uh, well, the sheathing, yeah. That's done." He checked his watch. "I'm on my own time now, right?"

She lifted one shoulder. "If you say so. You're the foreman."

"Yeah, well . . . what I want to bring up is strictly personal business, just so you know."

"Nothing you say will be used against you." She braced both hands on top of her cooler and leaned toward him. "What's on your mind?"

"Tell you the truth, it's you."

"Me?" she asked innocently.

"Yeah, you." He sprang away from the desk and shoved his hands into his pockets. "Don't act like you're surprised. You've been on my mind a lot lately."

"We've been around each other a lot lately."

"Yeah, I know. You have a way of appearing out of the woodwork." He lowered his voice. "Even when you're not really there."

"Am I giving you nightmares?" Her smile seemed whimsical.

"I might as well tell you, you'd be crazy to go out with me."

"Would I?"

"Yeah, you would. I don't know the first thing about dating." He turned to the window and stared at the toolbox in the back of his pickup. "It seems like I went from pulling girls' braids in school to pulling them down on the backseat of a car after buckin' out a bronc and downing the better part of a six pack. There weren't any dates."

"Then how did you get to know your wife?"

"I didn't. And I never let her get to know me." He faced her and leaned back against the windowsill. "Somewhere along the line, I just laid claim to her, I guess. I used to rodeo a lot, and she'd come along. When she got pregnant, we figured it might be kinda nice to get married." He gave a mirthless chuckle as he shook his head. "It wasn't nice. Neither one of us was any good at it. After a while, it seemed like all I did was argue with her or screw her." He saw her eyes widen, and he felt a little sick. He glanced away. "There's no other word for it," he said quietly. "After a while, that's what it was."

"I don't understand why you're telling me all this."

He sighed heavily. "Because at this point in my life, I'm about as backward as they come. I ought to be telling you I've just had bad luck with women, see if I can excite your caretaking instincts or challenge you to change my luck. But the truth is, women haven't had much luck with *me*."

"Your life has changed a great deal since you were married."

"Yeah, I know." He studied the toe of his boot. "That's why I was thinking . . . maybe if I went slow . . ."

The seconds ticked by, and he felt like an idiot. He was a *man*, goddamn it, not a choking-on-his-own-tongue kid. He looked up at her. He could almost hear her thinking the same thing.

"Are you asking me out, Sage?"

He gave a crooked smile. "Trying to."

She smiled back. "Then you really shouldn't tell me all your faults first."

"You mean I'm not going about this right?"

She clucked her tongue and shook her head. "About as backward as they come."

"I did pretty well at lunch, didn't I?" He straightened away from the window and approached her slowly. "We talked like friends. Two friends, just shootin' the breeze. And then we went back to work, and we're getting' the job done, and it's all good. Isn't it?" He saw the color rise in her cheeks, but she didn't back away. He took another step. "I don't know how you feel about seeing me off-site."

"*I* went to see *you* off-site."

"You did, didn't you?" She still wasn't backing away, but she looked like she might if he did the wrong thing. God, he wanted to reach for her. "I don't wanna screw anything up between us, Megan."

"Then let's keep it simple," she suggested. "How about a movie?"

He smiled at the idea of keeping it simple. That had been a survival tactic of his for the last four years. "You said you like horses," he reminded her. "I'd like to take you for a ride up in the Badlands, out by my place."

She gave him a bright-eyed smile. "Oh, I'd like that, too."

Chapter 9

THEY'D MADE A plan. Megan would pack a picnic lunch, and Sage would provide the beverages and transportation to the Badlands. She wasn't one to fuss over food, especially in her little motel kitchenette, but she took extra care with this meal. No sandwiches on this picnic.

Sage had been waiting for her. He hailed her from the corral and hopped down from the railing when she pulled up. She parked, grabbed her little cooler, and met him halfway.

"Ready to ride?" He was looking her up and down. Maybe she'd overdone the look. She wore a yellow knit tank top, jeans, and a pair of cowboy boots that had been sitting in her closet for years. "You'll be getting a good dose of sun today," he warned.

"That's exactly what I want."

He looked good in his straw cowboy hat. The wheat color contrasted sharply with his black hair and brown skin, and the loose weave of the brim created a pattern of sunlight and shadow over his face. He wore a blue chambray shirt with the sleeves rolled nearly to his elbows, and his jeans fit his long legs and slim hips as though they'd been tailored for him.

He ushered her through the narrow corral gate. "How much riding have you done?"

"I used to ride a little with a friend who had horses, but I haven't seen her since we were in college."

"I'm going to put you on the sorrel so you won't have to contend with mama's baby." He nodded toward the colt. "If she thinks he's having trouble keeping up, she might get broncy."

"Broncy?"

"She'll start balking. She might even offer to crow-hop a little. That sorrel is a nice trail horse, though. I use him all the time. I've also got two young mares out in the pasture." He gestured toward the hills. "They're only green broke."

The horses were saddled. Megan held the cooler up. "What'll we do with this?"

"Transfer it to the saddlebags." He took the cooler over to the sorrel's side and began filling the canvas pouch strapped behind the cantle of the saddle. "The plastic ice should be good for a while. I've got the drinks on the other side."

"I hope you like fried chicken." She peeked into the drink side of the bag. "Do you think it'll be okay in here?"

"If it's fried, I think it's past complaining." She saw his grin above the horse's rump. "I'm not going to let it sit too long. It smells great, and I'm hungry. Need any help getting up?"

"Oh, no, thanks. I'm a cowboy, too." But she found the stirrups had already been shortened for her, and the sorrel stood taller than she'd realized. She soon had her leg twisted up like one of the chicken wings she'd fried, with only the tip of her toe in the stirrup. She was grasping for any leather within reach when she heard him chuckle close behind her.

"A short one." His hands were on her waist. "And a hell of a contortionist."

His strength took her by surprise. She felt like a child getting swept off the ground effortlessly and tossed high in the air. Reaching for the saddle horn became an afterthought as she swung her leg over the horse's back, straightened in the saddle, and thanked him.

"Anytime." He led the mare through the gate. The colt pranced behind, eager for an outing. Sage closed the gate behind Megan, and she watched the fluid ease with which he swung himself into the saddle.

"It's only because your legs are longer," she muttered.

He flashed her a smile. "Eat your corn flakes, cowboy. You might stretch a little."

They'd ridden through three quarter sections of pasture dotted with cows and calves before the grass started giving way to weathered ridges of barren sandstone.

"Are we still on your land?" Megan asked. "I've seen more than fourteen cows out here."

"Really?" He turned and scanned the grassy flat. "They must be reproducing faster than I thought. How many do you think are out here?"

"Well, I'd say at least—" She frowned and peered past her shoulder at his deadpan expression. "I'd say you know exactly."

"Exactly a hundred and ninety-four," he told her with a smile. "I'm pasturing cattle for another rancher. Pays my lease and some of my other expenses."

"Your lease? I thought this was your land."

"Not all of it," he told her. "Some of it belongs to other members of the family, and I lease it from them through the BIA. I also have a grazing permit for some park land."

"Why doesn't the other rancher just lease the land himself?"

"This is one of the few instances where being an Indian is an advantage. White ranchers can only get the lease if no Indian wants it. I've got the lease, and he pays me to pasture his stock."

She peered ahead at the wall of worn rock stretching across the horizon like an ancient, craggy ruin. Beyond the first grassy steps and their eroded risers, there was no grass to speak of, not much plant life of any kind.

"I don't see how you could keep any cattle up there," she said. "You don't, do you? Nothing could live up there."

"Wait 'til we get closer. The only way to see the Badlands is to ride through them."

"I've only driven *past* them," she said.

"Then you're in for an experience," He grinned at her. "You seem to have an interest in things that might be just a little on the bad side."

They rode deeper into the Badlands. Megan felt as though she were being enveloped by draws lined with strange, striated tan and gray walls. Some of the eroded uprights supported grass-topped tables. Others were barren, carved by the wind to resemble the turrets and spires of gray and sandy-walled castles. Many of the walls were pockmarked with holes, as though they had been sprayed by a giant's machine gun. Sage explained that these were the burrows of a kind of bee, the solitary bee, whose larvae were hunted by pecking birds. Other rocky faces were visited by cliff swallows, who darted in and out of the clay blisters they'd fashioned on the sheer rock and tended their nests within.

"Some things live here." Sage pointed to the gray-green vegetation dotting the landscape.

"Yucca," she said. "And lots of sage."

"Tough stuff."

They followed the lazy curve of a mud flat, which seemed a poor excuse for a creek bank. But then, the narrow stream of water seemed a poor excuse for a creek. The animals that had been there earlier in the morning obviously found cause to disagree. Sage pointed to crisscrossing lines of tracks embedded in the mud. "Coyote," he said. "Rabbit. Couple of pronghorns." He pointed at the ground ahead and said in the same even tone, "Sasquatch."

Megan twisted in her saddle, studying the tracks as she passed. "Sasquatch? You mean . . . Bigfoot? Those look more like a horse's tracks."

"Sasquatch's horse. His big feet are killing him."

Once again she scowled at him. "Sasquatch, my foot."

"Yours are too small." He scowled back, and then he broke into another of his engaging grins.

"You're an awful tease, Parker."

"You're an easy mark, McBride." He reined his horse toward the hill. "Come on. There's a spot up here I want to show you."

They picked their way among the huge mushrooms of clay, undercut by the rushing water of spring storms, and climbed the puckers of rainwash toward a grassy upper level. They rode to the edge of the table, where Sage suddenly dismounted. "Let's eat."

He helped her down and handed her the saddlebags before picketing the horses several yards away from each another to avoid any competition for grass. The colt was free to romp, but like the toddler he was, he never strayed far from his mother. Megan was sorry she hadn't packed some sort of blanket, but Sage didn't seem to notice anything missing as he settled on the natural cushion of curly buffalo grass and broke out a bottle of mineral water and one of orange soda. She smiled when he offered her the lemon water, and he winked back. He'd remembered.

THE WEST WIND exercised unusual restraint, giving them only a pleasant midday breeze. Content with the company, they shared the food without much conversation. When they were down to licking fingers and draining drinks, Sage pointed across the chasm toward a higher wall and a higher grassy table. "That's where my grandfather's scaffold stood. That's the spot I wanted to show you."

"I thought scaffold funerals were illegal." Megan gazed at the high flat, and he wondered whether she saw—as he did—its special place in the sun.

"They are. But my grandfather said that beyond death, the law meant nothing. He told my mother his spirit would never rest unless his body went to the scaffold in the old way. She chose to defy the law rather than her father's last wish."

"How old was he when he died?"

"Ninety-four. He died in the cabin—the one I was born in." He plucked a single blade of little bluestem and stuck the end in his mouth.

Across the way, the grass moved gently, like pale water rippling in the sunshine. His mind's eye saw the scaffold standing above it. "I was only about six, but I remember hearing the death rattle in his throat. He crooned for days before he finally went. He spoke no English on his deathbed."

"Ninety-four. That's a long life."

Sage nodded, still gazing at the high ground, the hallowed place. "He outlived his sons and all but my mother, his youngest daughter. He said it was because he shunned the 'white sins'—flour, sugar, salt, and alcohol. My older brothers and sisters remember him better than I do, but I remember his death very well."

"It must have been terrible for you to watch him die."

"No, it wasn't. It was peaceful. He wasn't shut up in some antiseptic hospital with tubes stuck in his nose. Life went on as usual around him, and he was at peace when he slipped away from us." He leaned on one elbow and stretched his long legs out in the grass. "Then they prepared to raise him toward the sun. There was a lot of whispering and scurrying around to get it done quickly. I knew everyone was afraid the scaffold would be discovered, and I felt as though I was being trusted with an important secret."

"Did the talk of restless spirits scare you?"

"Of course." He looked at her solemnly. "It's supposed to. People around here have a healthy respect for spirits. My grandfather's most personal possessions were burned or buried with his bones after they were picked clean. The rest of his stuff was given away."

Megan drew her knees up to her chin and wrapped her arms around them. "But surely you wanted to keep some remembrances."

"It might be safe to keep things he'd shared or anything he'd given away himself."

"Safe?"

He looked into her eyes, searched for signs of a mind truly open here and now, in this place where the wind whispered secrets his ear couldn't quite catch. Her gaze was clear and bright. Curious, yes, but her eyes didn't ridicule him. He knew what it looked like, how it felt. Hell, he'd ridiculed himself for the old beliefs. He could mock them, call them superstitions, brush them away with an impudent gesture and call himself a modern man, but he couldn't help looking over his shoulder. He carried his ancestors in his DNA.

"They're called *wanagi*," he said. "Spirits of the departed ones. I've told myself when you live out here on the prairie, the night sounds alone will have you believing in ghosts. Comes right down to it, I can't explain them away. When I hunt, I still leave a piece of my kill for the *wanagi*."

"But have you ever actually run into them?" Her eyes were wide open, full of the eagerness of a child entertaining the thrill of fear. She hugged her legs tighter. "Personally, I mean."

He sat up and tossed aside the stem of grass he'd been chewing. "There was Jackie," he said quietly, feeling the risk in the pit of his stomach each time he said the dead man's name aloud.

"You mean, Jackie's ghost?"

"Something called me that day. I knew he was there, and I knew he'd been trying to tell me he was there." He watched her roll his claim over carefully in her mind. "You believe that?"

"I was there with you, Sage. Behind you. I mean . . . I was *right there*."

"Did you feel it, too? That weird tugging, that—"

"No. I felt scared. I could tell you'd found something terrible, and I just froze in my tracks."

He leaned closer. "What I saw *was* terrible, but what led me there wasn't part of it anymore. What do you think it could have been?"

"A spirit maybe? I don't know." She glanced across the chasm again. "I guess I believe there are some things that aren't easy to explain. Maybe they don't have to be explained. Maybe they just *are*."

He smiled, satisfied. Just that much margin in her thinking was enough. He got to his feet and offered her a hand. "Let me take you to another place where things 'just are.' Might save you a trip to the library."

THEY RODE THROUGH an eroded gully whose history was recorded in dark and light striations, which seemed to change color as her viewing angle changed. A hawk glided above them on an invisible current of hot air, and on a nearby plateau, a prairie dog barked a warning to its sprawling underground community.

"As beautiful as this land is, I can't imagine it's worth leasing for cattle," Megan said. "There isn't much grass."

"Not everyone sees its beauty, so you score a point for that. But there's more here than meets the eye. And there's good shelter in these breaks. It doesn't support too many head, but the lease is pretty reasonable. Besides, I like to come here. I don't have to try too hard to imagine what it was like here a hundred, two hundred, years ago. It was just like this." He nudged his mare with a boot heel and the sweet sound of a kiss, and she jumped across a narrow, dry stream bed. Her baby scrambled after her. Three pairs of eyes turned their expectations on Megan.

"You can do it."

"I could if I were on the ground."

"The horse is willing, and the creek won't rise."

Megan laughed. He looked pretty full of himself, grinning at her, sitting high in the saddle like he lived there. He didn't need paved roads or girder bridges. He was a horseman.

She tried to imagine what he would have looked like a century or more ago, without the hat, without the boots or Western saddle. It wasn't difficult. His hooded eyes were crinkled at the corners, and his cheekbones were chiseled and high—features made to protect the eyes of a man who faced limitless sky, sun, and wind every day of his life. Sage belonged to these stony, wind-worn hills as surely as his grandfather had.

He encouraged her with a nod, and she tried the boot and the kiss. They worked. She hung in there and—but for an abrupt bounce on the landing—did herself proud in the saddle. He rewarded her with a smile and that seductive wink.

They came to another stream and followed its winding path through a valley. The water was clear and inviting, and the sun overhead seemed to grow hotter by contrast.

"Are we there yet?" Megan teased.

"Are we where?" Sage chuckled. "If you need a bathroom, yeah. We're there."

"Can't we pull over and go wading?"

"One or the other. We don't pee in our pool."

"I'm okay." He wasn't looking, so she grinned. "Are we there yet?"

Up ahead on a sharp rise stood a dome-shaped willow skeleton. Megan felt her blood course a little faster as they drew closer. She knew what it was. Sage had told her about it, and he was about to show it to her. He was about to confide in her again.

They watered the horses before tethering them to either end of a fallen, sun-bleached cottonwood. Sage nodded toward the high ground. "We have to do a little climbing."

"Can't we ride?"

"Nope. We're holding our horses and using our own legs." Sage shook his head and gestured for her to go ahead. "This is why we leave the women and kids at home."

Megan scrambled up the steep, barren hill, her slick-soled boots slipping over sand and gravel. On a quick skid, she landed one hand on the ground. He landed one on her butt. "I should have worn my safety boots," she grumbled.

"You're safe. I'm right behind you."

"What kind of boots are you wearing?"

"Men's."

She laughed, straightened, and had her first close look at the small willow dome. A breeze teased her hair, and she closed her eyes, inviting it to cool her damp face as she started toward the structure.

He grabbed her arm. "Watch your step."

She'd almost walked into a shallow hole filed with charred wood and melon-size stones. "Tell me more," she said quietly.

"You cover the frame with hides and blankets to make the sweat lodge." He walked around it, drawing pictures in the air with his hands. "Or you can use tarps. You build a fire and heat the rocks outside. Then you roll the hot rocks inside, pour water over them for steam, and sweat buckets. When you've had enough, you run down and jump into the creek."

"What a shock that must be." She examined the way the slender, flexible willows were curved and lashed together. "You don't just sit there and sweat."

"Mostly you pray." He remembered when prayer had been suggested to Megan at Medicine Wheel, and she'd nodded like a student in class. He remembered a time when it had been suggested to him, and he'd laughed, said he wasn't much of a churchgoer. He hadn't been much of a student, either.

"What do you pray for?" She glanced up quickly. She hadn't meant to ask, but it just came out. "I mean, generally. I don't mean to pry, and I know there's no script, but I'm wondering if there's a sort of . . ."

"Liturgy?" He smiled and shook his head. "I don't know of any. If you have a holy man, he sings in Lakota. Not the songs you heard at the funeral. Those are church songs translated into Lakota. *Inipi* songs are much older. So you learn, you join in, and then everyone prays his own way. I'm still finding mine."

He ran his hand along the smooth curve of a willow rib. It occurred to him that this woman was important to him, and it made him a little nervous to speak of these things to her. It seemed more natural to tease her, to flash his smile and put them both at ease. But he wanted something else this time. It seemed right to do what she'd asked, to tell her more.

"I know what I'm looking for now. Healing. That's not something I could've said before. I never wanted to sound weak or, I don't know, needy." The word still tasted bad to him, and he swallowed hard. "But I'm trying to put the pieces back together, and I'm finding out that the pieces of me go way back. There's a spiritual connection that got short-circuited somewhere along the way."

"But so much time has passed, and so much has changed."

"Some things have shifted. I used to think they were total changes—the way we get our food and clothing, the kind of homes we have. But our basic needs haven't changed. We still eat. We still put clothes on our bodies and live in some kind of shelter. We've stuck by each other. We still have a community.

"The missionaries and the government denied us our ceremonies, and we've always been a very spiritual people. We tried to make do or do without. Everything got watered down and wrung out. Pretty soon, we were left with the desiccated remains of what we'd once been. We imitated ourselves for tourists, and we looked for something to kill the pain, something to fill the void. Alcohol seemed to be a ready cure for all that ailed us."

He squatted beside the cold fire pit and rested one knee on the cracked hardpan. "So I pray for healing," he told her as he lifted a fist-sized stone from the unused pile and weighed it in his hand. "I pray for the strength to put my self-indulgence aside so I can hold my head up." He looked up at her, adjusted the brim of his hat so he could stop squinting against the sun. "You know that End Of the Trail statue of the Indian on the horse? You see different versions of it everywhere." She nodded. "I hate it. I ain't goin' around hangin' my head like that. I'm not that guy. No Lakota man wants to be that guy.

"So I pray for strength. I pray for wisdom. Generation after generation has been stripped layer by layer. Some things are gone for good. We need to replenish ourselves. I want to know how."

"You need jobs," Megan said as she stepped closer. "In this day and age, in order to get the food, the clothing and the shelter, you have to have a job."

"Sure." He looked up, smiled, and got to his feet, bouncing the rock in his palm. "We need to do for ourselves, and the government payoffs aren't the answer. They're trying to pay for what we never agreed to sell. That's bullshit, and we know it. We have to look within ourselves, which isn't easy. Most of us are scared to death we'll find there's nothing there."

"Nothing there? That's ridiculous, Sage. Look how far you've come."

Uh-oh. She'd said the wrong thing. He stared at her for a moment, gave her an odd feeling that he was looking through her at the workings of her brain. He turned from her.

"Sage?" She waited. He was gazing off in the distance, and she wanted him back, so she waited. A second or two, at least. "What did I say? How can you feel—"

"I can feel whatever I feel." He turned slowly, looked at her as though he wasn't sure he knew her, was trying to place her in some remembered context. He shook his head once, giving up, maybe.

Or maybe not. His gesture was openhanded. "Listen, if I level with you about a real, deep and abiding fear, don't tell me it's ridiculous. Don't try to pat me on the head and say, 'You've come a long way, baby.' Because I'll ride off into the sunset, *baby*. And good luck finding your way home."

"I didn't mean that the way it . . . obviously . . ."

"And don't try to tell me you never in your life doubted yourself."

"Well, of course, I've—"

"Of course, of course. When you're right, you're right. When you're wrong, all it takes is an apology, maybe a little correction on your part, and everything's fixed. My God, you must sleep well at night."

She hated herself for lowering her gaze, but his emotion had filled his own eyes with such power that she couldn't bear the pressure any longer. "I only meant to say that *I* see a lot in you," she said quietly. "Skill, ambition, determination . . ."

"And *I* told *you* I pray for healing, for wisdom, for the strength to face another day without my children. What you see is what *you* want to see in a man. And what you want to see isn't enough. Not where I live. So don't . . ."

With one step, he closed the distance between them, lifted his hand, and placed it gently along her jaw, tracing the curve below her ear with his long middle finger. He rubbed her chin with his thumb, and the order became a soft plea. "Don't."

She stood her ground. "Don't what?"

"Don't look at me like that."

"I seem to say all the wrong things, and I don't mean to."

"I know."

She wanted him to kiss her. God, she wanted him to kiss her.

"Enough for what?" she persisted. "Singing your praises, I would have capped it off with *to name just a few* if you hadn't cut me off. Obviously, I believe in you."

"I appreciate that. I've laid down a lot of blacktop."

"*Obviously*, it's more than that."

"Really?" His smile was tentative. "If I get down off my high horse, will you name a few more?"

She lifted her shoulder. "Not until I figure out what was wrong with the few I named."

His smile spread slowly. "I'm still trying to understand what *I* believe in." He slid his hand the length of her arm and took her by the hand. "You've heard of *hanble ceya*, the vision quest?"

"Don't you see some kind of an animal or something after you starve yourself for several days?"

He looked at the clouds overhead and chuckled. "Yeah, right. Fast for three days so you can hallucinate herds of buffalo and skies full of eagles."

"Okay, don't get mad, but, yes, that's what I've seen in the movies. Mostly old ones on TV. Secondhand information, glammed up pictures."

"Secondhand?" He started leading her back down the hill. "You're giving them way too much credit."

"You've done a vision quest?"

"I have."

She didn't push. She was following his lead, seemed to be gaining in patience. They had come to the bottom of the hill. The mare was snuffling at a sparse patch of grass while her baby suckled on her, and the gelding stood hip-shot, half asleep. It was turning out to be a good day to speak of these things, as long as he didn't seek too much contact with her clear-water eyes. He knew he could drown in those eyes.

"Lakota tradition teaches that there are several aspects of the human soul. There's the part that lives on in the afterlife. There's also the shade—you know, the ghosts we talked about that haunt the living if they're not respectful. There's the earthly soul. That's the best part of you—your talents, skills. I don't know about *ambition*—more like your life's purpose, your ability to be noble and give love. It's that part of the soul that the vision quest is directed to. *Hanble ceya* is crying for a vision of your world and your place in it."

"Did you have a vision?"

He thought for a moment, glanced back up at the frame of his sweat lodge and then down at the crusty mud of the creek bank. There was some risk in answering her question. He hadn't gotten up this morning thinking it would be a good day to bring a woman to this place. One thing had led to another, and here they were. Maybe he was trying to impress her. Maybe it was a test.

Maybe it was no big deal. A walk in the park.

Without a park. But there was plenty of grass, some of it not half bad for sitting, and so he did, drawing Megan down with him.

"I went to the hill three times. Not here. A place chosen by a holy man." He smiled and shook his head as he recalled three fasts, three sweats, three days alone in the vision pit on each of three occasions. "I must have been a really hard case for the spirits to crack. The third time they saw me coming, they took pity on me and gave me a vision."

It was a confidence. She had no right to ask for more.

But, of course, she did. "I don't suppose you can talk about it. Your vision."

He raised his brow. "I'll tell you this much: it had me building a road. And there was a wheel." He leaned back to allow his hand access to his front pocket, from which he pulled a two-inch ring with four spokes all covered with red, white, yellow, and black quillwork. He handed it to her, saying, "It's a medicine wheel. I took it as my symbol and wore it for Sun Dance."

"The Sun Dance?" She sounded surprised. "With the piercing? Or is it more ritualistic nowadays, without real bloodshed?"

"You mean, is it all just a show?" She returned his medicine wheel, and he held it between his finger and thumb, considering. "It was done in secret for a long time because the government made it a crime. Even now, outsiders don't generally take part. But tradition says there must be witnesses, those who will care for the dancers, attest to the fact that the pain was endured and learn from what they see." He lifted his eyes to hers. "Wasn't it like that with the crucifixion? Without witnesses, no one would know. It would be as though nothing happened, nothing would change."

He reached out to pluck a blade of grass as he continued. "We've crippled ourselves by perfecting the cigar store Indian pose, silent and stone-faced. We're still around because we're too damn tough to die. If you have pain, you don't let it show. The alternative to stone-faced is shit-faced, and the witnesses, if they care about you, they mind their own business. Your trouble is embarrassing. It's just a damn shame, and shame trumps pain."

"I would be afraid to make that kind of sacrifice in public," she confessed. "I'd make a fool of myself. I'm a whiney wimp when I'm in pain."

"A whiney wimp?" He chuckled, tried to imagine Megan McBride whining and shook his head. "Pain is a warning. Something's breaking down. You have to recognize it and find the healing road. Through the Sun Dance, I accepted pain as part of life, and I made it a spiritual offering." He leaned to one side and pocketed his amulet. "It was the old way, and it was me doing it. So it was my way. It felt right. It made sense. Maybe not to you, but—"

"No, it does," she said quickly. "It makes a great deal of sense. Facing down pain when you're looking for healing. But the way they do it in . . ."

"The movies?"

She shrugged. "It just seems like such a drastic measure."

"It *is* a drastic measure." He smiled gently. "It's often done when someone in the family is very ill, or when you'd had a close call, whether on a battlefield or a county road, and you knew damn well it could have gone either way. You're still scared. I had a close call and—" He looked directly into her eyes, and his voice barely rose above the rustle of the wind in the tall grass "—sometimes I'm still scared."

"Like . . . when you saw Jackie?"

"Yeah." His eyes glazed with the memory. "When I saw my own face lying in the grass and felt a piece of him in me."

"Does it help?" she asked. "Are you stronger, having done the dance?"

"Yeah, I think I am."

"Were you pierced?"

She watched him unbutton his shirt. When he reached his belt, he pulled the fabric free of his pants and flicked the last two buttons open. He drew his shirt back to expose the scars—two puckered marks over his pectoral muscles. She wondered why she hadn't noticed them before. Identical and evenly placed, they were scars made by design, not by accident. He had borne them willingly in the hope of transcending the pain they caused.

Without thinking, she reached for his chest with both hands and placed her fingertips over the scars. His skin was hot, and the small cords of scar tissue felt hotter still.

He covered her hands with his and flattened them hard against his skin. "What's this about?" His voice was guttural, raw. "Tell me."

She had no words. She swallowed against a tingling throat, heard the catch in the deep breath he drew as he took her face in his hands. Their kiss came tentatively in a quick coupling of moist lips. It came again and lingered longer, mouths moving over one another, exploring possibilities. It came a third time with mutual insistence, hard pressure, a soft whimper, a needy groan. Sage slid his arms around her shoulders and lay back in the grass, pulling her down with him.

His scars seared her palms. She caressed them and kissed the lips that moved anxiously against hers. His belt buckle pressed against her stomach, and his erection grew quickly between her thighs. The sudden intimacy at once frightened and thrilled her, swishing a peppery feeling up and down her thighs. Then he rolled with her, tucked her underneath him, and invaded her mouth with his softly stroking tongue.

The heat of the sun diffused over his back and in his hair as he gloried in the way her hands felt against his skin. He made a conscious effort to transfer the sun's warmth to his kiss, to return the feeling of power she'd given him with just the touch of her hands. His body surged with it. His heart pounded with it. His soul was nourished with it.

He whispered her name, pressed his cheek against her breast, hugged her close. "God, you make me feel good."

She smoothed the thick, damp hair over the back of his neck. "I don't think we need any hot rocks to work up a sweat."

He shook with silent laughter as he shed his shirt. "Out of the mouths of well-kissed women." He lifted his head and kissed her once more before sliding down to pull off her boot. He had them both off before she had time to protest further. "Socks, too." He hooked his leg to work on his own boot. Then he grabbed her by the hand and pulled her to her feet.

"No way!" Digging her heels in was difficult. Resisting his strength was impossible. "Sage!"

He swept her up in his arms and strode into the water. "Defiance is useless, woman."

"I won't be kissed into submission, *man*." But her fist only play-pounded on his chest. She was ready for more fun.

"After the sweat comes the—" *Splash!*

Megan bobbed to the surface and sputtered into his face. "I thought this was a little stream."

He laughed. "It cuts a deep channel here. You can swim, can't you?"

"You'd better hope I can."

She could. After they'd traded splashes and displayed their best strokes, they emerged, laughing and dripping and shaking their fingers at one another in teasing admonition.

Megan pushed her hair back from her face. "Now look," she demanded, spreading her arms wide.

"I'm looking." He raised an appreciative eyebrow. "You sure are wet."

Her thin bra was a far cry from the ironclad number she wore on the job, her summer top had gone transparent on her, and the breeze was killing her softly. She folded her arms across her chest. "At least you still have a dry shirt, Mr. Parker, and if you were any kind of gentleman, you wouldn't stand there staring."

"You told me to look. I thought you were showing off." Grinning, he tossed his hair back and offered her his shirt. "Hell, I'm a man. Who thought up the rules for being a gentleman, anyway?"

"Probably Victoria."

"Figures. She sells you sexy underwear and dares us not to stare."

"*Queen* Victoria. I don't suppose she made all the rules, and it was more than a hundred years ago, but still . . ." She waved his shirt away. "I'll air dry."

"C'mon." He pressed with the shirt. "I'm trying to play the gentleman here. I'll turn my back, even."

She took the shirt.

He turned away and took a seat in the grass.

Megan turned her back, peeled off her top, slipped into his shirt and tied the tails at her waist. The bra was staying on. But the shirt—*his* shirt—felt good. It felt like part of him.

"I don't know about Victoria's rules, but I like her underwear," he drawled.

"A gentleman doesn't peek." She turned, eyebrow arched, corners of her mouth twitching. "But you did say *play*."

"That I did. And I owned up to the *man* part. As for the *gentle*, you be the judge." He patted the patch of grass next to him. "Take a load off, woman, and don't give me no more slybrow."

She gave in to his invitation and her itch to smile. "*Sly*brow?"

"It's pretty cute, actually."

"Does it look coy? I was going for coy."

"If you're going for me, it's working."

She glanced away. He was too straightforward by half. If she had any sense, she would be, too. She was trying too hard. Coyness wasn't her style.

"I've never seen the Badlands the way you've shown it to me today." She gestured toward the striated sandstone wall across the creek. "It's like a huge sand painting, the kind tourists buy in those plastic containers, all filled with layers of colored sand. One minute you think the wind and runoff have eroded all the life out of it." She leaned over to pluck a purple coneflower from a cluster rising in the tall grass. "The next, you come to a lovely spot like this."

"You would have ridden right past a spot like this," he said. "You have to get down and take a closer look. Here." He held up a sprig of white-striped greenery. "You know what this is?"

"Indian paintbrush."

"Let me color you beautiful." He feathered the tuft over her cheek. His eyes were made warm by his soft smile. "'Behold, my brothers, the spring has come. The earth has received the embraces of the sun, and we shall soon see the results of that love.'"

She felt dewy inside. "That's wonderful. Is it yours?"

"If I said it was, would you believe me?"

"Of course."

He shook his head, still smiling, and tucked the Indian paintbrush behind her ear. "You're an easy mark, Megan McBride. That was one of Sitting Bull's songs."

"It sounds Biblical. Old Testament style."

"Yeah, that wouldn't be me."

"But you know it by heart."

"I have a good memory for stuff like that, but I thought it was all in my head." He glanced back down at the bright water moving slowly past them. "Is it by heart?"

"Let's just say your delivery sounded heartfelt." Too serious, she told herself. Too much and way too far. She turned, injecting some sass into her smile. "*Deep.* You're a very deep, dark, and probably dangerous man, Mr. Parker."

He laughed. "You hit the mark, at least two out of three. I missed my mark altogether. I was going for romantic."

"You don't say." She leaned back, closed her eyes and lifted her face to the sun. "Maybe we're both right on target."

He glanced away. He had to. Take in the slithering water, he told himself, the soft green sage, the silver blue sky—anything but the invitation he saw in her eyes. If deep, dark, and dangerous attracted her, he was her man. He could come through for her on all counts and take pleasure in being somebody's hero for a change. He knew he'd had enough of being the villain.

He straightened the collar of his shirt—*his* shirt on *her* body—and lingered to touch the soft down on the back of her neck. "Does our employer have a policy on this kind of thing? Could I get fired for kissing you?"

She lifted her shoulder. "If you go down, I go with you. We're in this together, my friend."

"I don't have much experience with getting to be friends first."

"First?"

"Ain't gonna lie, Megan, I'm thinking about a lot more than kissing. But I want your friendship. I want you to accept mine, for whatever it's worth."

"It's worth—"

"Kissing for?" He hooked his elbow behind her neck and brought her close enough to make the discovery. Their friendship was indeed worth kissing for.

Chapter 10

SAGE CHEWED ON a toothpick and counted the shades of brown in the speckled linoleum floor of the Red Calf Community Center. There were fifteen people in the circle, and they were enjoying a time of reflection. To an observer, it might have seemed like a time of silence, but it wasn't. The voices of four children chasing one another on the far side of the room filled the adults' ears. The consideration of what had been said so far filled their minds. The scent of the burning sweet grass carried around the perimeter of the circle at the beginning of the meeting tantalized their nostrils. A steady rain pattered on the roof. The circle moved easily from talk to no-talk and back to talk again, but no one felt compelled to fill the air with chatter.

Sage's reflections turned often to Megan and the day they'd spent together in the Badlands. He had wondered whether their working relationship would become awkward once they'd shared kisses. It hadn't. Monday morning had brought business as usual. Megan had gone to Pierre on Tuesday and stayed for three days. He'd found himself missing her.

Initially, it had come as a surprise. He'd allowed himself to miss Brenda and Tommy, but otherwise, he'd generalized his loneliness. He missed women, family, even old buddies, but no one in particular other than the children. He was learning about real friendship through Medicine Wheel. Still, he spent most of his hours alone. Women, family, and old buddies were difficult to deal with, so he'd put them all on the back burner in his daily life. Now he faced a longing to be with one person, one particular woman, and it scared him. He wanted too much too suddenly. He'd made too many mistakes in the past, and he didn't want to repeat them.

He knew all the wrong ways to treat a relationship, and he wasn't at all sure about the right ones. If a man wasn't possessive, would a woman stick with him of her own accord? If he wasn't jealous, would she still be faithful to him? If he wasn't demanding, would she be inclined to give? And if he wasn't any of those things, who would he be? Would he appear weak? Unmanly? He knew how to attract her, but when she started admiring more than his looks and his skills, he had the feeling he was on shaky ground. Beneath the surface was a man who was learning to walk all over again, taking one careful step at a time. His experience had taught him how to build a masculine image and take refuge behind it. His newly developing inclinations told him to try a little trust.

"We can't trust Floyd Taylor."

Sage straightened in his chair, folded his arms over his chest and tuned his thoughts to Regina. No one stared at the speaker, but the circle assumed a listening attitude.

"He's saying he's willing to take a temporary license," Regina continued. "He says he wants a chance to prove himself. That's what he's saying to the council, anyway. Out of the other side of his mouth, he's calling in a lot of old debts. He's saying no more credit at the store. People are getting scared."

"It's crazy to borrow money from him," old Bessie War Shirt grumbled. "You never know how he figures the interest."

"Don't ask him to explain it, either," another woman advised. "All you'll get out of it is, you owe him more money than you've got."

"We got no bank." Marvin Bad Heart was a new member who wasn't convinced conditions could change. His voice was as expressionless as his face. "If we put Taylor out of business, we got no money. We've always borrowed money from the storekeeper. That's the way it's always been."

"We're gonna try it a different way," Sage said. "We can't be any worse off than we are now."

"Maybe," Marvin allowed. "But at least now we know what we've got. May not be much, but we know what it is."

"I got a little insurance money," Regina announced quietly. "I think he'd want me to use it to open a store. He told me I was crazy to try it, but I think now. . . . I think he'd like it if he could help me get it going."

The group allowed another quiet time to pass. They knew Regina was wise not to mention her dead husband's name, but they felt his presence. They had a sense that Jackie approved of Regina's plan. Before the group broke up, there was more talk of support for Regina's store. Members also offered to help her prepare during the coming year for the giveaway that would commemorate the first anniversary of Jackie's death. The gifts to be given to his friends, especially those who had helped with the funeral, would be gathered over the course of the year. Regina would need help, particularly with the quilting.

Sage stood in the kitchen doorway and watched the other vehicles pull away from the building one by one. The slanting rainfall glittered just beyond their headlights. He thought of the low spot in the roadbed filling up with water, sure as hell. He could haul a compressor down there, get a pump going and maybe save the project some time and money. The yard light illuminated the moat that was fast gathering around the community center. Poor drainage, Sage thought. In this country, there was never enough water except when there was too much.

He had put the chairs away, and Regina was taking care of kitchen cleanup. Sage paid no attention to the water running in the sink until it stopped. "Need any help?" he asked without turning around.

"The coffee pot's clean, and the windows are all closed." Regina closed a cupboard door. "My sister is watching the kids. We have time to talk if you want."

He turned now, smiling. "Aren't you all talked out?"

"You're not. You hardly said anything tonight." She leaned against the counter and waited, but he stayed where he was. His thoughts had strayed out into the night, and she was probably thinking it was a bad sign.

"I need to get going," he told her. "You ready?" It wouldn't be like Regina to press. Megan would, but Regina wouldn't. She would let him keep his thoughts.

But by the way she shouldered her bag, he knew she had her own thoughts. And she'd decided not to keep them to herself.

"You think it's a good idea, getting mixed up with another white woman?"

"Mixed up?" It surprised him to hear her use a term so direct and, for reasons that might surprise her, so appropriate. It made him laugh. He was mixed up, all right, but all on his own.

"We're trying to learn, not to repeat our mistakes," Regina reminded him as she crossed the floor.

He let his smile fade because she refused to return it. "I think of you as a sister, Regina. You know that."

"And I just lost one husband. I'm not looking for another one." Her boot heel skidded over the linoleum as she stopped beside him in the open doorway. "You're too important to this group. I don't want to see you getting your head messed up again by a white woman."

"My head was messed up long before I met Riva. Our marriage was a disaster, but it wasn't because she was white."

"She was no wife to you," Regina insisted.

"I was no husband to her." He dug his keys out of his pocket. "It was *my* head that was messed up." With the heel of his free hand he tapped his temple. "My *head,* not my heart. Somewhere along the line I guess I put my heart in cold storage."

"No one in this group cares more than you do."

He lowered his hand slowly. He could think of no greater compliment. "I *have* changed, Regina." He looked at her hopefully. "I have, haven't I?"

HIS HARD HAT and slicker were no protection against the downpour. Once again, he found himself kneeling in four inches of water and cussing at a pump. Nobody would have expected him to come back to the site after dark just to get a pump started. Rain was one of the inevitable impediments in road construction. If you dug a hole in a spot that held water and it rained, you lost time. Nobody came out in the middle of the night to rescue a roadbed.

But the changes Megan had made in her design had already increased costs. If this stretch washed out, it would mean more time, which would mean more money. While Megan was in Pierre, the project was Sage's baby. If the rain let up a little and the pump had a chance to catch up—hell, it was worth a try.

The rain and the compressor engine combined to drown out the sound of an approaching vehicle as another pair of headlights joined his own. The extra light illuminated the problem—a tangled hose—and was welcome, at least on that score. But ever since someone had tampered with his pickup, Sage had been wary.

"Anything I can do to help?"

Megan's was the last voice he'd expected to hear. He squinted into the bright lights at the top of the rise. "You already did," he shouted. "I think we're all set. Got any coffee with you?"

" 'Fraid not. I'll meet you back at the office."

The lights were burning in the trailer windows when he drove up. He leaped over the puddle at the foot of the steps and yanked the door open. He'd already abandoned his hat and slicker in the pickup, and he was drenched.

"Catch." A towel sailed across the room. Sage lifted his hand, and the towel flopped over this forearm like a horseshoe ringer.

He ruffled his hair with the towel, draped it around his neck and began unbuttoning his wet shirt. "When did you get back?"

"I got back to the motel a couple of hours ago."

Her hair was damp, but he could tell she'd just combed it. She wore a pink, V-neck cotton sweater and a nice pair of jeans. Her lips matched the sweater. Her feet were bare.

"My shoes got wet."

He looked up and caught her smiling. But she'd caught him first—taking inventory. "You didn't have to come out here on a night like this. You left me to take care of things. You checkin' up on me?"

He waited for an answer, but it was too slow in coming. *Give it to me straight. You trust me, or not? You want me, or not?*

"What are you doing here?" he asked quietly.

He knew. She could tell by his tone, at once heavy and soft like the rain on the roof. He knew how restless she'd been, how she'd been wondering where he might be and what he might have on his mind. There had been a good chance she would find him here. They shared this much, this river of gravel becoming blacktop. There had been a good chance of meeting him on this common ground.

He tossed his shirt over a chair. His scowl made her back away from the truth and turn to the file cabinets. "I needed some figures from the daily reports."

"Right." He moved in close behind her. She pulled out a file drawer, and he reached past her to stop it in its tracks. "Tell me why, Megan. Didn't you trust me to do the job?"

Her voice was small. "I knew you'd be here."

She let him push the drawer closed. He turned her toward him with a gentle hand. "Is this how it was with Karl Taylor? He backed you up against the files, and you—"

Cruel words. He wasn't sure where they'd come from or what he'd say next. Her anger flashed in her eyes, but he braced his hands against the file cabinet, trapping her.

"How can you even say that?" she whispered.

His chest tightened, and his brain did battle with itself. "I said it because . . ." Christ, what did he want from her? She knew he'd be here. He knew what was needed, knew his job, and, yes, he'd be taking care of things.

And here she was.

"Because it was the first damn thing that popped into my head. Walk away, Megan." He dropped his hands to his sides, and his plea became ragged. "Be smart. Walk away."

She stayed where she was. "Do you believe I led Karl on?"

"No." He shook his head, gave a dry chuckle. "Hell, no."

"Then why did you say that?"

"Old habits are hard to break." He couldn't stop himself from touching her, from pulling her against him and making it impossible for her to do as he'd asked. "They're so damn hard to break." He lowered his face into her hair and smelled the rain there.

"Maybe I can help," she whispered as she reached around his back.

"Maybe I can make you miserable."

"Maybe," she whispered again. His smooth shoulder was there for her lips to touch. "If I'm willing to let myself be miserable." She tipped her head back. "Is that how you want it?"

He showed her how he wanted it. He pulled her tight against his wet jeans and gave her a hard-driving kiss meant to make her go all soft. One hand slid beneath her sweater and caressed her back, while the other laid claim to her bottom. His kisses made more claims, and his tongue made promises. Megan spread her hands over the corded muscles in his back and her tongue welcomed his as she pressed him hard, made him harder, her whole body straining with the need he shared. He lured her tongue, sucked gently, and then chased it back where she could return the favor. When he finally broke their kiss, he realized she'd made claims, too. She'd taken his breath away.

"I'm not miserable yet," she whispered.

"I will be if we don't—" He pushed his fingers through her hair, shut his eyes and tipped his forehead against her cool skin. "—go somewhere."

"My room's closest."

"My pickup's even closer." He cursed himself under his breath. Dragging her down on the seat of a pickup had been his first suggestion, even when he knew damn well that kind of a scene would be bad for both of them. "But let's take your room and your truck. I'll leave mine, and we'll come back early."

Megan retrieved her shoes from behind the desk. Sage grabbed his shirt and saw her shiver when she slipped her slicker on with unsteady hands, watched her try to fight her way into wet shoes.

"Carry the shoes, and I'll carry you."

She offered a tentative smile. "Is there a river out there I might get dropped into?"

He stuck his head outside and ducked back in, smiling. "Wide as the Missouri. Come on."

He lifted her easily into his arms, bounded down the steps, sprinted through the puddles, and they laughed like mischievous children setting out for an adventure on a stormy night. He opened the door on the driver's side and handed her into his pickup. She slid all the way over to the far side of the seat, and he wanted her closer. She read his message and scooted back, and he reached for her. Once he had her in his arms again, he kissed every drop of water from her face.

"God, I'm thirsty," he whispered. "Got anything to drink at your place?"

"There'll be more water where that came from." She gave him a saucy smile. "I might be out of glasses."

He smiled back. "Maybe you'd like to take a shower."

It was only a ten-mile drive, but it seemed to take forever. Sage thought the whacking of the windshield wipers would drive him crazy. He watched the rain slash across the beams of light ahead.

"It's this one," she said, as though she'd just come awake. Blue and yellow neon tubes made the words Arrowhead Motel jump out from the roadside. Then the U-shaped motor court came into view, with its zigzagging neon trim along the overhang.

The overdose of neon had never bothered Megan before. This was just a place to stay. But then, she'd never brought a man to her room before, and she wished the neon would evaporate. She wished her apartment wasn't so far away. Sage had taken her to places that were part of him, and she was taking him to the Arrowhead Motel.

"Uh, Megan, do you think Kessler's would be open?"

They passed the motel, and she turned to him and stared. He was suddenly aware of everything about himself that must have looked ridiculous. His pants were wet, his shirt was lying on the seat between them, he was overdue for a haircut, and he had about thirteen dollars in his wallet and nothing else. *Nothing else.* It all came together in such an absurd package, it had him laughing aloud.

When had he last needed anything else? Thank God he had the thirteen dollars. It would have been embarrassing as hell to have to borrow money from her. It was going to be bad enough when he walked up to the cash register looking like he'd just been let out of some cage, with that single purchase in his hand. But anyone who tried to peek outside to get a look at who was with him risked a swift kick in the ass.

"What's so funny?" she asked.

Damn if she wasn't just as uneasy as he was. He tried to smooth things over with a smile. "I'm sorry. I know these things are supposed to be spontaneous." He lifted one shoulder to shrug away that expectation.

"A proper gentleman would be prepared to be spontaneous, right? A guy with class who knows enough to take his girl someplace nice, order fancy wine, check out the cork. What's with the cork?" He was spouting nonsense. It took the sight of the lights still on at Kessler's Dollar Store to make him quit. "I may be short on class, but I haven't run out of luck. It's still open. I need a candy bar or something. How about you?"

It felt good to laugh with her when he parked behind the building.

"Sage, it's raining. Look how far you have to walk."

She looked so damn cute, he had to kiss her. "Do I have to remind you, you've got your name emblazoned on the side of this pickup?"

"It says South Dakota Highway Department."

"Right." He planted another quick kiss on her mouth and grabbed his shirt. "Don't tell me what kind you like. Let me surprise you."

Megan slid down in the seat and grinned at the rain splattering the windshield. No one could accuse Sage Parker of being irresponsible. Megan McBride, maybe, but not Sage. Within minutes, he was back with a small brown paper sack, from which he produced a Hershey's with almonds.

"Was I right?" He brushed the water off his forehead with his wet sleeve as he turned the pickup back onto the street.

"Excellent choice." She tore open the wrapper and took a bite. The creamy chocolate melted on her tongue. "Where's yours?"

He gave a chin jerk. "It's in the bag. Mine's for later."

"Have a bite of mine, then." She held it up to his lips, and he bit off a mouthful.

HER ROOM SURE didn't look lived in. It was little more than a double bed with a picture of the Eiffel Tower hanging above the headboard, a little dresser, a tiny table with a couple of chairs jammed in one corner with a small stove and refrigerator. Megan flicked the switch on a pole lamp stretching floor to ceiling between the TV and a saggy-cushioned armchair, and Sage wondered where she kept her stuff. Not much on the dresser, no clothes on the chair. Her neatness put his spare living to shame.

"I don't know why they call this the Arrowhead Motel when they have Paris on the wall." She kicked her shoes off quickly.

He heard the high note of nervousness in her voice. He closed the door behind him, took off his muddy boots, and set them near her shoes. The light was dim, but he stilled her hand before she turned another on. She glanced up at him, then at the room. "It's pretty dingy, isn't it?"

"You've seen where I live. At least you've got room to turn around."

"Your trailer is very masculine."

He lifted one corner of his mouth in a half smile. "Is that a polite way of saying it's got no style?"

"No. It's a polite way of saying it's functional."

"Same as this."

"But it's not feminine."

"You're feminine, Megan, and I swear to God, you're all I'm looking at right now. I want to make love with you." He hooked his arm behind her neck and leaned closer to whisper, "Are you scared?"

"Of course not." She'd spoken so quickly, the three words ran together.

"You tell me what you want. With words or some other way, I'm pretty perceptive. I want to be good to you. We can just—"

"I'm not scared, Sage. A little nervous, but not scared. Are you?"

"Of course not," he whispered, mimicking her quick answer. "A little, maybe. If I screw up, I won't get invited back."

"That's right." She slid her arms around his waist. "So don't screw up."

He buried his lips in her hair and inhaled her scent. He wanted her, and he knew he would want her again. That alone was probably a screw-up. With things going pretty good right now, why take the risk? Why risk his job, their friendship, maybe even his sobriety? Because his blood coursed through him like river rapids, and if he didn't get inside her soon, he was going to bust wide open? Hell of a reason. He wanted to believe himself capable of having one tender, unselfish reason somewhere in his mind. This woman was good to him, and he wanted to be good in return.

"I need a shower," he said hoarsely. "I've been down on my hands and knees in the mud, and that's not the way I want to come to you."

"They have coin-operated machines here. I can wash your clothes for you while you—"

He shook his head. "I'll let you take care of me, just for tonight, but not that way."

"What way, then?"

"By sharing with me." He tossed the paper bag on the bed and took her in his arms. "The best water I ever tasted came from your face,

Megan." He dropped his voice close to her ear. "I need another drink."

"Sage . . ."

"Start by sharing a shower with me."

His kiss came hot and hard, but his clothes felt cold and soggy where he pressed himself against her. Her answer was to slide her hand between them and unbutton his shirt. She slipped her hand inside.

"You're cold," she whispered.

"Yeah." He nuzzled her neck. "Warm me."

She pushed his shirt off his shoulders, but she wouldn't let it go until it was draped over a chair. His wicked laughter sounded deep in his throat.

"I don't care about my clothes," he whispered. "I care about yours." She stole a glance at him. "I want to undress you and touch every part of you while I do it. I want to give you pleasure, do the things I never used to take the time for. And I'm not real sure . . ."

"Let's find out." She laid her hands along his smooth cheeks. "And let's agree that we can feel whatever we feel."

He smiled.

She raised her arms slowly, and he peeled the pink sweater away. He kissed her while he unfastened her jeans, slid his hand beneath the waistband and made the zipper crawl down tooth by tooth as he moved his hand over her firm belly. There was a band of lace and a triangle of cotton, but he felt the satin softness of skin it covered, and his fingertips found the upper fringe of springy hair. It was like plotting a course. He'd assured himself of his destination, but he didn't want to shorten the journey. He retreated as delicately as he'd advanced, pushed her jeans over her hips, and she lifted one foot at a time so he could remove them.

She looked smaller now than he'd imagined. His hands could almost span her waist. He dropped one knee to the floor and tried it, and he wondered at her worry about feminine frills. She had a female waist, female hips. He moved his hands over them and rested his forehead between the lacy cups of her bra.

"You're so small," he whispered.

"Is that bad?"

"It scares me. I've never been with such a small woman."

"Small but strong. I build roads."

"*I* build roads. You plan 'em, I build 'em. And I have a habit of blasting my way through."

She raked her fingers through his thick hair. "I'll show you where to set the charges."

He unfastened the clasp between her breasts, pushed her bra aside and stood, taking her breasts in his hands. He claimed her mouth with a caressing kiss, moved his lips over hers as he moved his thumbs over her soft skin.

She put her arms around his neck and lifted her chest on a deep breath, offering him more to hold and touch. Like ragged pieces of polishing cloth, the roughened pads of his thumbs whisked over her nipples. They tingled and tightened, and she groaned into his mouth.

"Don't ask me to set charges on such perfect little peaks," he whispered, still favoring her with his exquisitely tender touch. "I never knew a woman could be so—"

"Please don't say small."

"Delicate."

"I don't want to be delicate."

"What do you want to be?"

"Voluptuous."

He lifted her high off the floor and kissed the valley between her breasts. She closed her eyes and enjoyed the ride—three quick steps and a slow, sensuous slide over Sage's half-dressed, fully aroused body. Her toes touched down on cold tile, and the light came on as she opened her eyes.

"I want you to be wet, the way you were by the creek." He reached behind the clear plastic curtain and turned on the shower. "But *naked* and wet this time." He shed his jeans and tossed them behind him, watching her all the while.

"Buck naked, you say?" Her eyes never left his face.

He smiled. "That would be me."

He slid his hands over her hips and removed the last of her clothing, and then it was he who orchestrated the shower. The water was pleasantly warm, and the soap made them slick. Back slid against belly, thigh against thigh, bottom against cock. And randy cock was more than ready to bang his head against this woman's door.

But Sage was in control. She could boss him all she pleased—and she would be pleased—with Sage Parker holding the reins. He moved his hands over her, making small swirls of suds, moving slowly up and steadily up and listening for the catch in her breath when he finally touched her nipples. She moaned softly, dropped her head back against his shoulder and expanded her chest on a breath. He became her sole support, and the feel of her weight against him gave him pleasure. He looked down, saw brown fingers rubbing reddening nipples, watched her lips part, the lower one quiver, and, God, he wanted in. But he could hold off. He could wait for instructions.

And if she gave none, he could always improvise.

"Turn to me and let me kiss you," he said, and she did.

He licked into her mouth, let her suck on his tongue while he rolled her nipples between thumb and middle finger and used forefingers for flicking their tips. She reached back and gripped his ass, tried to dig her nails in, but his cheeks were rock hard. Any other time, he would have crowed like a vain cock, but his hands and his mouth had better things to do, ways to convey her to a higher plane, right where he wanted her. She gave herself over to his levitating touch, the sleight of a powerful hand. Her body quivered, and his kiss became a knowing smile. There would be more where that came from.

He slipped one hand between her thighs, and she gasped and relied on his arm for support. Ah, she was a handful of soft and warm down there, and the fragile, feminine feel of her took his breath, lightened his head, gentled his laborer's hand. He slid a finger inside her slowly and drew sweet music, hungry mewling from deep in her throat. He thumbed the sensitive, secret bit of flesh tucked in the harbor between her legs. She drew a shallow quaking breath when he tickled her there. He knew he was on the right path. He mounted a bold assault with his tongue, sweetly tormenting her until she shuddered uncontrollably in his arms.

Sage slammed the water off and drew her from the shower. Steam filled the tiny room. He held her in his arms, and she rubbed against him like a cat while he sipped water from her face and neck. He backed her against the bar hung with thick towels, anchored his hands on either side of her, and moved his mouth over her breasts, suckling each nipple in turn until she gave a sultry moan. Then he kissed his way down the middle of her belly.

"Brace yourself on my shoulders," he said, brushing breath and lips over her dewy skin. "Let me take you for a ride." She was slick, like a water slide, and he'd begun his descent. "So good," he whispered at her threshold. "Nourish me, Megan."

His lips tugged at the springy curls that trimmed her womanhood. With finger and thumb, he spread curls and cleft, and then he dipped his tongue to taste her deeply. His tongue became a flame that danced for her. When she drew a ragged breath, he sucked her and licked her until she arched and came, calling his name. He rose through the mist and pinned her to the wall, sliding his body over hers.

"Was it enough?" His lips drifted through the damp sheen on her forehead.

"Not by half." She rolled her head back and forth against the wall. "Good start, though."

"You want me to double it?" He lifted his head and saw the glaze in her eyes, the wistful smile on well-kissed lips. His laughter started deep within his chest and emerged as a wicked sound. He took her hand, slid it down the front of his body and pressed it to his cock. "You ready to try this on for size?"

"I am."

She tried to press him down and herself up, but all she could do was rub the tip of his penis over her engorged bundle of nerves. It felt splendid and selfish and undeniable. "Sit down," she pleaded. "Let me put you inside me right here, right now."

He groaned, shutting her up and cutting off his own curse with a hungry kiss. Steam followed them into the bedroom. She lay down, and he prepared himself for her quickly, and then he went to her, straddled her on hands and knees, covered and kissed her belly, breast, parted her thighs as he nuzzled her neck, nipped her earlobe, and finally claimed her mouth with his.

His body alone filled her senses—its hard planes and sleek skin, the heat of his breath and the pounding of his heart in time with her own. She reached for him, guided him to her as he raised her knees to ease his entry. He filled her so far beyond the physical bounds that she wept for his tenderness even as she arched her hips to help him make the explosion happen again, this time for both of them.

When it was done and he had caught his breath and cleaned up a bit, he kissed away her tears. In the silence, he thought of all the things that might have brought them on. Was she thinking of another time? Missing somebody? Sorry, sad, what? His throat tightened up on him, and he didn't want to speak at all. But tears, *Christ*. A guy had to say something.

"I didn't hurt you, did I?" It came out sounding a little gruff, which wasn't the way he felt. He felt a whole lot of *hallelujah* mixed in with a baffling bit of *what the hell?*

"No." Her voice was small. He wasn't sure she meant it until she touched his cheek and said, "Far from it. You couldn't hurt me."

Then who did? He wasn't going to ask now. Not now, when he wanted whatever she was feeling, good or bad, to be about him. So he turned his head and kissed her palm.

"I'm not crying," she said. "I don't cry."

His smile followed his kiss, right into her hand. "Your eyes were leaking."

"I'm leaking everywhere." She laughed. "I'm mel-tiiing."

"Mmm." He found a crease in her palm with the tip of his tongue and followed it to the crotch between her first and middle fingers. "Sweet. Like creamy drips on the cone."

"That tickles." She laughed again. "Who knew it could be like that?"

He still didn't get where the tears had come from. "What could be like what?"

"Sex could be like heaven. A little bit, anyway."

"*Little* bit?"

"Well, yeah, if heaven lasts forever."

"Hey, I lasted pretty good. At least I knew better than to punch in right away." He gave her ass cheek a quick squeeze. "So don't go docking me, huh?" She giggled, and he squeezed again. "Cut me some slack."

She reached down and cupped his penis. "I think you've taken care of that."

"Backing off to recoup. Not that you'd understand. You don't have to back off." He slid his hand over her belly on its way to lifting her breast. "You can just keep on coming."

"Can I?"

"In the right hands, you sure can." His thumb circled her nipple, and he could feel the catch in her breath. "You like this, don't you?"

She rested her forehead against his and nodded.

"Feels good?"

She nodded again. He slid down, took her other nipple with tongue and suckling mouth to put two points on her, proving that the right hands were only the beginning, and that in the end, there was no end. She could just keep on coming.

Her little squeal made him smile against her soft breast. "Half again more, or enough for now?"

"Oh . . ." Slowly, she drew a deep breath, and so did he, and the rising tide lifted all breasts. ". . . yesss."

He took her nipple gently between his teeth. "Which is it?"

"Just hold me," she whispered. "I don't want to float away."

"I like your hair." He touched his nose to it, rubbed back and forth. It was cool and soft, still damp. "It smells like rain."

"I like yours, too." She lifted her hand to his hair and combed her fingers through it. "I like everything about you. Should I let my hair grow?"

"Why?"

"So I don't look boyish. I mean, I'm feeling very womanly, but I stopped trying to look the part because I don't want it to be the first thing that comes to mind."

He chuckled. "Good luck with that."

"Well, I am lucky in some ways. My boobs are small, hips pretty straight, and if I were just a little taller . . ."

He groaned, rolled to his back, and gathered her in his arms. "I thought my heart would bust wide open when I saw your body and how small and pretty you are."

"You were expecting . . ."

"I don't know. The boss, maybe. Come right down to it, I wasn't expecting you to be shy." Another chuckle. "I guess I wasn't expecting you. But I was sure as hell wanting you. Just you. Every inch of you." He kissed the top of her head. "Don't sign up with any matchmakers. You'll sell yourself short."

"Not signing anything." She bit his shoulder gently. "Not selling anything."

"Not bossing anybody?"

"Not off the clock." She kissed the place she'd nipped. "I wouldn't know how."

"You can tell me what you want, how you want me to . . ." He lifted her chin and kissed her. ". . . please you."

"I want to please you, too," she whispered.

"Pleasing you pleases me."

"I got lost. I left it all up to you and didn't do anything."

"Yeah, you did. The sound, the feel of your pleasure excites me."

She tucked her head under his chin.

"Lost in what?" he asked.

"What you were giving me. What you made me feel. Pure pleasure."

"I was there with you. Couldn't you tell?"

"You were perfection." She lifted her head, looked into his eyes, touched his face. "Almost scary."

"Far from perfect. Nobody's perfect."

"Nearly perfect, then." She traced a line along his jaw. "I've never known anyone like you, Sage. The way you work, the care you take with people and with . . ." She kissed him softly. "I thought my heart would bust wide open, too."

"Don't give me too much credit, Megan. A little is nice, but don't go crazy with it." He smiled. "You know what's crazy? I've never made love to a friend before. Hell, I'm not sure I've ever made love before. Now *that's* almost scary."

"What do you mean? You were mar—"

"I've had sex," he said quickly. "I've had me some women. But I made love to you."

"I know."

"I did, didn't I?"

"You did."

He held her close and tucked her head back under his chin. "I made love to someone I care about. God, it felt good." He swallowed hard, trying to soothe the burning in his throat. "Your tears scared the hell out of me. I thought I'd done something wrong."

"You were so gentle, Sage." She kissed the base of his throat. "You keep telling me how bad you've been, but all I see is good. You've wrestled with the bad things, and you've won."

She made him feel so good, he couldn't argue with her. He couldn't bring himself to tell her just then how he struggled every day, and how he would go on struggling for the rest of his life. He wanted to be good to her always. That much he knew.

"I still want your friendship first," he told her. "Without that, we've got nothing."

"I know." She leaned back to look at him. His good looks always stunned her—his black hair, still damp from their shower, his dark, enigmatic eyes, and his deeply tanned face with its hard, angular features. She touched his lower lip with her forefinger. "So tell me things friends tell each other. Tell me about Sage Parker. From the very beginning."

"From the beginning, huh?" He nipped at her finger, and then he smiled. "In the very beginning—beautiful day, springtime—there was a harrowing buckboard ride. My mother was in labor, and my father was trying to get her to the clinic. She'd already delivered at home six times, and the doctor had warned her not to try it again. She was getting too old for that stuff."

"A buckboard ride?" she asked. "We're talking about your mother, now, not your grandmother."

"A buckboard ride," he confirmed. "We were between cars. Maybe you go by who was alive when whatever happened—like, after Grandpa died, before Junior was born. With my dad, you had to know the order of cars. Indian cars, you know? Classics, he called them, but they were just old, and he drove 'em 'til they died. I came along between the Rambler and the old woodie."

"The *woodie?*"

"Not . . ." He scowled. "You've been around road crews too long. An old woodie station wagon, for God's sake." He reached for the chenille spread at the foot of the bed, and he tossed it over them. "Too many road crews, too few rez roads. When a car dies, you make do with what you've got, and we always had horses. Now, this is the true story of my birth, so show some respect."

She pillowed her head on his shoulder. "Okay. Your father was driving the buckboard."

"And my mom kept yelling at him to go faster, and he kept saying they should have stayed home." He used his free hand to follow the motion of the story in the air above their heads. "So, they're bumping along, and the back wheel falls off the axle." The heel of his hand skidded to a stop in the middle of his chest.

"Are you sure you're not confusing this with the pickup?"

"Of course I'm sure. I've heard the damn story a hundred times. Between contractions, my mom had to get down from the buckboard and shove the wheel back on while my dad held the axle up. 'Course, he couldn't drive it 'cause the burr was busted. He set the brake, unhitched the team, and got back up there in time to catch me coming out of the chute."

Megan laughed so hard she could barely speak. "You're making . . . all this . . . up."

"Hell, I could never invent anything this good," he assured her. "So my mom says to my dad, 'Husband, I have given you another son.'"

"Oh, come on."

"Well, words to that effect." His shoulders shook with silent laughter. "By the time the whole scene was edited for the retelling, that was her line. She never thought the story was too funny until it came to that line."

"I can imagine."

"So then he says, 'What name have you chosen for this lusty, strapping man-child?'"

"Give me a break," Megan groaned.

"So that's when she always turned to me with the real solemn look and said, 'I had your name all picked out, my son. It was going to be Sampson. But you didn't lift a finger to help me with that wheel. I looked around me—blue sky and native prairie as far as the eye could see—and I looked down at you, and I knew who you were.'"

She shifted toward him, laid her arm over his chest and savored the sound of his name. "Sage."

"Uh-uh." He put his lips close to her ear and whispered, "Jackrabbit."

She groaned again. "You're so full of it, Parker."

"Straight up, woman. I speak with straight tongue."

She pinched his side and discovered he was ticklish. "A-ha! Now I know your weak spot."

He held her hand still and flashed his wicked grin. "Use it against me and I'll find every one of yours."

"How come you weren't this funny when we first met?"

"How come you weren't this friendly when we first met?"

The softness they saw in one another's eyes only hinted at the answers each chose to keep for the time being.

I would have been, if I had trusted you as I do now.

I would have been, if I had loved you as I do now.

Megan snuggled against him again. "Seriously, how much of that story is true?"

"Nearly every word. It was my mother's favorite kid story. Except she didn't give me the nickname. Little brothers get pet names, right? I was a fast runner. And nobody calls me that anymore, so don't you try." He kissed her forehead. "That's like my baby name. Another weak spot. If you use it against me—" He gestured with a flat hand. "—we are no longer friends."

"The name or the ticklish spot?"

"The name." The flat hand curved around her breast. "You tickle me, I tickle you."

"Mmm."

"You know what we call that?"

"Uh-uh."

"Tit for tat."

"Of course."

"So what was yours?" He thought better of going for the nipple. She'd gotten some history out of him, and it was her turn. "Your baby name."

"I was always Megan," she said quietly. "Your story is so much better."

"You know what I just discovered?" He turned the thought over in his mind for a moment just to be sure of it. "I can tell that story just as well sober as I can half-shot."

"Better, maybe."

"Better, maybe." He turned his head and kissed the top of hers. "You're the best damn audience a guy could ask for, Megan McBride."

"Most gullible?"

"Most fun," he told her. She lifted her head as if to see whether he was laughing at her, and he made sure she found only the softness in his eyes. "This is the first I've told that story in bed." He combed his fingers through her damp hair. "I really like this."

"What?"

"Lying here with you. Holding each other and just talking. And touching."

"But, like you said, you've been with—"

"No." He laid a finger over her lips and shook his head. "No. This is new for me. I'm not buzzed and cocky as hell, and I wasn't looking to get laid." He slid his hand over her shoulder and down the length of her back. "I already did that, and you're still here."

"This is my room," she reminded him. "*You're* still here."

"Time for me to go?"

"Don't you dare." She snuggled down again. "I really like this, too. It shouldn't be rushed. Unless you're tired."

"Are you?"

"Sleepy." She tightened her arms around him. "But I don't want to go to sleep yet. Do you?"

"I'm in no rush," he whispered.

"I wish I had met you first," she said, and she kissed his shoulder. It was hers to kiss, she thought recklessly, and it should never have been anyone else's. "Before your wife. Before the other women."

"Don't." He groaned. "If I'd had you then, you wouldn't be here now."

"Things might have been different."

"You couldn't have changed me. I have to do that for myself." He lifted his head to look at her face. Her pretty face. She was so confident in her ability to make things right. "I'm glad you came along when you did. Maybe I was ready for you."

"Well, almost." She propped her chin on his shoulder and hiked a teasing eyebrow. "You were after you stopped at Kessler's."

With a chuckle, he dropped his head back on the pillow. "I'm doing good." Rolling his head to the side allowed him to see her face again. "See? That's a prime example. Years ago, I would have knocked you up without thinking twice."

"No, you wouldn't have. I wouldn't have let you."

He frowned. "You're not on the pill, are you?"

"N-no. I . . . had no reason to be."

"You got something else stashed around here?" She shook her head. "It was my idea, then, wasn't it?" She nodded, feeling foolish. "See? I really am doing good." He touched her cheek and whispered, "I hate the thought of hurting you."

She closed her eyes and laid her cheek against his shoulder again. "I didn't think. I just wanted us to make love."

He hugged her close, pleased with himself for proving trustworthy, at least tonight. "Tell me your story, Megan."

"Mine isn't as good as yours."

"It must be. Megan sounds like somebody they should write a song about."

"It's my grandmother's name," she said matter-of-factly. "My sister got my other grandmother's name. My parents live in Pierre, but I don't see much of them anymore."

"Why not?" He figured he knew why, but he wanted her to tell him.

"I wish my father could go to a Medicine Wheel meeting," she said quietly. "He doesn't see it. He's never lost a job, never gotten arrested, but it's every night until he goes to bed. Talk about busting wide open, he has health issues."

"Heart?"

"Among other things. If he met someone like you, your group, your . . . maybe he would just stop drinking once and for all."

"There is no 'once and for all,' Megan. There's no 'happily ever after.' There's just one day at a time."

She smoothed her hand over his chest. "Four years is a lot of one days."

"Sometimes, a day is too much. Sometimes, when it's really bad, when all you can think about is where the nearest bottle is—sometimes, you tell yourself to hold on for another minute. And then you figure maybe you can go one more."

"Do you have days like that?"

"Not as often as I used to, but, yeah. Some."

"What do you do?"

"I go to a meeting. I find someone to talk to, someone who's like me. I try to sweat it out in the lodge. I pray."

"Could you ever . . . come to me?"

"Uh-uh." He felt her disappointment, and he rubbed her back, hoping the disappointment would melt away. He needed her acceptance.

"You're not an alcoholic, Megan. You can't take care of us. But you can care. Don't cut yourself off from your father. Don't expect perfection. If your father's anything like me—and it sounds like he might be—we can be hard-headed. Hard-hearted. Don't be afraid to tell us the truth. Tell him you want him to get help. And then step back."

She was quiet for a time, and then. . . . "I was 'Eggie.' I guess my sister started it. Isn't that awful?"

He smiled. "No worse than Rabbit."

"It's a lot worse. My mother had the good sense to stop calling me Meggie, so Megan it was. But every so often my sister drags out the . . ."

"What did your dad call you?" He knew there was something else. He had a daughter, too.

"Baby. My sister was Princess, and I was Baby. Not very original." She drew a ragged breath. "He doesn't think. . . . It would hurt his feelings if I suggested anything like that. And he wouldn't listen anyway."

"Maybe not, but all you can do is tell him your side. His side is up to him."

"Look at all *you* do." She rose up as though she were going to accuse him of something. "You're trying to make big changes. *Big* changes. Aren't you looking out for other people?"

"I just want us to look out for ourselves. You know, as a community. When I came back from treatment with the idea for Medicine Wheel, I couldn't shut up about it. I needed to do something or I knew I'd start in drinking again. I probably sounded like some damn missionary for a while there, but I figured we'd find our way if we looked to our own traditions. Pretty soon, we had a little group. We're growing, and we're getting healthy enough to try to make our community healthy."

"When's the next hearing?" she asked. "I want to be there."

He pulled her toward him, and she lay back down in his arms. "I don't think that's a good idea anymore, Megan."

"Why not? I just want to stand by you. That isn't caretaking, is it?"

"There have been . . . threats. Taylor stands to lose some of his business. If we're lucky, if Regina gets the store going, maybe a lot of his business. I don't want him to try to get to me by. . . . He might try to hurt the people around me."

"He threatened you?"

"It's just something you should know." He cupped her breast with a protective hand. "This kind of sharing is nice, but I don't want to share my enemies with you."

"I'm going to that hearing," she insisted.

"Whatever you say." Turning on his side, he adjusted her in his arms. "It's stopped raining," he told her. "If we went to sleep right now, we might get in about four hours before daybreak. I don't know about you, but I've got work to do."

She nuzzled his neck. "I could make do with three and a half. I've been going to bed early all my life."

"What for?"

"Resting up for tonight."

He rolled on top of her and hooked his leg over hers. He was more than ready. "If you were so damn sure of yourself, why didn't you stop at the drugstore before you came to get me?"

"Came to get—"

Megan's protest was lost in Sage's kiss.

Chapter 11

SAGE'S CRYPTIC comments about the threats against him worried Megan, but he showed no concern for himself. His only fear seemed to be for her. She decided to pay Pete Petersen a visit. He understood local politics, and she thought he was probably within earshot of most of the local rumors, as well.

Pete still hadn't oiled the springs in his desk chair. They creaked as he leaned back, linking his fingers over his stomach. "Sounds to me like you've developed more than a professional interest in Sage Parker."

"We've been working together all summer." Megan uncrossed her legs and resettled herself in her chair. "It's no surprise we've become friends." She recrossed her legs from the other side.

"No surprise at all." Pete's smile reminded her of a card player laying down a winning hand.

"Besides that, Sage's pickup was sabotaged on the site."

His eyebrows shot up, his interest piqued. "Sabotaged?"

"The lug nuts were loosened on one of the tires. The whole wheel fell off."

"Anybody hurt?"

"Sage might have been. He nearly went over an embankment. Frankly, I think he knows more about it than he's told me."

Pete picked up a pencil and tapped the eraser against his desk pad. "Well, you asked me if I thought somebody might be out to get him on this liquor sales thing, and I guess you've answered your own question. Sounds like somebody is."

"Taylor?"

"Could be." Pete tossed the pencil aside. "Taylor's an opportunist. A taker, like so many of the people who've beaten a path to the reservations to make a buck. They've cheated these people out of land, food, program money, lease checks—you name it. It's been going on for over a hundred years. And they always seem to be taking with one hand and peddling whiskey with the other."

"If someone stands up to them, is he likely to be . . . punished somehow?"

"Your friend might be found dead alongside the road." He punctuated the news with a sigh and a *tsk*. "I've been here almost thirty years. I remember one guy who tried to blow the whistle on a fishy cattle-buying deal. Government program, tribe was buying cattle, some of the records didn't jibe. After this guy got shot at on the highway a few times, he decided he'd forgotten how to add. And the tribe figured if they didn't take what they got, they wouldn't get anything. That's the history of this place. That's why people tend to just let things go."

Megan tightened her grip on the arms of her chair. "How much support do you think Sage has? Do you hear any talk about—"

"Oh, yeah, Sage is the talk of the town. He's either a saint or a sinner, depending on who you're talking to. Some people are standing neutral on the issue itself, but there's no neutral ground where Sage is concerned."

"He's worried about. . . . He thinks I might be threatened, too."

"Why? Because you've gone to a couple of council sessions? A Medicine Wheel meeting or two?"

Megan shot him a scowl.

"I'm the one who gave you the information, remember? I haven't heard too much talk about you, but everybody knows who you are. Around here, people see a man and a woman together more than once, they draw conclusions."

Good, she thought. Let them. *If they want to shoot at him, they can shoot at me, too.* She caught Pete's intuitive smile, and she returned it with pride.

"He's no saint, Megan, but he's a damn good man. He's been working at it for a good long time now, and he's doing fine." He bobbed his head and repeated the conviction. "He's doing just fine."

"He's helping people. I saw that at the meeting."

Pete leaned back in his chair and clasped his hands behind his head. "What else did you see?"

She gave him a quizzical look.

"It's a different world, isn't it? A community like no other, and you're drawn to it, even though you're the minority here. But that doesn't bother you, does it?"

She shook her head.

"Maybe you'd be interested in a civil service job with the BIA. I've got a guy transferring out in September, and I'm looking at retirement soon myself. Be a good future in it for you."

Megan raised a speculative eyebrow. "But, as you point out, I'm not Lakota."

"Neither am I. There's Indian preference, but you've gotta qualify otherwise, and you do."

"This was my first big assignment, but I'm still pretty low on the totem pole with the state highway department. I'm open to other options." She couldn't help smiling. "I guess it wouldn't hurt to fill out an application."

Pete took her to the local café for hamburgers. It was after seven when she unlocked the door to her pickup and she caught a glimpse of a stern face in the side mirror. The unfriendly look in the dark eyes was chilling. Megan turned slowly, her mind spinning with possibilities she didn't much like.

"Hello, Regina."

"I'm looking for Sage."

Megan frowned. "He isn't with me."

"I thought you might be with him," Regina said flatly. "We have a meeting scheduled for seven-thirty tonight. We're helping them start a group here like the one we've got going in Red Calf."

"Then I'm sure he'll be here. I left the site early. Sage did say he had a meeting tonight, but he didn't mention where."

The look on Regina's face betrayed her doubt. Let her think what she wanted, Megan decided. She wasn't following Sage. If she had known Sage planned to be in Big Thunder, she would have planned her visit for another day. He might ask questions about her reason for visiting Pete, and her answer might be construed as "caretaking." Megan was tired of trying to figure out what the word really meant.

"He's always early," Regina said. "He always makes sure there's coffee, and we set up the chairs."

Megan laughed. "You could float a battleship in the coffee that man consumes." She touched Regina's arm, hoping the gesture would be taken as friendly. "I'm sure he stopped off to change his clothes, and he probably had a couple of chores to do or something. He's bound to be along soon."

Regina lowered her gaze and stood quite still. "I just thought you might have come to town together."

"We didn't." Megan dropped her hand, but she felt something more genuine reaching toward the woman from within herself. "Medicine Wheel is something I would never interfere with, Regina. Never. Sage asked me to go to a meeting and see how it worked. I'm glad I did.

I understand why it's so important to him."

"It's his lifeline," Regina said. "It can't be replaced by a woman."

Megan felt a tightening in her throat. "I know that."

"Good."

Regina turned to walk away, but Megan spoke her name, and she turned back. "How are you doing?" Megan asked gently.

Regina nodded, and the tension dropped from her shoulders as she sighed. "Okay. It's hard." She swallowed and glanced away. "With the children especially. My two older ones took it hard." Her eyes grew cloudy with emotion. "I'm doing okay."

"Your husband was a good worker," Megan offered, choosing not to mention any exceptions. "I enjoyed having him on the crew. And I'm so sorry." Regina nodded again.

Megan backed her pickup away from the curb, but before she had it in gear, she heard someone call her name. Pete left his car idling on the opposite side of the street with the door standing open. His awkward attempt at a jog would have seemed funny if he hadn't had such a grave expression on his face.

He braced himself in her open window and struggled to catch his breath. "I just heard some bad news. It's about Sage."

THE SMELL OF IT was the worst part now. Flesh on fire. It was more pungent than the acrid smell of wood smoke or burning hay. Sage's eyes stung, and his gut roiled. The air around him was heavy with that smell. He dropped his forehead against his fingertips and rubbed his eyes with the heels of his hands, hoping to find enough moisture in them to relieve the stinging. The heat had left them dry. It had left *him* dry.

With his eyes closed, there was only the swirl of sounds—the crackle and hiss, the call for water, the shifting of timber. And the smell. He saw Jackie's rotting flesh behind his eyelids and imagined the wild-eyed mare with her spotted hide ablaze. She wasn't shrieking anymore, thank God. He tasted the bile rising in the back of his throat, and he wished his stomach would settle down. He would have been grateful just for that.

Another beam gave way behind him. He turned to see the charred bones of his dream house clatter one against another. Like dominoes, they finally knocked each other down. The subfloor gave way, and the smoking rubble collapsed into its own cement grave. At least no one was in it.

He wished he could say the same for the barn. His mare was someone. She was also someone's mother. He turned again and watched the rural volunteer fire department reorganize its efforts to attack the barn from a different angle. There was little left to save. They'd kept the fire from spreading across the prairie, which was a commendable feat. The house had gone quickly, but bright orange flames from the barn still licked the evening sky. With the hay inside, it had become an inferno, and the part that was metal held the heat. Twilight gave the horizon a shrinking red rim, and the first few stars claimed their places in the heavens.

Sage wondered where his place was. Obviously, heaven had no use for him. He'd tried to change. Places inside him were still raw from the effort. But he'd *made* the effort. He'd shivered and sweated with it. He'd stumbled and dragged himself on his belly until he found that his legs could hold him again. It must have been a disgusting sight. Unmanly. Unforgiveable. Why else would God have turned His head while some damn sonuvabitch set a torch to the only real dream Sage had left?

He lay back on the hood of his pickup, where somebody had insisted he sit and rest for a while. He'd seen the smoke on his way home, and he'd had a sinking feeling well before he saw the blaze. Several neighbors and one of the fire pickups were already on the scene. Despair had turned to rage, and he'd been a madman for a while there. He'd probably scared the hell out of them at first, when he'd tried to get into the barn. Then he'd settled down and helped with the hoses and the buckets until the nausea had overwhelmed him. He'd nearly puked his guts into his mouth.

What had he done? There was supposed to be forgiveness up there, wasn't there? A single star winked at him. It was all a terrific joke, wasn't it? It was the ultimate tease. Destiny enjoyed letting you think you had a say. He'd had the audacity to believe things could change. If people wanted to drink, they'd drink. Hell, he knew that.

And he knew better than to think a good woman could love Sage Parker. He'd had his chance, and he wasn't supposed to get another one. He'd been a shitty husband, a worthless father, and a few years later, he'd let himself get all puffed up with pride just because he'd nailed a few boards together and bought a few cows. And then he'd taken a woman. He wasn't supposed to have a woman. He wasn't good enough for any woman. Women meant family, and he wasn't supposed to have that, either.

The stench was proof. He was fond of saying he'd been to hell and back. Now he knew different. Hell was the end of the line.

"How're you doing, Sage?"

He sat up. It took him a moment to think of his neighbor's name. Old Bernie Richards. He'd known the man since he was a kid. Bernie's gray hair was covered with soot; maybe that was why Sage hadn't recognized him. And he hadn't really heard the question.

"You okay?" Bernie laid a hand on Sage's shoulder, looking to cut through the haze. "This is a hell of a thing. I think you oughta stay with somebody for a while, son." Bernie waited for a reaction. Sage had none to give. "How 'bout your brother George? He still around?"

Sage shook his head. "Moved to Montana." He covered the old man's hand with his own. "I'm okay, Bernie. I appreciate your help."

"You can sure stay with us," Bernie offered.

"I've still got the trailer." His eyes felt like rocks, and his stony gaze rolled back to the barn. "I'll be fine."

"Well, I just wanted to warn you. A couple of young fellas got a bottle going around over there." He nodded at a trio taking a break near the corral. "You keep your head on straight, son. You hear?"

Sage stared at the small party going on in honor of his barn-burning.

"You got any insurance, Sage?"

His gaze was riveted on the three men. "No. No insurance."

"That's the hell of it. Who can pay for it nowadays?" Bernie patted Sage's shoulder. "Not much more I can do for you tonight then. This is gonna burn itself out now. Lucky it didn't spread."

"Yeah. Lucky."

"Anything you need, you just—"

"Thanks, Bernie."

Sage had no idea what they were drinking, but he could taste it. His throat was raw from the smoke, and his mouth was dry. He turned his head quickly and tried to fix his mind on something else. There was the trailer. One of his saddles was in the bedroom. Most of his tools were in the back of the pickup. He still had a job. He needed Medicine Wheel. Now. There was a meeting going on right now, and he needed . . .

"I'll bet you could use a drink right about now."

It cut deep, like an electrical shock. Sage pressed his lips together and turned slowly, trying to remember how to refuse. He wasn't even sure who this man was, but he knew one of the guys he was drinking with. Lonnie Crow. Sage remembered drinking with Lonnie, too.

"You've had a tough night. One drink won't hurt."

Sage tried to ignore the bottle. "Did you come with the firefighters?"

The man stuck out his hand. "Gordon Brown. I came with Lonnie. He's a friend of Chet's, and Chet's a volunteer."

Sage caught himself watching the man take a long pull on the bottle. In the dark, it was hard to tell much about him. He wore a cowboy hat and sounded pretty South Dakota. Sage could feel some high-octane hooch slide down the man's throat as he watched him swallow.

Gordon wiped his mouth on his sleeve and leaned on the hood of the pickup, setting the bottle in front of him. "This is a damn shame, Sage. Lonnie said you did most of the work here yourself. And the way that poor horse screamed . . ."

Sage took a deep breath and held it. Wicked spirits. The screech of the crow would drown out everything else, and he'd take the smell of aged piss over burning horseflesh any damn day. He watched his hand close over the neck of the bottle.

The first taste singed his tongue and burned going down. He filled his mouth with it again and made his peace with it. He'd fucked up big time, and he was being punished. He thought he'd changed, but his insides were still filled with scum. Something that tasted like lye might clean it all out for him.

IN THE DARK, THE barn looked like a hulking black creature trapped in a pool of embers. The basement of Sage's unfinished house had become a firepit. Megan turned her pickup toward the dark little trailer. Was it the smell of charred dreams or the prickle in her eyes making her feel physically sick? She remembered Sage's imposing figure on the rooftop and the halo the sun had made for him. With two separate fires, there was no pretense of an accident.

She parked beside the trailer, shut the pickup door quietly as though she didn't want to disturb anyone. Gloom rank with smoke hung in the air. There was nothing to be done. Two or three shadowy figures shifted near the barn. A couple more backed away as a charred timber groaned and sagged in their direction. Like funeral goers, they spoke to each other in low tones, heads down, respectful of the loss. None of the shadows was Sage. She would know. She wouldn't call out, but she would find him.

HE SAW HER COMING. His first instinct was to hide the bottle. He had a good buzz on, but it hadn't drowned out the voices yet. He wished they'd leave. He really wished Megan would leave, but here she came. He couldn't see her face yet, but he knew her shape, her walk, her purpose. He wouldn't enjoy having her see him this way. It would be like getting beaten up right in front of her. But his instincts were overruled by a greater need to be honest with her, to let her see the truth. He was no hero.

He felt it when she spotted him. He could see her moonlit features now, and his heart skidded a little, the way it did when he was a kid caught hiding. He didn't like the feeling—he was a man, after all—and he nearly tipped the bottle to his mouth just to show her. But she mouthed his name and hurried toward him, her look of distress fixed on his face. Waves of regret washed over him. He would have given any-thing at that moment to be the man she thought she was running to. Then he remembered he had nothing to offer up in trade.

He slid down from the pickup hood, leaving the open fifth standing at his back in plain view. Still, she saw nothing but him as she slipped her arms around him and laid her head against his chest. She asked no ques-tions, gave him no words of sympathy. She simply held him.

Tradition said there should have been an argument right at the outset. The sooner he could get angry and stay angry, the sooner he could stop feeling like garbage. If he worked it right, he could convince her that his failure was hers, too, and he could add her contempt to his list of reasons for getting wasted. But she was ignorant of the tradition. In her mind, she was still holding the man she'd said goodbye to earlier in the day.

There was no place to put his arms but around her shoulders. He felt her shudder against him and hoped to God she wasn't crying. He didn't want anyone crying over him. He had no comfort to offer. He wanted to crawl inside her and shut the rest of the world away, but he had nothing for her in return. He was empty.

Maybe he could walk away from the bottle. Stand up straight, hold his head high and walk away. Maybe this woman would give him a pass if he did that, forgive him his trespass, and take his pain away by that very act. Not that he'd done her any harm. Yet.

HIS SHIRT REEKED of smoke, but she buried her face against it anyway. If she'd been there sooner, she could have helped him fight the fire, and then the smoke from his home would have been in her clothes. They were a good team and maybe she could have made a difference.

"Are you hurt?"

"Hurt?"

He sounded confused. She looked up at his soot-smeared face and saw the glazed expression in his eyes. She ran her hands along his arms, and he winced when she came to his hands. They examined them together, finding scrapes and blisters.

"You're burned. We need to get you to a doctor."

He stared at his hands as though he didn't know where they'd come from. He shook his head. "Must've happened when I tried to get the barn door open. The horses . . ."

"Horses," Megan echoed.

"I always leave that side door open during the day so they can go in for shade. There's a latch that holds it open. I *always* . . ." He tipped his head back and searched the sky for help, but none was there. Blinking hard, he swallowed the sting in his throat and told himself to hang on to what was left of his dignity. Finally, he risked looking down at her face. "The mare was in the barn. Her colt was outside, and they were calling to each other. Crying. *Screaming.* The door had to be bolted from the inside."

"Oh, my God," she whispered.

"I know I didn't shut that door." He'd gone over it in his mind a dozen times, retracing his steps, but this was the first time he'd said it aloud. "It was open to the corral. I know it was. I filled the water tank this morning. I fed them, locked up the storage closet, and secured the latch." He'd broken a sweat just talking about it. He wiped his brow with his sleeve. "You could smell the kerosene. Hell, I don't even keep any kerosene out there."

"The colt is okay?"

He nodded. "I opened the gate, and he took off. But he'll be back, looking for his mother."

"Sage, it was set. Somebody locked the mare in, and, oh my God. . . . We'll tell the authorities. They'll find out who did this." She had both his shoulders in her grip when her nostrils flared. Her eyes widened as she stiffened. "Sage?"

He reached behind him and slid the dark bottle to his side, watching her all the while. She blanched. He was sure of it. There in the darkness, she lost all color in her face. Some sinister need to shock her overcame him, and he tipped the bottle to his mouth and sucked the stuff down greedily.

"Sage, what are you doing?"

He set the bottle down, wiped his mouth on the back of his hand and gave her a cold smile. "I'm getting drunk."

"You can't do that."

"It's been a while, but I think I remember how it's done."

He started to raise the bottle again, and she grabbed his arm. "You don't need it, Sage. You're through with all that."

He transferred the whiskey into his other hand and took another drink. Pressing his lips together, he stared her down. "Don't ever try to separate a drunk from his bottle, Megan. You can get hurt that way."

"You'd never hurt me."

"You can't be sure of that," he warned. "You can't be sure of any-thing or any*one*."

"And you're *not* a drunk. Don't call yourself that."

"Oh yeah?" His laughter sounded cruel. "That's where you're wrong, darlin'. You're in way over your head, and there's a hell of a storm brewing." He latched onto her upper arm, and the pain in his eyes had nothing to do with his blistered skin. "I know you can swim, Megan," he said, desperately struggling with the gravel in his throat. "Re-member? Head for higher ground. There's nothing left here."

"You're here," she whispered.

He touched her cheek with raw fingers. "I'm going under."

"You've got a lot of friends, Sage." They both turned toward the voice of reason, which came from Pete Petersen. "They're not going to let you down. This doesn't end here."

Sage looked back at Megan, his eyes suddenly cold again. "What? You brought reinforcements?"

"Pete was the one who told me—"

Another car arrived, and two doors slammed shut. Sage peered over Megan's head. "Christ," Sage muttered between clenched teeth. "What's next? The cavalry?" He dropped his hands and sidled away from her, glaring. "Where's your bugle, baby? Let's have the whole show."

The approaching feet swished in the grass. Megan turned. Regina approached with another group member. Lonnie, Gordon, and Chet were converging from the opposite direction.

"Sage, let's get your hands taken care of," Megan urged. There was no disguising her anxiety anymore. It rolled down her cheeks in glitter-ing tears.

"Yeah, let's." In defiance, he splashed whiskey over the worst of his burns. He sucked his breath between clenched teeth and took masochistic pleasure in the wild stinging. "There. All taken care of."

"Hey, don't waste it," Gordon called as he sauntered through the tall grass. "That's good stuff."

"Give it back to them, Sage," Regina said quietly. "Talk to us. Let's have the circle right out here."

Sage glanced from one face to another, then past them to the volunteers, one still soaking the smoldering timbers of his barn. He felt like an animal caught in a trap. They all wanted pieces of him, and if he stood there much longer, they would get their wish. He'd shatter.

"We're gonna take off, Sage." Sage swung his head toward Lonnie. *Take off* reverberated in his brain. "Thought we'd hit some spots. It's been a thirsty night."

Gordon's offer rolled off his tongue like a bolt of silk. "We got room for you, if you wanna come along."

Sage made his move.

"Don't go, Sage."

Words he'd heard many times before, coming at him now in a small, sweet, tearful voice. The threat of buzzkill. Fuel for a drinking man's flight. He got behind the wheel of his pickup and kept his eyes on the remains of the barn as he shut the door.

THE LITTLE GROUP huddled together and watched the lights of one pickup trail the other.

"He's in no condition to drive." Megan eyed her pickup. "He won't be hard to find. There aren't that many bars—"

"Don't do it, Megan," Pete warned. "He's on his own now."

"But he'll get into trouble."

"He's in trouble now." Regina's resignation was chilling.

"We can't just stand here and watch him do this to himself," Megan insisted.

"You can sure call the police," Pete said. "They'll stop him from hurting himself, or someone else."

"I . . . couldn't do that to him," she said.

"Then you haven't learned anything." Regina turned and headed back to her car.

Megan watched her go. The woman had just lost her husband. Had *she* learned anything? This was madness. "Pete, I can't sit idly by—"

He laid a hand on her shoulder. "Go home. Get some sleep. I'll take care of the call. And if he comes to you, don't try to talk to him when he's drunk. You won't get anywhere."

Feeling shell-shocked, Megan allowed herself to be escorted to her pickup.

THE FACE IN THE mirror was ghastly. A night of little sleep had left its shadows beside traces of soot. Cavernous eyes lacked any sign of a human soul. A puffiness reminiscent of death made Sage turn his eyes downward toward the sink. The sight would drive young children to hide behind their mothers' legs. His own often had. Bracing his knuckles gingerly on both sides of the sink, he lowered his entire face into the basin of icy water. Much to his dismay, he hadn't drowned during the night. He had half a mind to correct fate's error there in the sink.

On his way back up, he bumped his head on the faucet. He muttered a curse. The bump was only a small insult to add to the injury he'd already heaped on himself. His hair was plastered around his face, and the water rushed to form a single stream over his square chin. He looked down and considered his hands, which reminded him of rashers of bacon. The aching intensified as he eased them, palms up, into the water. His fingers trembled, and he saw the bacon curling, bubbling up in a cast-iron skillet. The image of cooking conjured a smell that turned his stomach.

Minutes passed. The cold water dulled the pain in his hands, and he caught himself half listening to Elmer Fudd harangue the "cwazy wabbit." He must have left the TV on all night. He pulled the black rubber stopper up by its chain, leaned his forearms on the edge of the sink, and watched the water eddy toward the drain. Then the pint bottle on the back of the toilet caught his eye.

It was in his hand before he thought about reaching. Funny he hadn't drained the bottle the night before. Apparently, it hadn't taken as much as it once did to put him down. He studied the label. He didn't know a damn thing about wine, but he had good taste in whiskey. Not that he could tell by the taste in his mouth. He was afraid if he opened his mouth in front of the mirror, he would find a coating of mold. Didn't whiskey kill bacteria? His mouth yearned toward the bottle. A little hair of the dog.

Little dog.

Pint-size dog.

Officer, I was bitten by a pint-size dog named Whiskey.

He struck the bottle against the side of the sink and watched the brown liquid slide over the shattered glass and down the drain. He hadn't been stopped this time. Wasn't sitting in jail, hadn't lost his job, hadn't been kicked out of the house on his ass. Yeah, he'd been burned out, but he was still kickin'. And he'd keep on kickin' if he could stay away from the dog that never failed to bite him in the ass. Whiskey would kill him.

He did not want to die.

The realization made him quiver. He wanted life. Despite all the losses he'd sustained in one chaotic night, he would live.

He *would* live.

Picking up the pieces might be almost as tricky as cleaning up the mess he'd just made. He sliced his hand with the first shard of glass, and he saw that he was bound to bleed. What did he expect? Bleeding was part of living. That's what Band-Aids were for. Besides, the fire had rendered him a little short on dexterity just now. It might be a week or so before he could handle a hammer again.

The knock at the door echoed the clatter of glass as he tossed it in the waste basket. He jerked his head around and took a quick survey. Hot Springs. Easy Rider Motel. It was definitely a couple of stars down from the Arrowhead. No satellite TV. Bugs Bunny was squiggly, and the picture was rolling. A lot like his gut.

After the second knock he yelled, "Yeah, I'm coming." He was going to add "Keep your shirt on," but he realized he was missing his. He'd slept in sooty jeans, and the bedding showed it. He flipped the bedspread over the sheets and picked his shirt up off the floor. No doubt the manager had come to give him hell over the TV, which he switched off on his way to the door.

It was Megan. He stared at her dumbly, unable to draw breath. She looked tired, but her eyes were clear; her face looked fresh, and everything about her struck him as immaculate. The Easy Rider Motel was not her turf.

"You look like hell," she told him.

"Thanks." He wanted to laugh, but he hadn't rallied that much yet. Getting enough air into his lungs for a one-word response had been a major accomplishment. "Come on in."

He stepped back and took his first notice of the room he barely remembered renting. Small, dark, and oppressive. Faded flowered wallpaper was peeling above the bed, and the shit-color carpet had been worn to fuzz. The place smelled like some fool had spilled his whiskey. He checked his jeans. Zipped and dry.

Count your blessings, Parker. You checked yourself into a room, and you're standing up this morning.

"How did you find me?"

"You flatter yourself." She had her back to him now, no doubt taking the same inventory. "I wasn't looking for you. I was on my way to work, and I saw your pickup. It's one of a kind." She turned to him, but she kept her distance. "Frankly, I'm surprised you're not in jail."

He saw the judgment in her eyes, saw how the sight of him sickened her. He felt cold. His shame stripped him naked, and her eyes chilled him. He groped for a comeback.

"Just lucky, I guess."

"Pete said we should call the police and tell them to get you off the road."

"He was right. You should have."

"I thought he was going to."

"Maybe I was flying under the radar. Or maybe he called the Indian police. They don't have any jurisdiction off the reservation." He raised his hand to offer her a chair, and blood dripped on the carpet.

"Oh, God, Sage, what have you done?" Her hands shot out reflexively, and she grabbed his arm.

"I cut myself on a bottle."

She claimed eye contact as she took charge of his hand.

"Not on purpose," he said. "If I wanted to do myself in, I'd cut off my aching head."

She reached for his other hand. He stood there like some needy kid, letting her turn his palms up and see more evidence of his shame.

He'd failed his horse. That was the worst part. He had no right to act like he was the one who'd suffered.

"Sage, your hands need attention. Have you washed them?"

"Yeah, sort of." He let her lead him into the bathroom because it was her attention he craved. Even if she cared only for his hands, it was something. She liked his hands.

"I have a first aid kit in the truck. Let me get it."

By the time she returned, he'd washed his hands with soap and water. They hurt like hell, and he didn't want to touch them with a towel, so he stood making a puddle near his bare feet. He almost laughed when she stood in the doorway and ordered him out of her way with a wordless jerk of her chin. In his world, it was a man's gesture, even when a woman was in charge. And this one was.

He sat on the bed, elbows braced on his knees, hands dangling like rags, blood dripping off his thumb. Megan pulled up a chair and sat facing him, knees to knees. She covered her lap with a threadbare bath towel, took his hands palms-up in hers and blew his blistered skin dry.

"Feels good," he said, but she wouldn't even look up.

He didn't blame her. He knew he could get a little sympathy out of her if he could catch her eye. She knew it, too, but he'd made the mistake of warning her off pity, and clearly she'd taken his advice to heart.

Damn, he was smart when he wanted to be.

And Megan was at her calm, cool best when she had a job to do. She painstakingly dabbed some kind of ointment all over his hands and bandaged him up.

Finally, she sat back and looked him in the eye. "This is the main reason I stopped when I saw your pickup."

He had to laugh, even if it hurt. "You wanted to make sure I washed my hands?"

"You should see a doctor."

"It took guts for you to stop here. You didn't know how bad off I might be or whether you'd find someone else in this bed with me."

She scowled at him. "I wasn't thinking that way."

"Neither was I. But you had no way of knowing."

She lowered her eyes and shook her head. "I tried to stop you. I didn't know how."

"What we had the other night felt right. It felt real."

"I know. That's why—"

"I lost my head last night. Once I started down the dark road, nothing was gonna stop me from making a run for it. So you can't be running after me. There's no point. Before long, you'll be as crazy as I am."

Megan took a deep breath as she covered his wrists with her cool hands. "This is something I can do, Sage. I can see the injury here, and I can tend to it. The other . . ." Her eyes betrayed her fear. "I want to help you, but I don't know how."

He lifted his hands, and she let hers slide away. "This much is fine. I would have had a hard time doing this on my own. Otherwise . . ." He shook his head. "You can't fix it for me, Megan, any more than you could for Jackie."

"You're not like Jackie."

"I *am* like Jackie. Look!" He held his hands up in front of her face. "I'm flesh and blood, just like he was. I'm an alcoholic, just like he was.

And if I choose to, I can lie down in the grass and die, just like he did."
He laid his hands back on the towel in her lap and looked into her eyes.
They were like big windows, open to him, inviting him in. *Tell her something good. Something true.* "I can also choose to live. I don't like to say I
have a disease, but sometimes it feels like it."

"Like now?"

"Right now, I feel like a fool." He shrugged. He didn't know why he
was talking so much. "A sick one. But the sick feeling will pass, and
nobody calls foolishness a disease. Like it or not, I'm—"

"You made a foolish choice last night, but the fire was a horrible
disaster. *Horrible.* And you couldn't make it stop." She blinked back
tears. "So you ran off with your friends."

"Hardly know those guys. Did a few shots with them, bought my
own bottle, brought it here, and drank until I couldn't smell burning
horseflesh anymore."

"Sage . . ."

"You saw how it is with me," he said quietly. "I can't be the poster
boy for the recovered alcoholic for you, Megan. There is no *recovered.* I'm
recovering. I'm not the poster boy for anything."

"You're not a boy."

"A holy man once told me to stop being a boy in a man's body." He
tipped his head back, remembering. "It doesn't work, he said. Walk tall.
Think before you speak. Use your strength for the good of your family.
Act like a man and soon you'll be one. Act like *Iktomi,* and soon you'll be
crawling around on all fours." He offered a tentative smile. He really
ought to quit bullshitting. It was a true story, but he was using it to sound
like he knew something. "Under construction, right?"

"What's *Iktomi?*"

"He's a trickster. He's a spider sometimes, a coyote—he finds all
kinds of ways to fool people."

"Like the Joker or the devil?"

"Nah, there's no devil. We don't see things that way. *Iktomi* is usually a troublemaker, but he's a lot more complicated than that. He can
cause good things to happen, but he doesn't plan it that way. He's generally all about having his way, getting what he wants. What's the term?
Instant gratification? A lot of times, he trips himself up, ends up like
this." He held up his bandaged hands. "But he's immortal. He keeps on
coming back. People aren't so lucky."

"Are you back?"

"I had four years of sobriety. I really worked at it, Megan. But I sat there watching everything I'd worked for burn to the ground, and I thought, what's the use? Why fight it, you know?" She kept looking at him, waiting. He straightened his back and sighed. "No, you don't know."

"I was there last night. I saw what happened, and it was horrible. Worse than I can imagine, even though I was right there, but that's because I've never lost everything I've worked for. No, I don't know how that feels." She laid her hands on his knees. "But, Sage, you're a strong man. I know that much. Maybe—*definitely* the strongest man I know."

"Okay, then know this. I have no power over alcohol."

"None?"

"That's right." He watched her digest that bombshell. Her hero had toppled. He couldn't help feeling a pang of regret.

Her eyes narrowed. She was already trying to figure out how she could put the pieces back together. Women were a wonder to him. Born to restore.

"Last night was heartbreaking," she said. "I don't think last night counts. Not against you and the progress you've made. It would have taken a superhuman effort. . . . What's so funny?"

"You are." He flopped back on the bed and rolled his head from side to side, chuckling. "You're so beautiful, it's funny. And what makes it even funnier is the fact that you're absolutely serious. God, how I'd love to let you make excuses for me, Megan, but I'm afraid last night *does* count." He lifted his head and caught her eye. "If we're keeping score, last night counts."

"You mean, no do-overs?"

"I've done it over. And over. And—"

"Try-agains, then. You've still got a head on your shoulders." She took a try-again. Tried to lift his spirits with a smile. "You didn't cut it off."

"Not yet." He rubbed his forehead. "The day's just getting started."

"What happened yesterday can't be changed. What happened last night—"

He jackknifed into a sitting position again. "Is an old story. The Indian gets fucked over, so he goes out and gets fucked up. Which doesn't change the fact that he got fucked over, and it limits his chances of making a comeback. So last night counts. If I don't deal with it, I'll be back where I was four years ago."

He stood up, facing her with more conviction than he'd had when she'd arrived. "I've decided I don't like getting fucked over, pardon my French. Is it French?"

She shrugged. "Pretty sure it's English."

"It ain't Lakota, that's for damn sure. Whatever language they're doing it in, I'm not letting them have the final say. It wasn't the barn they wanted, or the house. It was my power, my *life*." He turned a hard glance on the wastebasket in the bathroom. "And they damn near got it, because I *damn near* started in again this morning."

She followed his glance, then reached for his arm. "Sage—"

He backed away. "I'm not done, Megan. There's something else I don't like. I don't like it when you look at me like I'm some orphan kid in a TV commercial. What do you get out of that? Does that boost you up above the masses? Do you look at your dad that way, too?"

"My father?" She stiffened, tilting her chin up. "My father has nothing to do with this. I don't think my father is really an alcoholic. Not like . . ."

"Not like me?"

"I'm not comparing. He's just not . . ."

"He's not? Then why do you want him to quit drinking?"

"I just think he drinks too much, that's all. He's getting older, and I just . . ." She crossed her arms over her chest, as was her custom. "I don't feel sorry for you, Sage. I'm sorry about the fire, and I truly feel sick about that beautiful mare, but I don't feel sorry for you. Okay?"

"Okay." They stared at one another through several silent moments. Finally, he asked, "So, without your sympathy, do I still have a job?"

"Are you back?"

"Gettin' there."

"If you don't show up for work today, you get a warning," she told him. "That's policy. If you have a medical excuse, of course, that's different, and you should have a doctor look at those hands."

"And you should stop telling me what I *should* do. I'll be a little late, but I'll be there."

"You can't come to work with hands that are all blistered like that."

"Or a face that looks like hell?" He snatched his shirt off the bed. "Calling in sick is less embarrassing than walking in with a flashing neon hangover, right? If we cover it up carefully enough, maybe we can convince ourselves that I really didn't get drunk last night. Maybe we can run up my score so the strong man can claim the trophy." He nodded toward the bed. "Right now."

She took a step closer to him. "Maybe we can stand around in this dump and argue about it all morning."

"Arguing gives me a hard-on, and I love the smell of sex in the morning."

She gave him the slybrow. "It smells like victory?"

"Yeah," He gave her the smartass smile. "Smells like win-win." He moved closer, putting them almost nose to nose. "Maybe you can get out of here so I can get myself together and get to work."

"Excellent suggestion." They watched each other ease off slowly. He took a step back and let her walk past him. She turned at the door, apparently unable to resist trying for the last word. "I don't care what you do to your hands. And you're going to be late anyway." In a huff, she jerked at the door.

"I've got news for you, lady." She hesitated, and it amused him that she had to hear *his* parting shot. "So are you."

Chapter 12

SAGE FACED A steep uphill climb, and he found his first handhold in his job. He made it through the first day on a pair of work gloves, a box of gauze bandaging, and a bottle of aspirin. That evening, he saw a doctor, who told him he shouldn't use his hands for a couple of days. He stocked up on gauze and antiseptic and decided his hands shouldn't be idle except during sleep. And he worked. After work, with some help from friends and neighbors, he hauled rubble from the ruins of his buildings. After dark, he met with the members of the Medicine Wheel. No matter how small the circle, he needed to be there. And the others knew it, so they came.

Megan's attitude toward him was guarded. She seemed to be afraid to laugh around him, as though there had been a death in his family and his feelings might be fragile. They had always worked well together, and that hadn't changed. They let the road be their focus, the visible thread that bound them together. They discussed layers of compaction with such studied interest that any concern for the levels of their relationship was imperceptible. When Sage felt her eyes on him, he held his breath and allowed the moment to pass. He was glad when his hands started healing. Once, she'd discovered him washing them after they'd cracked open and begun to bleed, and he'd waited for her comment. It hadn't come.

So they were both recovering. He figured her recovery from her close call with a risky relationship would be healthy for both of them. But it was good to see her, good to be near her so much of the time. By the time the job was over, maybe he would be content with a friendly parting, some straight-up exchange about how working together had been a real pleasure. By that time, he hoped the need to touch her would have dulled and the memory of love's pleasures would actually feel like part of the past.

It bothered him to have to take time off from work to attend another council hearing. This thing had gone on long enough, had played enough havoc in his life. It bothered him most of all because it meant bringing the issue up with Megan. She knew immediately why he needed an afternoon off. This time, when her eyes glistened with the soft light that said she was looking at Sage, the man, rather than Sage, the co-worker, he held her gaze. Despite the knot in his stomach, he knew it was time to talk.

"Pete tells me they've arrested someone in connection with the fire," she said.

He laid his clipboard aside and leaned against the desk, resting his thigh along the edge. Megan took the cue and sat beside him.

"A guy named Gordon Brown. He was the guy who decided the barn burning was bring-your-own-bottle."

Megan shook her head slowly. "I thought for sure it was Floyd Taylor."

"I'm sure it was, but it looks like he used Brown. And so far, Brown isn't talking."

"And you didn't know this Gordon Brown?"

Sage turned his mouth down and shook his head. "Never saw him before. Some guy who hired on for the summer with one of the local ranchers. I knew one of the guys he was with—good-time Lonnie. I don't think Lonnie knows anything."

"I wish they could get Taylor."

He chuckled. "A woman after my own heart." She glanced at him quickly, surprised, and he looked away. Awkward silence.

"How are you, Sage? I mean . . ."

He turned his palms up to show her the healing.

"I mean, how are you doing otherwise?"

He lifted his eyes slowly and let her see inside himself, if she cared to look. "Otherwise, I'm doing okay. I went back on Antabuse." She questioned the word with a look. "It's a drug I took for about a year after I got out of treatment. If you drink any alcohol at all while you're taking it, you puke your guts out."

She winced. "That oughta cure you."

"Careful how you throw that word 'cure' around." Smiling, he lifted a forefinger. "Remember what I told you. There is no 'recovered,' only—"

"Only recovering. I know. And you are. I'm glad."

Her smiled warmed him inside. "I've started over before. It wasn't as tough this time. I had Medicine Wheel."

"What made you decide to quit the first time?" she asked. "Was it losing your wife?"

"The divorce was a long time coming. It was a relief to have it over. For both of us. But I wanted to be able to see the kids. I told her I'd fight for that much, at least. I told her—" He studied his hand and the healing that had already taken place. Healing up inside was slow going.

"My daughter Brenda was just six years old, but they grow up fast, which is what kids do. Anyway, the judge asked her how she'd feel about living with her dad. She told him she wanted to go with her mother." His voice became gruff, and he grimaced as he spoke. "She said she loved her dad, but she didn't want to be around him anymore because he liked to get drunk." His eyes burned with his pain, and his voice echoed in his ears, as though he'd forced the story from the bottom of a well. "That didn't leave me with any delusions about fighting for my kids. Kids don't like watching their parents get drunk."

Megan's eyes widened. "So you made the decision to stop drinking for your daughter's sake."

"Hell, no." His chuckle was self-derisive. "I made the decision right then and there to drown the memory of that sweet little face in a long-neck bottle. I ended up in treatment when one of my sisters had me committed because I wasn't making my lease payments."

"Oh." She glanced away.

"Hey." He caught her chin with two gentle fingers and turned her face back to him. "If it's any consolation, you can't drown out the memory of disappointing someone you care about. It's still there when you sober up."

"So you start in again?"

"That's the way addiction works." He drew his hand back reluctantly. It felt good to touch her. "Something has to break the cycle, and it's usually not the addict. In my case, it was the wrath of a sister who wanted her lease check."

She caught his hand, touched her fingers to his palm, and moved them slowly to the tips of his fingers. "Through it all, you worked so hard, even with burned and battered hands. When I saw how sore they were that time, I wanted to . . ."

"I know," he said in a raspy voice. "I know what you wanted to do."

"But you're healing *yourself.*"

He shook his head. "I'm letting the healing take place." He sought understanding in her eyes. "So are you, Megan. By letting go. By not claiming you have the power to *make* me get well."

"It's hard to believe doing nothing is all I can do to help."

"You were pulling for me, weren't you? In your heart you were saying, 'God, I hope he makes it.' "

She nodded and offered him a sweet smile.

"See how that works? I need a lot of that."

SAGE HOPED A FEW of the people in the crowded council chambers were pulling for him as he adjusted the microphone. There were people all around him—a clerk distributing papers to the council members, and a man offering coffee refills, a couple of women talking about things that had nothing to do with him. But they were his people, and they were all around him.

He found he'd missed a snap on his cuff, and he pressed it together. He'd hurriedly unrolled his shirt sleeves moments before, and now he wished he'd thought to wear a sport jacket. His tarnished image needed some polish.

He glanced over his shoulder to reassure himself that Regina and Bessie were still there. They were, but the fact barely registered as his eyes met Megan's. Why had she come? This was not to be his finest moment. He'd come forth with all the mortification of the prodigal son, and some of those present would take satisfaction in that. Why the hell did she have to be there? He took a deep breath and turned back to the microphone. The chairman gave him the signal to speak his piece.

"Mr. Chairman, I'm not going waste your time repeating my position on this matter. You've heard it before. Mr. Taylor wants to continue to do business with us, and I want us to send him and all his goods packing. His way isn't our way.

"Mr. Taylor wants us to believe we've lost our way, that denying him his way won't change anything, won't prevent anyone from getting drunk. And he made a point to look at me when he said it." The room grew very still as Sage scanned the faces of the councilmen. "I had a relapse. It was nobody's responsibility but mine. The last time I spoke to you, I was able to say it had been four years since I'd had a drink. Today, I can only tell you it's been fourteen days. But those fourteen days were just as hard-won as the four years, and they tell me Medicine Wheel works if I work.

"So I'm working. I'm finding out that what tradition tells us about ourselves is true. We're Lakota. We're a community that's older than the state, older than the United States. We're a circle of people whose lives are interconnected no matter where we live. The circle can be a strength for us. It can also be a weakness. When we allow alcohol to eat away at the circle, we lose our way. We look for easier ways, find ways to tear each other down.

"We need to stand up. *I* need to stand up. I believe we need to say no to the way this man, Taylor, operates. Alcohol is taking too high a toll on us. For whatever reason, we're too susceptible. It destroys us.

"It was brought here and given to us a long time ago, and we had no more resistance to it than we had to measles. Then, later, they said, 'No, you guys better not drink that stuff. It's bad for you.' And they passed laws against selling it to us. But by that time, we were saying, 'Who the hell do you think you are? We'll drink it if we want to.' So we did. And we're suffering for it. And now it's time to say, we *don't want to.*"

MEGAN LISTENED to Sage's voice as it came through the microphone, filling the room with a rich, deep rumble. He slipped one hand beneath the table and wiped his palm on his thigh, and she rubbed her own palms together. They were sweating, too. No longer her image of an iron-willed hero, here was a man who was even more dear because he struggled with his imperfections, more courageous because he was not without fear.

"I know I said I didn't want to," Sage continued. "I said it loud and clear, and then I weakened. I know you won't forget that. I don't ask you to. I only ask you to accept me the way I am today—sober and speaking straight. Whatever the council decides, I'm going to keep saying it." He looked directly at Floyd Taylor and fought to control the anger he felt at the sight of the man. "I'm going to keep urging you to turn people like Floyd Taylor away. I've started rebuilding my barn. If it burns down again, I'll build it again. You can't stop me, Taylor. There's only one person who can destroy me, and that's *me*."

Taylor nearly tripped over himself trying to get to his feet. "If you're accusing me of anything, Parker, you damn well better have proof!"

"That's all I have to say, Mr. Chairman."

There was more testimony. Taylor had hired a glib attorney, and the proprietors of other businesses were allowed to speak. In the end, Taylor was reminded that his business permit would soon be up for renewal, and he was admonished to clean up his act. Megan stood aside as Medicine Wheel sympathizers gathered outside the front doors of the tribal office building, some shaking Sage's hand, some shaking their heads.

When Floyd Taylor and his associates appeared, heads turned and heated looks were exchanged. Taylor postured as he walked past Sage, throwing his shoulders back and looking around to be sure this was, indeed, the proper moment for a parting shot.

"You haven't changed, Parker. You come on over to the Rooster tonight. Your first one's on the hou—"

Sage's left fist hit Taylor's gut like a cannonball. Over the man's breathless grunt, Sage muttered, "I *want* to change, Taylor." As Taylor's chin dipped, Sage caught it with a cracking right. "I've been working pretty hard at it, trying to keep my cool." Taylor's big frame toppled into his buddies' arms, while Sage's friends moved to restrain him. He grinned broadly as he shook the tension out of his right hand. "Guess I've still got a ways to go."

Megan's heart pounded as she watched his friends spirit Sage away. She pressed her own right fist into her left hand and gave a secret smile.

After a solitary supper at the local café, she left town. The sun was August-evening gold hanging low in the western sky. She came to a junction. If she took the west fork, she would be squinting into the sun most of the way. The north fork would take her the long way around with less eyestrain. It would also take her past Sage's place.

His pickup was parked near the trailer. She turned onto the approach and took a deep breath as she neared the empty places. She remembered the house as a work in progress, the barn as the pride of a man with a dream. She remembered the flames, the embers, and the charred beams. The rubble had been cleared away. Part of the corral had been saved, and the enclosure had been repaired with new lumber.

Sage stood on the small wooden platform that served as his front step. His white T-shirt was a beacon in the waning light.

"Checking up on me?" he asked quietly as she approached the steps. The pointed end of a wooden toothpick peeked out the corner of his mouth.

Megan rejected *just passing by* as quickly as it came to mind and smiled up at him. "I was hoping you'd be home."

"I just got back." With a sweeping gesture, he offered the wooden step. "Have a seat. It's cooler out here."

"You've done a lot of work already."

"I've about had my fill of the smell of charcoal." He sat beside her on the step and stretched his legs. His boot heels rested on the ground. "I saw your pickup at the café. I thought about stopping, but decided I'd better get out of town before sunset." With a dry chuckle, he leaned back on his arms and tipped his chin up. "I really blew it, didn't I?"

"Not at all," she protested. "You were eloquent."

"Eloquent?" He shifted the toothpick from one side of his mouth to the other and hiked a teasing eyebrow. "An eloquent gut-buster?"

"Oh, that." She laughed and hugged her knees. "That part was magnificent."

"The lady's got a real mean streak."

"Only when somebody's got it coming, and I can't think of anyone who deserves it more than Floyd Taylor."

"That's probably the extent of the satisfaction I'll get anytime soon." He sat up, looked across the yard at the little corral and draped his forearm over one knee. "Gordon Brown's white, so they can't try him in tribal court."

"It's a federal charge, isn't it?"

"Yeah."

"Isn't that better?"

"We'll see. Better than county court, I guess. Taylor's got too much local influence." He shrugged. "I'm not a big fan of the court system. Seems like Lady Justice has a hole somewhere in her blindfold." A slow, sinister smile spread across his face. "How 'bout an old-fashioned trial by fire? I've got some charcoal in the basement. Turn Taylor and Brown on a spit, and if they get crisp, we pronounce them guilty as hell."

"Sage!"

"No, I was thinking salt, maybe Tabasco sauce."

He watched her eyes brighten with laughter and considered how pretty she looked in pink. "Why did you come to the hearing today?" he asked quietly.

The laughter died. "Not out of curiosity," she assured him. "I'm allowed to pull for you, remember? That's all I was doing. Didn't you tell me there had to be witnesses? Somehow, I think today's ordeal was as difficult the Sun Dance."

"Megan . . ." He sighed heavily, glanced away, and then looked back at her. "The night of the fire, when I saw you drive up, I wanted to crawl into a hole. Not just because I was ashamed of the drinking, but I was . . . I was . . ." He groped for the words. Defeated? Beaten? He didn't like any of the words that came to mind. "A man feels totally emasculated when a woman sees him pinned to the ground like that."

God*damn*, that sounded pitiful.

"They've never pinned you to the ground." She put her hand on his shoulder. The warmth of his flesh under the soft cotton T-shirt stirred warmth in her. "They take clumsy potshots at you. As long as you keep coming back, they can't touch the man you are."

She could, he thought. She could touch the man he was, and he would never stop coming back. But he had to be careful.

"Why did you come here tonight?" He had to know.

She stiffened and drew her hand away. "Just to see you."

"To see if I was still sober?"

"I didn't think you'd . . ."

"I could have. I thought about it. It's always there, standing in the shadows with *Iktomi*."

"I *didn't* think you . . ."

He hiked her a slybrow.

"Okay, it did occur to me. Standing in the shadows." She shook her head. "But I wanted to see you. That's what brought me here. I needed to see you here, off the clock, just you and me."

"I'll buy that." He leaned back on his elbow and admired the way the rosy sky behind her turned her into a softly shaded silhouette. "After that amazing speech I made—" He shook a finger at her. "—and you get the blame for that. Or the credit, however you wanna look at it. I wasn't such a big talker until I started hangin' with you.

"Anyway, it's crazy, but I had it all pictured in my mind that I'd make this amazing speech, cut myself open and bleed all over the table for all the world to see, and—" He snapped his fingers. "—problem solved. I was actually disappointed it didn't happen that way. But I was already back to work. All kinds of work. Or maybe *work* isn't the right word. *Life.* I was back to living my life. I'm not going to get drunk over those two assholes. There are other ways."

"Keep talking. See?" She grabbed her earlobe and stretched it like frybread in the making. "I have ears."

"You sure do." She smacked his shoulder, and he chuckled. "So Regina's going to be able to open her store soon. If people are as tired of being jacked around by Taylor as they say they are, they'll take their business to Regina. If not . . ." He took the toothpick from the corner of his mouth and tossed it into the night. "If not, the hell with them."

"Really?"

"Really. You've gotta learn to recognize when enough's enough."

"You?" she asked. "Or the others?"

"Both. All of us." He offered a quick smile. "I'm not much of a host, am I? Would you like coffee?"

"If I can help you make it."

He laughed as he got to his feet. "Will you let *me* take care of *you* for once? Besides, it's made."

She took the hand he offered and followed him inside. "I'm not sure I understand this 'caretaker' thing. I'm far from domestic, but I can make coffee." She closed the screen door behind her. "It just seemed polite to offer to help."

"It was." He pointed to a small overhead cupboard. "Get the cups. I hope you like it black, because I don't have anything to lighten it."

"Black is fine," she said. She set the cups down, and he poured from an aluminum percolator.

"Tell me about your dad," Sage suggested almost off-handedly. "Does he handle the checkbook, pay the bills?"

"Oh, no, he's no good with money. My mother takes care of that."

"Because she wants to?"

"She hates it." He nodded toward the door, and she swung it open. "But when he does it, he has it all messed up inside a week. She says he does it on purpose so she won't even suggest he take a turn. I think if she could get him to stop . . ."

The conversation stalled as they settled on the steps again. Sage watched Megan hide her face behind her coffee cup. "Stop what?" he asked gently.

She flashed wide, wary eyes. "I wasn't going to say 'drinking.'"

His patient smile was lopsided. "What else weren't you going to say?"

"I wasn't going to say that I don't ever have any thought of taking care of you. Because I guess that wouldn't be entirely true."

"Fight the urge, darlin'. Fight the urge." The light from the kitchen illuminated the doubt in her eyes. He set his cup down and leaned closer. "It'll make you crazy. It'll make you just as sick as I was when you saw me the morning after the fire. Sure, I needed a friend, but I didn't need a crutch. I can't drink, and that's *my* problem. When I do need a crutch, it's got to be a wooden one. Not a human one."

"Like my mother?" Megan lowered her cup to the step slowly. Her back stiffened. "That's not fair, Sage."

"You said it. I didn't."

"You brought it up. You don't even know them."

"I know you."

"You're taking things I've confided in you, and you're blowing them out of proportion."

"Will I ever meet them?"

She glanced away. He could see the answer. She was swallowing it.

"Because you don't want them to know me, or me to know them?" She kept right on swallowing.

"I never liked the word *alcoholic* either. *Problem drinker* sounds a little better. You wanna use that? Go ahead. It changes nothing." He struggled against the edge in his voice. All of a sudden, he was taking offense to the way she sat up in front of him, so prim and perfect. "It's a family disease. The whole family suffers. Why should your family be granted immunity? What other diseases *can't* you get? It's killing my people, and if you've got a vaccination against it, you damn well better—"

"I don't need any more of this." Megan pushed herself to her feet, tottering a bit as she reached her full height. "I have never said anything . . . unkind or . . ."

Sage set his cup down. "I'm not trying to be unkind, Megan," he said evenly. "I just want to understand the terms. Here we've got drunks. Winos. Off the reservation, you've got your problem drinkers. What difference does it make? Does it look prettier? I mean, you haven't seen me when I'm *really* wasted, so it's probably not fair to compare terms yet."

She'd begun to tremble inside, and she wasn't sure why. She opened her mouth for a crisp goodbye, and it didn't come. Her throat burned, and she couldn't catch her breath. When he stood up gradually, she had the terrible feeling that he might hit her over the head, not with his hand, but with something worse, something that would hurt far more. She searched for some defense, and it came, sadly, in a high-pitched retort.

"I've seen you with a hangover, and it looks the same on you as it does on anyone else. An old man's face, and sick to your stomach like a child!"

FOR A MOMENT, his boots were nailed to the step. He'd had no right, he told himself as he watched her turn and run. He'd pushed her too far. When he could move, he vaulted over the side of the step and caught up to her just as she reached her pickup.

"Megan." He reached for her, but she jerked her arm away. "Look, I'm sorry. You're right, I don't know—"

"You know all about it, Sage. You're an expert." The last word was nearly lost in her wild-eyed frenzy to get into the truck.

In one word, she'd thrown everything he'd confided in her back in his face. *An expert.* He grabbed the door. She tried to pull it shut, but her strength was no match for his. They eyed one another through the open window, black irises glittering, blue glinting back. Megan's chest heaved with each shallow breath as she waited for him to relinquish his hold.

"You can become an expert, too, Megan. You might as well. You're up to your eyebrows in it." His voice was soft and smoother than he'd thought he could manage. "Come to Medicine Wheel. They've listened to me for two solid weeks, and they're ready for somebody else. Or find a group that meets your needs. All you have to do is own up to the problem."

With that, he shut the door and backed away. He watched her fumble with her keys and go through the steps of putting the pickup in motion as though it were a new skill. She ground the forward gears, turned the headlights on as an afterthought, and put thirty yards between them. The red brake lights came on. Sage gave her a few seconds, and when he was certain she was going no farther, he followed. He found her slumped over the wheel, her shoulders shaking.

"Slide over," he said as he pulled the door open.

She fought with the gear shift, choking out, "Shit." The pickup surrendered.

"It's okay," he said quietly. "Just let it go."

LET IT GO. HE meant the pickup, but she heard more. The words were inviting, the concept incredible. It was a relief to let him take over, and when he took her in his arms, there was deliverance. She gave herself over to the tears and the awful quaking, trusting him to shield her while she did, indeed, let go. The solid flesh beneath his soft shirt offered support, and she leaned all her cares against it as she wept.

"He's not a bad man, Sage," she whispered. Such a thing could not be suggested aloud.

"Am I a bad man?"

"No. Oh, no."

"I've done some bad things," he said. Aloud.

"He's my father." Her voice tripped over tears as the words tumbled out. "I can't not like . . . not love . . ."

"I know," he whispered. "It's okay, Megan."

"I can't help loving him," she choked. "I *do* love him, and it hurts because . . ."

"Because . . ."

"Because I love you, too, and I don't know what's wrong with me." It all came out in a breathless rush.

"Nothing." His heart soared. He held her tighter and cherished the feel of her tears against his neck. "There's nothing wrong with you that I can see."

"There must be something the matter with me." She tickled his neck with the tip of her tongue. "I should know better."

"Who says?" He coaxed her with kisses at her temple and in her hair. "It's okay to love me." He wanted it to be true, and he wanted her to believe it. "I'm not a bad man. It's not enough reason, but . . ." He poured small kisses over her face. ". . . it's a start."

"I don't need a reason to feel what I feel."

"Who says?"

He knew the answer, and he smiled when she gave it to him the way she did.

"Sage Parker says."

His mouth was close to her ear, and his heart wedged itself in his throat. "Is it okay that I love you, too?"

"Yes."

"Will you stay with me tonight?"

"Yes."

"Sleep where I sleep?"

"Yes."

"Make me believe I deserve to be loved?"

"I can do that."

"It won't be easy. I haven't been feelin' it lately." He took her face in his hands and kissed the salty corners of her smile. "But give it a try. I'll make it worth your while."

He took her to the trailer, and for the first time since he'd lived there, he delighted in the walls' closeness. The little fan whirred in the dark as they undressed each another, maneuvering in a small warm space that reminded him of the sweat lodge. The earth's womb. Small and feminine, like the breasts he covered with his hands. Persistent, like the nipples that formed hard pebbles to tickle his palms. Round and smooth, like the hips that housed the hearth of his heart's choosing.

The walls kept him close, as snug as a cocoon his body had nearly outgrown. She slid her skin against his, and he couldn't have moved away no matter what.

What matter? Tight quarters, heat, health, rhyme, reason? There was only her skin sliding against his and his body straining to enter hers. He didn't care why she loved him. She loved him because she loved him because she loved him.

The scent of musk filled her head and drove her to touch him with boldly seeking hands. He was moist satin skin over hard muscle everywhere she touched, and he would fill her with power before they were through. The thrill of anticipation rippled along the insides of her thighs in a trail blazed by his fingertips. She spread her hands over his chest and made his nipples tighten with her thumbs as she pressed him back upon the bed.

"You deserve to be loved." She took him in hand, and her hands worked magic.

"Sweet Jesus. Sweet, sweet . . ." Her lips drove him mad. Beyond rhyme, beyond reason, beyond pride. She tended to him with her tongue, and he couldn't hold his. "Suck me," he whispered. "Please."

She didn't know what she was doing, but it didn't matter. She was everything he needed, and he didn't want her to stop. But he was rigid and ready, and he wasn't where he needed to be. He reached for her, drew her up and up and filled her slowly, drew down and pushed up and filled her quickly and held and held while she quivered enough to let him know he'd better reach for the condom now. Right now.

"I want too much of you," he whispered. He pulled out, flipped her on her back, and slipped his slippery self into the condom. "Now more," he said, and he filled her again. "Show me your secret self." He rocked within her, made his search and made his find and made her cry out and shudder and whisper his name over and over and over again.

His seed was contained, but his tears were not. They touched her shoulder with the gentle beauty of a warm rain on rich earth, newly turned and springtime fertile.

Chapter 13

MEGAN'S ROAD LAY like a shiny licorice whip over the small stretch of South Dakota prairie to which she would always lay some sentimental claim. It was mid-October, and although the evenings had grown cold, Indian Summer warmed the tawny hills through the afternoon hours. Her little white Honda chased the broken yellow line from hollow to crest as she pushed past the speed limit to keep her date. She'd been invited to a picnic.

Sage was driving nails in his new subfloor when the white car turned into his long driveway. He'd been waiting for her, checking his watch every few minutes and keeping his hands busy with the hammer. The floor was nearly finished. He hopped down from the plywood deck, untied the leather apron, and stashed everything in his tool box.

"Is this one of those working dates you're so famous for?"

He took her in his arms and answered her question by kissing her smile away. She wound her arms around his neck and said hello her way.

"If I'm famous for them," he muttered between nibbles, "it's because you've been bragging them up."

"I can't help it," she murmured into his mouth. "I love to be envied."

"Me too. One of these days, you can get dressed up, and I'll take you out to some big event. Make every guy in the place jealous of me." He lifted one corner of his mouth and sassed her back. "Soon as the high school basketball season starts."

"Promises, promises."

"Aren't you going to say anything about the barn?"

He took her hand from the back of his neck and turned her around.

Her face lit up. Behind the original site in the shade of an old burr oak stood the new pole barn. And beyond that, four horses grazed in the late afternoon sunlight.

"It's finished!"

"Almost. I've still got to get shingles and doors."

"But how did you . . . I mean, the last time I saw it, there were just . . ."

"Just a few poles. I know. A couple of the women from Medicine Wheel employed a time-honored Indian custom." He grinned, and golden sunlight glinted in the warmth of his autumn brown eyes. "They raffled off a couple of star quilts. Then they rounded up a bunch of people, and we had most of it done inside a day."

"You had a barn raising, and you didn't call me?"

"It was a surprise."

She slipped her arm around his waist and gave him a squeeze. "I think we should celebrate."

"I think so, too. I hope you didn't bring a bunch of food, like you usually do."

"Why not?"

"Because I told you I'd cook."

"And I hope you did."

The aroma of the freshly deep-fried bread she'd come to love in recent months filled the little trailer. It had been served at every function she'd attended on the Big Thunder Reservation, and she'd attended quite a few. "I don't believe you actually made frybread," she said as he opened the door for her. His proud smile said he'd just opened a package full of surprises. "Did you really?"

"You think I can't make anything but cold meat sandwiches? I learned a secret." He tossed her a conspiratorial wink. "Frozen bread dough."

"It works?"

"Pretty well." He handed her a stack of paper plates and a roll of paper towels. "You take the china." He reached for a cardboard box. "I'll take the picnic basket. I already set the stage. Romance in the shelter belt. You gonna be warm enough?" She glanced down at her fisherman knit sweater and nodded. "I'll take an extra blanket anyway. When that sun goes down, you really know it's fall."

He'd spread a star quilt over the grass amid the rows of cottonwoods. Its burst of orange, yellow, and red gave the scattering of withered brown and pale yellow cottonwood leaves a taste of what autumn color should be. Megan giggled when she noticed the plastic ice-cream pail at the corner of the quilt. Two green bottles of Perrier were planted in ice.

"I spared no expense for this occasion." He set the picnic box next to the blanket.

"I did bring a little dessert."

"Did you, now." He took the paper stuff from her, pulled her down beside him and cupped his hands over her breasts. "A little dessert? I always love your little desserts."

"You might not get any if you say *little* one more time." She gave him a sweet kiss, which held out some promise.

"Keep that up and we'll have cold frybread."

She settled on the blanket and watched him open the first bottle. "Frybread and Perrier make a very interesting combination."

"Oh, it gets better." He poured a small amount of the sparkling water into a plastic glass. "How do Indian tacos and Perrier strike you?"

"Sounds heavenly. I won't have to worry about being little much longer with this kind of feasting." She lifted the plastic glass toward the setting sun and smiled as the tiny bubbles became glinting jewels. "Excellent clarity."

"Well, hell, it's French. What can I say?"

She swirled, sniffed and sipped. "Tangy. It has a life of its own. I believe you can actually taste the granite from the spring."

Sage poured himself some and tossed it down. "Not much kick to it," he judged. "Let's try the tacos."

The flat pieces of frybread were piled high with hot, spicy hamburger and fresh salad. Megan held the plate just inches from her mouth, stretched wide to accommodate the layers of chili and Cheddar cheese and warm, chewy bread. Spicy red juice dribbled down her chin, and Sage tossed her the roll of paper towels. When the same thing happened to him, she tossed it back. The messiness was part of its appeal.

It was impossible to talk with their mouths full of shredded lettuce and heavy bread, but when they were down to the Perrier and the prospect of dessert, Sage told her his news. He'd sold his calves and gotten a good price. He'd bought seven bred heifers, which brought his herd up to twenty-one. Calving out first-calf heifers could be dicey, so she could expect his call for help when the time came. He'd teach her how to use a calf-puller.

"I kept one steer calf," he told her. "I'll feed him over the winter and donate him for the dinner when Regina has her giveaway next summer."

"How's her store doing?"

"She's taking a big cut out of Taylor's business, *and*—" He gave her his signature wink. "Ol' Floyd isn't selling as much booze these days as he'd like to."

It had been slow in coming, but Sage's victory was beginning to taste sweet. Gordon Brown had been indicted on charges of arson, and he was awaiting trial in federal court. There was still hope that he might implicate Taylor.

"The Medicine Wheel program is growing, isn't it?"

"They've got a strong group in Big Thunder, and we're running a meeting just about every night now in Red Calf."

She held her cup out for more water. "Do you think I'd be welcome, sort of on a regular basis?"

He gave her a puzzled look. "Sure, you're always welcome, but that's a long way to drive from Pierre. I thought you'd found a group there that you liked."

"I did." She studied her glass. She hadn't told him, because she didn't know how he'd react. She suspected the distance between them might be a safety valve for him. "I'm moving," she announced finally.

"Moving," he repeated slowly. "Moving . . . here?"

"I'm going to work for Pete Petersen at the roads department in Big Thunder."

"You didn't tell me you were applying for a BIA job."

She made herself look up. "I applied last summer. I didn't know whether I'd get it, and when it was offered, I didn't know whether to take it. I talked to Pete and Bob Krueger, and then I gave it a lot of thought." The look in his eyes didn't change, and it was hard to read. She had to keep talking, piling onto the explanation. "It's a good opportunity for me. I can learn a lot from Pete. When he retires in a couple of years, who knows?"

"I don't understand why you didn't tell me."

She sighed. "I didn't tell you because, well, I needed to look at the job apart from us. It had to be good for me, for my career."

"It could be good for the time being, but more Indians are qualifying for those jobs nowadays. Couple'a years, you might be out of a job."

"Big picture, Sage. You have to be open to opportunities you haven't thought of yet. Maybe I don't want to work in the field for the rest of my life. Maybe I'll go back to school. Maybe I'll teach." She helped herself to more water. "Maybe the one-day-at-a-time philosophy is beginning to make sense to me."

He held his glass out for a refill. "It does bring you . . . within easy reach."

"It does," she said quietly.

"I don't know about you, but I like that idea." A broad smile slid across his face and touched his eyes. He lifted his glass. "In fact, I'll drink to it."

When the glasses were drained, he pulled a letter from his shirt pocket. "Here's something else I've got to celebrate. It's from Brenda."

"Your daughter? She finally answered your letters?"

He nodded as he pulled the lined notebook paper from its envelope. "You can read it. It's not like she's dying to see me or anything, but she remembers me, and her mom said it was okay to write to me if she wanted to." His eyes glistened as he handed Megan the letter. "She wanted to."

Two small school pictures slipped out when she unfolded the paper. There was a dark-haired boy whose new permanent teeth were still too large for his little-boy face and a dark-eyed girl who, in a few short years, would be a lovely young woman. Megan knew how much older they must have looked to Sage, and her chest grew tight at the thought of all he'd missed.

"They look so much like you," she said.

"You think so? I kinda thought so, too."

Megan unfolded the letter and read the message written in the carefully rounded hand of a twelve-year-old. "She says she remembers riding double with you, and she remembers how you used to call her 'Shorty.' And she says . . ." She looked up as she folded the letter and tucked it back in the envelope. His eyes were filled with a bitter-sweet mixture of emotion. ". . . she's so glad you've stopped drinking."

"I told her I was working hard at it. I didn't tell her about . . ."

"You told her the truth, Sage." She reached for him, putting her arms around his neck. "I need to hold you," she whispered, pressing her palm over his soft sweatshirt.

"I need to hold you, too." He pulled her into his lap and crushed her to him. Their needs had nothing to do with pity. There was pain to be acknowledged and joy to be shared, but there was no bid for sympathy and no caretaking.

"I went to see my father," she told him.

"How did it go?"

"I just told him that I was participating in a group for adult children of alcoholics."

"What did he say?"

She leaned back, holding his head in her hands. "He said he'd never heard of such a thing, and my mother said that groups were the in thing these days. I think he was hurt. I think she was a little angry."

"You're not doing it for him," he reminded her.

"I'm doing it for me."

She was learning. He grinned as he sneaked his hands beneath her sweater. "That's right. Now, how about doing something for me?"

"I suppose you want dessert."

"Right again." He lowered her back against the cotton quilt, and she heard the crackle of the bed of leaves beneath it.

"I really did bring some, you know."

He pushed her sweater out of the way and nuzzled the ivory satin that covered her ivory skin. Both soft. Both powder-scented. "I know you did." He nudged at the satin with his nose. "Little tart."

"I warned you about—"

"Mmm, two little tarts." He sucked at her through the satin.

She took a deep breath. "That word *little*."

"Two for me," he muttered as he moved to taste the second one. "And none for you."

"I brought . . ." He released the clasp between her breasts, and she sighed. ". . . something that probably isn't very . . ."

"I'm stealing these tarts," he whispered, "with these sweet little berries."

He unbuttoned her jeans and inched the zipper down while he feasted.

". . . very good . . ." Megan breathed. She buried her fingers in his thick hair for support as her thighs went slack. "Oh, Sage, that feels . . . very, very . . . good."

"You like that?"

"Mmmm."

"You hungry?"

"Mmmmmmmmm."

"How about an éclair?"

Her hand crept under his sweatshirt and over his belly, and he sucked his breath in when it reached the waistband of his jeans. "Do you have one for me?" she whispered hotly.

"Mmm-hmmm. Somewhere."

"I know how to find it."

PALE WHITE STARS were beginning to make their appearance in the great Dakota sky, and a pumpkin-colored harvest moon hung low above the jagged horizon. Wrapped together in a blanket and in each another's arms, two lovers shared dreams and intimate touches and listened to the last of summer's cottonwood leaves answer the night breeze with a dry rustle.

"Do you think we'll ever build another road together?" Megan asked.

"I think I'm supposed to build roads," he said absently, enjoying the feel of the soft down on the back of her neck as he stroked her. "All kinds of roads."

"If I did a vision quest, do you think I'd find out what I'm supposed to do?"

He dipped his chin and feathered his lips across her forehead, wondering what she dreamed about now when she closed her eyes. "What if you did one and it told you to go back to Pierre and find some guy who's already got his act together? Then what?"

"How many times did you say you went back to the vision pit?"

"Three."

"Then I'd try again." She levered herself up on one arm and traced the lines across his brow with her thumb. "I've learned a lesson from you, Sage Parker." Care lines, she thought. She cherished each one. "You're only beaten when you stop trying."

"I love you."

"And I love you."

The End

Author's Note

Big Thunder, Red Calf, and the Medicine Wheel program are fictitious. The Lakota people are not. Those who no longer make their homes in the Dakotas still have their roots there, roots that are as native to the land as prairie grass. But the road to Indian Country, particularly in the West, remains a road less traveled.

The concept for Medicine Wheel was partly inspired by the story of Alkalai Lake, a community of the Shuswap people in British Columbia. There, the courageous decision of one woman led to recovery for herself, her husband, and, eventually, almost the entire community. Native American people in a number of North and South Dakota communities are designing their own recovery programs, revitalizing an ancient heritage of spirituality as they attack the problem of alcoholism with new self-confidence and a tradition of wisdom as old as the rolling hills of the Dakotas.

About The Author

Kathleen Eagle published her first book, a Romance Writers of America Golden Heart Award winner, with Silhouette Books in 1984. Since then, she has published more than forty books, including historical and contemporary, series and single title, earning her nearly every award in the industry. Her books have consistently appeared on regional and national bestseller lists, including the *USA Today* list and the *New York Times* extended bestseller list.